White Girl Problems

White Girl Problems

BABE WALKER

HYPERION
NEW YORK

Library of Congress Cataloging-in-Publication Data

Walker, Babe.
White girl problems / Babe Walker. — 1st ed.
p. cm.
ISBN 978-1-4013-2454-4
1. Young women—Fiction. 2. Women, White—Fiction.
3. Chick lit. I. Title.
PS3623.A35886W47 2012
813'.6—dc23
2011046462

Hyperion books are available for special promotions and premiums. For details contact the HarperCollins Special Markets Department in the New York office at 212-207-7528, fax 212-207-7222, or email spsales@harpercollins.com.

Book design by Chris Welch

FIRST EDITION

THIS LABEL APPLIES TO TEXT STOCK

We try to produce the most beautiful books possible, and we are also extremely concerned about the impact of our manufacturing process on the forests of the world and the environment as a whole. Accordingly, we've made sure that all of the paper we use has been certified as coming from forests that are managed, to ensure the protection of the people and wildlife dependent upon them.

For me.

Problems

"People want you to be a crazy, out-of-control teen brat. They want you miserable, just like them. They don't want heroes; what they want is to see you fall."

—Leonardo DiCaprio

Day 26

I've been thinking a lot about what Jackson said in our session yesterday—fuck that guy. And fuck his stringy hair, and his fisherman hats, and his almond breath. How many times do I need to explain to him that I'm here because I spent $246,893.50 at Barneys during an afternoon of mental unclarity? What does he not understand?

During our first session, Jackson told me I could trust him, and that recovery was about accepting help from others. Quick question: how am I supposed to trust a man who works at a rehab facility in Utah? Does he not realize how creepy that is? He talks to psychos 24/7. I'm not going to just open up to him all of a sudden, so he needs to give it up. He keeps telling me that I'm approaching treatment from a place of anger. Well guess what? He hit the nail on the fucking head, because I am angry. I'm angry that I picked this bullshit, sauna-less rehab facility. I'm angry that, out of all of the counselors at this stupid place, they paired me with Jackson: the least chic one. And I'm angry that, after four weeks of being here, he still insists I've made zero progress. This past month was supposed to be about me relaxing, getting my emotions to a less fragile place, and losing a few pounds. Jackson, however, has made it his mission to ruin my chances of achieving peace with his constant nagging and prying.

Gosh, you're so fucking *smart*, aren't you, Jackson? With your "theories" about the "underlying issues" that brought me to rehab. I don't even know what you're talking about half of the time. Surrender, borderline, acceptance, boundaries, anorexia . . . blah, blah, hugging, crying, chanting, BORING. You need to relax. I'm addicted to shopping, not meth.

Everyone makes fun of me during group sessions. Their nickname for me is "White Girl Problems." I know that Jackson and the rest of the cast of *Trainspotting* think that because I grew up in Bel Air, they know what I'm all about. They don't. My life is not a joke, and that nickname is actually so fucking rude. Sometimes Jackson defends me, which I appreciate, but I've seen him laugh, which means I've also seen his teeth. Sick.

The truth is, *Jackhole*, that even though I'd rather talk about the inconsistencies in your hairline during group, I *do* actually have a lot of real problems. I always fuck the wrong guys, I hated my vagina for eleven years until I had it replaced, my dad's British, I can't hold a job, Alexander McQueen is gone forever, and even though I love Sarah Burton—and I really do love her—it will never be the same. Also, I just met my mom for the first time last week, which was a real mindfuck.

Is that good? Is that enough? Do you need more information to make your grand diagnosis? Do you need to know my entire life story? Is that what you fucking need, because I will go there, Jackson. I WILL GO THERE.

You know what I'm gonna do? I'm going to smoke two Marlboro Lights, brush my teeth, pull my hair into a chic/grungy little bun, put on my black shawl and a pair of Lanvin flats, walk down the hall to that smelly girl from Arizona's room, steal ten Adderall from her stash, come back to my room, and write down all my life's problems from start to finish. I'll show all you cunt-faced bitches what *White Girl Problems* really are.

Love,

Babe

WHITE GIRL PROBLEM #1

All I want for my birthday is for you to know what I want for my birthday without me having to tell you.

In a cruel twist of fate, every birthday I've ever had has been a complete and utter disaster. I'm cursed. And as much as I try to be a good person and put positivity out into the world, the birthday gods continue to piss upon me.

My first year of being on this earth was somewhat hectic. I was born at Cedars Sinai Hospital in Los Angeles on June 10, 1987. My mom then opted out of motherhood altogether, leaving my dad to deal with the pressures of raising a supercute kid on his own. So there we were, alone in a mansion in Bel Air.

The thing about my dad is, he's *the* entertainment attorney in Los Angeles. If you are important, aka a celebrity, chances are you've worked with him. He's also from England, which is great for me because there's nothing chicer than having a European parent, and having two passports really puts you on a whole different social level. Also, everything sounds better with a British accent. Not that I have one myself, but I've been known to pull a Madonna if the occasion calls for it.

Just after I was born, my grandmother (whom I call Tai Tai because she thinks the word "grandmother" is an ageist slur) moved from London to LA and set herself up in a wing in our house so she could "help out with that adorable little accessory." The truth was, she was excited at the prospect of living in a city where she wouldn't have to apologize for making her appearance her number one priority, and she figured that pushing a newborn baby around in a stroller would make her appear younger.

When my first birthday rolled around, Tai Tai took it upon herself to host a cocktail reception on my behalf at the Peninsula Hotel in Beverly Hills. The guest list included my dad and all of her new Hollywood friends (producers, directors and their Asian girlfriends, and Elizabeth Taylor). Everyone was shocked when they arrived to find the party Babe-less. Yeah. Somewhere between lunching at La Scala and getting her hair done for the party, Tai Tai had managed to leave me in a dressing room at Neiman's (while trying on a pair of sling-backs, I'm sure). Thankfully, some kind soul found me wandering around the jewelry department clutching an Hermès bangle (the only time I've shoplifted, I swear) and decided not to involve the authorities.

This accidental misplacement inspired my dad to hire Mabinty, a Jamaican baby nurse, to keep tabs on my every move. Mabinty's been with us ever since. She's a total bitch but in the best way possible. I guess I technically benefited from this first birthday party by getting a mother figure, so happy birthday to me.

The years passed, and I had a slew of shitty birthday scenarios, but I convinced myself that by my tenth, the curse would be lifted. Not so. I hadn't even seen the worst of it . . .

I had always wanted to do a movie-themed party, so when the film *The Lost World: Jurassic Park* came out in theaters just before my tenth birthday, I knew I'd found the perfect fit. I was obsessed with the entire Jurassic Park franchise, so I decided to really go for it and transform our entire backyard into a lush dinosaur jungle. My dad even made a call to Steven Spielberg's lawyer and got him to personally lend us some animatronic velociraptors. It was going to be major.

I kicked off the birthday festivities by screening a short film that I had written, directed, and starred in. This was my moment. At its core, my short film was an homage to *Jurassic Park* but way more political, and it was shot from the perspective of a dinosaur. I think it went over the heads of a lot of my guests, but when you're pushing the boundaries of storytelling you're gonna lose some people along the way. Looking back, I really admire the passion that I put into that film.

After the credits rolled, I made my grand entrance by busting through the movie screen on a go-kart that had been painted to look like a Jurassic Park Jeep. I was wearing a really chic safari number, complete with a hardened straw safari hat, and I announced to my guests that they were about to enter a "new world with endless possibilities."

I led the first group into "The Lost World," and within seconds it became clear that the animatronic dinosaurs were a huge mistake. The dinosaurs were so realistic-looking that every kid there was paralyzed with fear. Two boys from my class immediately pissed their pants when a velociraptor leapt at them from behind a tree. Children were literally freaking out. Three kids (including one epileptic) passed out completely, and one of my guests went into a catatonic state and had to be rushed out on a stretcher. I heard she spent seven years in therapy dealing with post-traumatic stress disorder and is now addicted to crack. (Sorry, Brooke! xoxo)

After a calamitous eleventh birthday (my boyfriend at the time had a crazy peanut allergy) and a controversial twelfth-birthday-party performance by Marilyn Manson, in which he tore out pages of a Bible and ate them, burned an American flag, and threatened to "make Satanic love" to my Tai Tai (who was into it), I decided that the best route to take for my thirteenth birthday would be a low-key pool party. So I threw a basic BBQ/swim/sleepover and invited the girls in my grade who were still allowed to come to my house, which basically just meant the nerdy, acne-faced girls to whom I'd barely ever spoken. But I needed seat fillers, it was my birthday for fuck's sake.

Of course, I wasn't going to partake in any barbecue *food*, but if my guests had such little respect for themselves that they wanted to clog their veins with cholesterol, the option was on the table, literally. In order to make a point that the Walker family could host a normal teenager's birthday celebration, everyone attending was encouraged to bring food, making for a potluck scenario. (Let it be known that I vehemently oppose potluck ANYTHING, but I'd been branded a Satan worshipper thanks to Marilyn's antics, so I needed an image overhaul.)

My dad had to be out of town for work on the day of the party, so Mabinty and Tai Tai were in charge of overseeing the festivities. Mabinty (my nanny/maid/BFF/party planner/project manager) and I have a tradition of staying up late on the night before my birthday and watching a movie that came out the year I was born. The night before my thirteenth birthday we watched *Dirty Dancing* while splitting half a slice of cake. Mabinty and I must have both fallen asleep during the movie, because I was jolted awake at 8:30 A.M. by loud snores and realized she was still in my bed. I got up and ran to the window, ripping open the curtains, expecting to see the beautiful Bel Air sun shining down on my backyard, but instead I was met with a gloomy, gray morning. And not only was it cloudy, but it was starting to sprinkle. *Fuck.* I couldn't deal with a weather malfunction, so obviously I panicked.

"Mabinty! Mabinty! 9-1-1! 9-1-1!"

I ran over to my bed and pulled back the covers. I could tell by Mabinty's breathing patterns that she was pretending to be asleep, so I started whispering in her ear.

"Mabinty, we have a code red emergency. Clouds. Rain. How are we going to pull off this party if there's a hurricane today? This is supposed to be a pool party! What are the chances of tenting the entire pool/hot tub zone in the next three hours? I'm calling the architect."

Mabinty pulled the covers back over her head.

"Yuh know yuh cyan't be wakin' mi up before nine in di morning, Babe Walker," she said in her native Jamaican dialect, Patois (Patwa). "Every day ina di month of June begin with a gray sky. Mi promise yuh, dis afternoon it'll be sunny fi yuh party. Mi gwahn down to mi room. Mi need to sleep so don't yuh come a bahderin' mi till at least eleven."

I assumed that Mabinty knew what she was talking about or

could see into the future, because by the time all of the guests arrived there wasn't a cloud in the sky. Tai Tai, on the other hand, brought the shit storm. A week before my party, she'd gone under the knife for her second face-lift, and even though she was in a lot of post-op pain, she'd agreed to show up and bring some desserts. Due to her tendency to drink six to eight glasses of champagne a day no matter what's going on, Tai Tai's plastic surgeon had advised against taking any pain medication, so she was smoking lots of marijuana during the first few days of the healing process. Then she got sick of "smelling like an artist," so she had her French pastry chef start making edible weed treats for her. On the day of my party, she mistakenly walked out the door with a tray of "Mary-Jane Macaroons" and "Petit Four-Twenties" instead of the vegan cupcakes I had requested.

When Tai Tai arrived at my party, I screamed in horror, then kindly greeted her and asked if she wouldn't mind participating in the birthday celebration from the safety of our panic room. I don't know if you've ever seen a face-lift after one week, but let me tell you, it's really fucking scary. Her head was bandaged in such a way that only her eyes, nose, and mouth peered out, all black and blue and swollen. She looked like a dead Teletubby. I didn't want her creeping out my guests. They'd been through enough over the years. Tai Tai was a little angry, but she relented once we set her up with a bottle of her favorite rosé and queued up all the surveillance cameras so she'd be able to see what was going on.

I'm not proud of what happened next.

Every year on my birthday I give myself the gift of eating one treat. Sometimes it's a little piece of cake or a cookie. This year

I went with one of Tai Tai's macaroons. It was so fucking good that I couldn't stop myself from eating two more. My guests followed suit and went to town on the tray of sweets, raving about how delish they were. About an hour later, everyone at the party was unknowingly stoned. My hot tub was filled with twelve tweenage girls, blazed out of their minds, discussing whether or not their moms' fake tits were a bad thing. One girl was so paranoid that she locked herself in a broom closet and was never seen or heard from again. I was so high that I even let it slide when I opened my presents and discovered that two girls had bought me the same Kate Spade book bag. Mabinty knew something was up when she saw me lurking around the food table, murmuring, "I'm so hungry," to myself and eating a plate of Kobe beef sliders with blue cheese dipping sauce. She cornered me.

"Babe Walker. What yuh dun now? Yuh smoking weed? Yuh too young to be stealin' from mi stash."

"That was one time. I was nine, okay? It won't happen again. What are you even talking about?"

"Yuh eyes are red, and yuh eatin' like it's yuh last meal on eart. Don't try and tell Mabinty yuh nah high as a kite right now."

She was right. Thankfully, no parents were around, and since we were all high, none of my guests thought anything weird was going on. Everyone had a blast, ate a ton of food, and we were all asleep on the living room floor by 8:30 P.M., so I guess it wasn't *that* bad of a party, but I will never forgive myself for eating those little hamburgers. Or that hot dog. Or those sprinkles. Or that frosting on a spoon. Or that leftover pad thai that I found in the fridge that wasn't even part of my birthday party. I mean, it's fine for all of those regular people to eat that shit, but not me. Whatever, moving on.

My Sweet 16 was possibly the most epic disaster of all, and the only party that ended in death. That year was all about a tacky party, so my big idea was to transform the guest house into Studio 54. I had the interior of the house temporarily gutted and remodeled to resemble the club at its peak in the late seventies, obviously. Black walls, booths, ceiling-high shafts of neon lights—it was the perfect balance of grotesque and gorgeous. To add character, and to keep in theme with the era, I had small mounds of faux cocaine (vitamin B powder) scattered around the house. A lot of kids were so high on actual coke that they ended up snorting it anyway. The Studio 54 effect wouldn't have been complete without a huge mass of people waiting in line to get in, so I hired one hundred extras to do that all night. One of them actually fainted because the polyester suit he was wearing was superhot, and I guess he was too old to stand up for five hours straight. Looking back, his near-death experience brought a certain authenticity to the party, which I can now appreciate.

I wore a blue, off-the-shoulder, vintage Halston jumpsuit and a pair of red Manolo Blahnik pumps that I regret to this day. I mean, it was 2003, everyone and their mother was drinking the Manolo Kool-Aid at that point. Thanks, *Carrie*, for convincing us that simple, boring pumps were chic because they're expensive and kind of comfortable! Anyways, I arrived to the party on a white stallion, flanked by two white Bengal tigers on chains. Huge moment for everyone. Things were going so well that it seemed like everyone had forgotten the mishaps at my many previous parties. I was on top of the world.

Halfway through the party my dad took out a bullhorn (so embarrassing) and instructed everyone to come to the front yard so he could give me my birthday present. Once we were all in position, a big truck pulled into our driveway. My dad had actually gotten me the all-white Range Rover I'd secretly been praying for! I was freaking out, and all of my friends were screaming in anticipation.

The door of the trailer opened, and there was no Range Rover to be found. In fact, there was no car at all. Instead, a huge fucking *peacock* came strolling out of the trailer and onto my driveway. A PEACOCK. Like, an actual bird, with feathers and a beak. The crowd fell silent; I was beyond confused. I wanted to flip, but I pulled it together and pretended that a peacock was exactly what I'd been hoping for. I didn't want any of my guests to see how deeply saddened I was by the sight of this fucking piece-of-shit bird, so I allowed the party photographers to do a mini photo shoot of me and my "gift." The pictures turned out really gorgeous, but if you look closely you'll notice that both of my hands are balled up into fists.

After the photo shoot, I pulled my dad aside to have a little chat with him.

"Dad, why did you get me that bird thing? It's not a car," I whispered.

"That's a Burmese green peafowl with golden plumage. Do you know how rare that is? Who wouldn't want that? Plus, I overheard you on the phone a couple of weeks ago talking to your friend about how you are 'obsessed with owning a crocodile or a peacock.' I certainly wasn't going to get you a bloody crocodile, now was I? That would have been completely irresponsible, Babe."

"That's really sweet, Dad, but I was talking about Hermès bags, not pets. There's a fantastic *crocodile* Birkin in *peacock* blue coming out soon that I would kill for."

"Well, I guess I misunderstood you then. Look at the bright side, now you have a beautiful pet to take care of. And looking after this fine specimen will teach you some damn responsibility, you'll learn to love the little bugger. Who of your friends can say they have a Burmese green peafowl? Answer me that!" he said with a huge grin.

After staring at him for about fifteen seconds, I simply said, "Hello, I'm Babe Walker, your daughter. Clearly we've never met." And walked off.

I knew my dad was into weird animals and stuff, but the fact that he thought it was okay to get me this peacock for my birthday was baffling—misunderstanding or not. At that moment, two cater waiters dressed as Andy Warhol and Bianca Jagger brought out a birthday cake and all the guests started loudly singing "Happy Birthday." As I blew out the candles, a huge fireworks display began in my front yard. It was so loud and so scary that the peacock was losing his shit and flapping his huge wings angrily. He was running around in circles through the party, knocking over my friends and the extras and destroying the decorations. Mabinty was chasing him around, which only seemed to make the peacock more frantic. The animal was even emitting a high-pitched bird scream, which added to the mass hysteria.

In a last attempt to escape the loud torture that had become my sixteenth birthday party, the peafowl ran for the wooded area next to my house. He sprinted through the fountain and across our circular driveway, and ran straight into the arms of one of the Bengal tigers that was chained to a statue in the yard. Best day of that tiger's life.

It was horrifying. The peacock exploded in the grip of the tiger's jaw and was being whipped, lifeless, all around the driveway. Feathers and bird guts spritzed a crowd of screaming kids who were standing close by. You really have no concept of how many feathers can actually come off of one bird until they are scattered around your front lawn. It was disgusting, but at least it was quick.

The brutal demise of the peacock really killed the party. All of my guests and extras left shortly thereafter. The biggest travesty was that Maroon 5 were the surprise musical guest, and no one was there to see them play. They ended up doing a private show for my dad, Mabinty, and me, but they weren't even really singing, so that was annoying.

That was the last birthday party I ever had.

WHITE GIRL PROBLEM

#2

If I like him, he's probably gay.

The question "How did I end up losing my virginity to my gay best friend, dressed as Sandy from *Grease*, while my maid taped us from inside my closet?" is one that most girls never ask themselves. It all began a long time ago, when I was a little baby Babe, running around the garden in Pampers. Just kidding, my nanny would've been fired immediately for even saying the word "Pampers." My skin is sensitive. I required cloth diapers.

When I was six, my father sent me to a very chic elementary school. At the time, La Maison du Petit Étoiles was the most forward-thinking school in the States. I think they invented the dry-erase board or something. To this day, I believe my education at Maison set the tone for my entire relationship with the world. In other words, it bestowed upon me a high level of taste and a low tolerance for processed kids' food. We only ate certified organic greens and root vegetables direct from *le jardin*.

It was at La Maison that I first met Roman Di Fiore. From day one, Roman was a total mo, as well as my partner in crime. I thought he was the coolest kid in our class. He said what he wanted, dressed how he wanted, and did whatever he wanted, and I loved him for it. When we were ten, in honor of Princess Diana's death, Roman wore a purple three-piece suit for a week and I wore a series of custom purple Versace children's dresses. Although I didn't know it at the time, the boy I played house with, the boy who would only let me pretend I was his wife if I let him wear my sequined scrunchie around his ankle, the boy who on the jungle gym politely asked if he could touch my "wee wee," would eventually take my virginity.

But that was much, much later. Tragically, Roman and I were ripped apart when his family moved to Las Vegas. Roman's dad, Mauricio, was a movie producer who decided to leave the film business and compulsively invest in commercial real estate/ his gambling addiction. He now owns half of Vegas.

I was devastated when Roman moved away. Who would braid my hair? Who would tell me I looked like Christy Turlington? Who would go to ballet class with me? It wasn't easy, but I moved on, and resigned myself to hanging out with the girls in my class who were obsessed with me.

Growing up lonely and beautiful in LA without a gay best friend to lean on, I quickly learned that even the homely girls in my seventh grade Social Studies class, whom I thought I could trust, were psychos. Especially at Archer, which is a private, all-girls school in Brentwood, where every girl's main objective was to out-slut the next. Parading my A cups around in a tube top and hooking up with Mark McGrath at MTV's Spring Break was not my style, so I stuck to shopping.

By the time I was a B cup (sophomore in high school), I had finally started to entertain the idea of having sex. I knew it was time I took my vagina out for a test drive. She was ready for her maiden voyage. Yeah, I had given a couple blowjobs and done the whole "let's get drunk and make out and maybe get naked in your parents' room" thing, but I wasn't the type of girl who was about to give my virginity away to a guy I barely even knew just because he drove a Range Rover. Even though most of my friends had done it and gossiped about it, sex still seemed sloppy and gross to me. Which is why it came as a total shock when I laid eyes on the new boy at school and instantly wanted to fuck him.

It was the first day of school, and I was about fifteen minutes late to first period Geometry. I mean, who gives a shit about shapes if they're not part of a Pucci print? Am I right? I settled down in my desk, turned to the left, and there he was: a tall, sinewy, Burberry Prorsum ad. Studded leather jacket, ripped white tee, perfectly skinny black jeans, and filthy black Dior Homme ankle boots. A true fashion punk. His look said "Fuck me, or fuck off. Your decision." His skin was flawless, his hair was calculatedly disheveled, and I wanted to kiss him. On the dick. I swear he winked at me and I literally melted.

Babe, I thought to myself, *Do not fall in love. Do not listen to your stupid body. Your body is a nutcase, you're puffy from those three beers you drank over the summer, and your skin is an 8 right now, at best. It's first period of the first day of sophomore year and already you're eye-fucking this strange boy-man. Sit the fuck down. But you* are *sitting down! Shut up.*

I mentally slapped myself and kept my eyes locked on my teacher's depressing red clogs, never once looking at the street prince sitting next to me. I was trying so hard to not completely lose my shit and break down in a tsunami of teenage sexual angst, and doing a pretty decent job, until he turned and put his hand on my shoulder.

"Did you have a good summer? I heard Turks and Caicos had one of its most beautiful seasons this year, which would explain your perfect tan."

I'm sorry, what? Did anyone else just hear that? How did he know my dad and I go to Turks and Caicos every August? My heart was pumping so hard. I swear I could feel my knees sweating. A single tear fell from my eye. Was he confused? Then I said something stupid.

"Do you love me?"

I started full-blown crying. I never thought I'd be the kind of girl who would meet her husband in high school, but apparently I never think a lot of things.

At this point, our geometry teacher kicked us both out because I was literally sobbing and clinging to my desk. I was able to pull myself together by the time we were in the hall.

"Do you have any cigarettes?" I asked my soul mate.

"Totally. They're French, is that okay?"

"Of course. Get out of my brain, pre-cog." (I have a major sci-fi obsession. You'll learn this about me.) "Do you think I'd smoke them if they weren't ?" We walked out behind the Math building. Roman handed me a cigarette and lit it.

"How'd you score that bag? It doesn't show in Paris until next month," he asked, smiling.

"My dad is an attorney and his firm represents Louis Vuitton, so I've known about the collaboration with Steven Sprouse for months. It's a finished sample. Whatever. You're ogling."

He stopped and turned to me, grabbing both my hands. Butterflies.

"You still don't know who I am, do you?"

As soon as I took a close look into his big dark eyes, I remembered.

"Fuck off! ROMAN?!" We hugged and I died a little on the inside. It was a horrible combination of excitement to see him again mixed with the devastation of remembering that he was totally into dudes. There was no chance in hell that my body, which included breasts and a vagina, would ever be of any interest to this queer beacon of chic.

From that point on, our friendship picked up exactly where it left off. We would do all kinds of fun things, like weekends in Palm Springs, waxing, dieting, making fun of frisbee players, etc. I mean, he totally understood my need to change clothes three times a day and completely supported my blowout habit, and I completely supported his blow habit.

One night, we were making a list of guys at our school who I could potentially have sex with, categorized by hand size. I wanted to be into it, but I kept coming back to the sad truth that Roman was the only one I wanted. I couldn't let go of my initial attraction to him from that first day in Geometry.

I didn't say this out loud, obviously, but in a stroke of genius, I realized his gayness was *exactly* the reason why he should be the guy I lose my virginity to. Roman was an amazing dancer, his skin was softer than mine, he was sweet and attentive, and he was completely gay, so I could eliminate the fear of him bragging to his "homies" and spreading any miserable rumors around school about the true circumference of my thighs or my less-than-perfect vagina scenario (more on that later).

I decided to confront him. "Roman," I said plainly one day while we were floating on pink rafts in my pool, drinking oxygen water, "on a scale of Pam Anderson to your grandpa, what's your blowjob style?"

"What do you mean?"

"I mean when you're giving a guy head, are you, like, aggressive or gentle?"

"I guess I don't really have a style. I kind of just go with the flow. It's more about what the guy likes, ya know? I just like making people feel good."

Roman seemed to know way more about sex than I did, which was superhot.

"Yeah, yeah, totally. Oh my God, I'm the exact same way. Totally. Just, like, pleasing guys is my main thing. So, you've never wondered what having sex with a girl is like?" I asked, praying that this would inspire him to jump off of his raft and de-virginize me on the spot.

"Yeah, I've thought about it. And it weirds me out. I mean, no offense, Babe, but I just don't have any interest in vaginas. They seem really soft. Too soft for me. The whole vagina thing is just unclear."

I had a feeling he was playing games with me, so I said, "But if the moment is right, could you be into it?"

"Yeah," he said. "Maybe. I guess."

What I heard was "If I'm drunk enough, I will fuck you. P.S. you look superthin in that bikini."

I decided then and there that I was going to get Roman drunk. And fuck him. I set up an epic *Grease*-themed date night for the two of us. He lived for that movie, and I totally understood the fetish. At the time, John Travolta was his personal icon. We met at Mel's Diner on Sunset. I'd had my hair dyed the most beautiful shade of honeycomb blond (I was born a brunette) and teased and curled to perfection, and I wore a push-up bra, black tank top, vintage Versace leather jeans, and red pumps, obviously.

I should mention that as a very young girl I became obsessed with fashion. At age seven I started drawing sketches of myself in all of the outfits I would wear. Drawing just came naturally to me and I really enjoyed doing it. I realized that the best way to put a look together was to draw it out on paper and see if the ensemble worked. When you look in a mirror, it's easy to get distracted by other objects in the room or problem areas on your body, but when you sketch, you really punctuate the important aspects of your look: you and you and your clothing. Sketching can help you discover something completely new about a piece of clothing that you thought you knew inside-out. Highly recommend.

Anyways, back to the *Grease* date. Roman was a vision in black Fendi leather everything. He looked so fucking sexy that night. He looked like the kind of gay who would have no issue breaking your nose if you called him queer, especially since his hair was slicked back and he was on a fucking motorcycle.

I ordered a side of fries but substituted celery sticks for the fries. They were delish. Roman ordered a burger and a malt, as

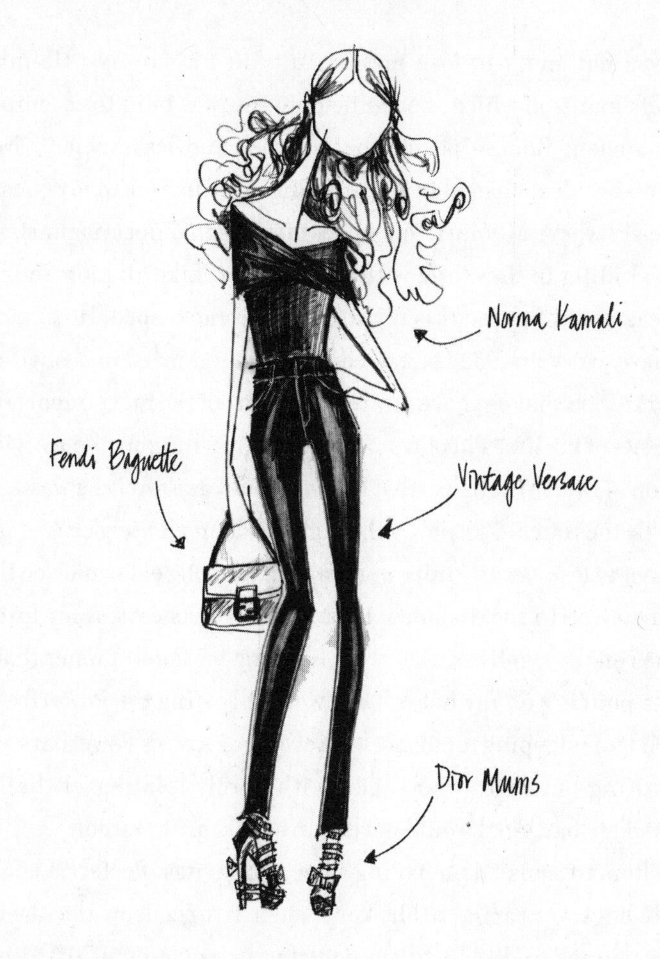

a joke (he would never eat that in public). We spiked our Diet Cokes with Jack Daniel's under the table and made fun of our lazy-eyed waiter. The date was shaping up perfectly, our conversation was supercute, and Roman was starting to get buzzed and flirty. God, we were so happy then.

Roman wanted us to go back to his house after dinner, but

I was not about to lose my virginity in his family's Holmby Hills mansion which, not coincidentally, was built to resemble an ancient Roman palace, but smaller and less ancient. Not chic. Besides, I had planned on bringing him back to my guesthouse, where Mabinty (my maid/bff/personal documentarian) was hiding in the closet with a camcorder. Like all momentous occasions, I figured this night should be videotaped. How could I have every birthday taped, edited, and organized on a shelf in our library and not have any record of one of the most important events of my life? Plus I'd stocked the bar in the guesthouse with a ton of liquor to ensure that Roman would definitely be wasted.

By the time we sashayed through the door, all the pieces of my quest to lose my virginity were falling into place. I could see the finish line in the distance. I could hear the cheers of my loved ones on the sidelines; they were handing me cups of water that I was pouring on my head. They were throwing me PowerBars, and I was slapping them, because everyone knows PowerBars are nothing but carbs and sugar, with barely less regret than a Snickers bar. P.S. I would never run a fucking marathon.

Roman insisted on having a few margaritas. Perfect. I could tell he was nearing a blackout when I turned on the *Grease* soundtrack and he legit screamed with excitement, lifted me up, and threw me on the bed. We danced on the bed for a little bit, and when the moment seemed right, I went in for a kiss and simultaneously grabbed his dick. I wasn't expecting him to kiss me back, but when he did, I went with it.

"Romie. Let's make love."

"Babe that's gross. Stop. Wait—is there somebody in your closet?"

"Huh? No! What? Of course not. You're shitfaced!"

I lifted Roman's shirt over his head, lay down on the bed, and peeled off my leather pants. A note: vintage Versace leather jeans are really sticky once you've let yourself sweat in them, so if you think you're going to be in a heated situation, you should preempt by dusting your legs with baby powder before you put them on. It will save you twenty minutes when you go to take them off. Trust me.

By the time I had my pants off, Roman was lying next to me wearing nothing except his Calvin Kleins.

"You look really thin. Are you okay, Babe? Sometimes I worry about you. I mean, you ate celery sticks for dinner."

Obviously my adherence to the Atkins Diet had been paying off. I smiled.

"Roman, I'm fine. I want to have sex. With you. Right now."

"Babe, I—"

"I don't care what you say. You are going to have sex with me. Look. I'm naked and you aren't turning away or anything. You're staring at my boobs."

This was true. I'd wiggled out of my underwear while Roman was going on about my weight. Nothing makes me want to get naked more than someone telling me how thin I look. I was starting to feel really free with my body. Isn't sex amazing?

"Take your pants off. We're fucking," I demanded.

"Babe, I'm not into you like that. What are you doing?"

"This is going to be fun! Trust me. You'll like it."

"No I won't. Vagina scares me. I don't even know what to do with it."

"Well, let's make a safe word that we can say if things get too intense. If either of us says it, we'll stop. But honestly, Roman, just man up and don't say the safe word."

He agreed. And we decided that the safe word would be "Tom Ford." Roman took his pants off and lay next to me. His dick was huge. Honestly, I felt kind of scared, but we'd gotten this far, and there was no way I was going to back out now.

"Okay, get on top of me," I said.

"I hate you, Babe."

"No, you don't."

"I know."

"Now, when we start doing it, I want you to really go for it. It's probably going to hurt me a little bit, and I might scream, but you need to just keep going."

"Okay. But Babe—"

"What?!"

"I'm not sure—"

"Just fuck me, Roman!!"

He thrust his hips forward, and all of a sudden it felt like a fire had been lit inside my vagina.

"TOM FORD!" I screamed, slapping him across the face.

"Oh my God! I'm so sorry!" He looked terrified.

"It's okay. Sorry for slapping you. Just kidding with the safe word, keep going."

He started thrusting again. At first it felt sharp, then the pain eventually went away, then it felt rhythmic and good-ish. By this point I think I was in such shock that I was actually having sex, that I kind of allowed myself to bliss out and go with it. It became apparent that Roman had gotten really into it too, when all of a sudden he flipped me on my stomach and started fucking me from behind, moaning, "Danny! Danny!" I was moaning too, and kind of laughing. And kind of screaming "Sandy!!!" I figured that I had gotten mine and it was only fair that he got his, for what it was worth.

All in all, having sex for the first time with a gay guy was, like, totally weird and totally hot. It didn't feel anything like I had expected, but I guess sex is one of those things that you need to try firsthand to understand. Like a facial. After it was over, we both hung out naked and watched *Clueless* until we fell asleep. The next morning, I woke up to a note from Roman on my bedside table. It said:

Dear Danny,

I will never do that with you again, but just so you know, I fucking loved it. Pedicures at 3?

Love, Roman

We don't talk about that night very often, but sometimes, when we're drinking whiskey at my place, Roman and I watch the tape. Despite the Led Zeppelin tattoo situation that was going on on my ankle at that point (removed last year), and Mabinty laughing so hard that the camera is shaking uncontrollably, you can clearly tell that we both looked amazing, young, free, and in some sort of love. Even if it wasn't traditional. Or natural.

Who am I, and when did I gain a pound?

In addition to filming my sex tape and all of my birthdays, my maid, Mabinty, has also been my closest confidante. She basically raised me. Growing up, my dad was always at work, and my grandmother, while an amazing role model, had a tendency to pop in and out of my life at her leisure. Mabinty has been with me since before my little baby brain could form memories.

Mabinty moved to LA from Jamaica and was hired as my night nurse when I was two days old. She went from being my night nurse, to being my nanny/maid, to being my assistant/mother. Whenever I heard a new curse word at school, she was the person I went running to looking for the definition. Mabinty ushered me into womanhood. She taught me about sex by sitting me down in front of the TV and playing every episode of HBO's *Real Sex*, while giving me a play-by-play commentary. Once, to teach me about the dangers of woman-on-woman violence, Mabinty directed my friend Genevieve and me in a staged version of *Single White Female* in our backyard.

For as long as I can remember, Mabinty has encouraged me to express myself through clothes. She allowed me to leave the house in whatever outfit I wanted, without judgment. Therefore, I credit her for my unique sense of personal style. I've never known my real mom, so she's the closest thing I've got, for better or worse.

One morning, during my junior year of high school, I woke up feeling bloated. I got out of bed and looked in the mirror to see a monster zit forming on my chin. *Fuck*, I thought. *I must be PMS-ing.* Whenever I'm about to get my period, I turn into a nightmare, and all it takes is one off-color comment to send me spinning into a rage. During high school, I would always have Mabinty call in for me and tell them I was too sick to come to class. During moments of uterine compromise, my presence on campus would put faculty and students at risk. Think Columbine, but in a Burberry trench.

I decided to spend the day de-puffing in a sea-salt bath, watching episodes of MTV's *Making the Video*. I was in the middle of a deep-breathing exercise when Mabinty came rushing into the bathroom to tell me that my dad was on the phone. He'd been out of town on a business trip, so she and I had the house to ourselves for the week.

"I don't want to talk to Dad today," I said, waving the phone away. "I don't feel good. I told you that."

"It's been tree days, deary. Yuh gotta check in wid him. Tell him 'bout yuh new dress. Yuh know, di slutty one."

"Fine," I relented.

Then, as she handed me the portable phone, she looked me straight in the eye and said:

"Mi not sure if yuh a do sumting diffrent wid yuhself, but yuh a look real healthy, gyal."

Then she turned and walked out of the bathroom, as if nothing had happened. As if she hadn't just ruined my life. I was in shock. I dropped the phone to the floor.

I'd have rather had someone tell me that I looked sick, sad, miserable, starving, or dead, than have someone tell me I looked healthy. *Healthy? Are you fucking kidding me?* Why would Mabinty call me fat? She knew I was PMS-ing, so the only logical explanation was that I'd actually gained weight.

After sitting in silence for a few minutes, I mustered up enough energy to stand up and stare at myself in the mirror for fifteen minutes, searching every square centimeter of my body for the fat that Mabinty must have been referring to. When I got to my midsection I noticed a tiny bulge in my belly. Was this bloat? Was it fat? Was I, like, a fat pig and I had no idea? I'd always read about women being pregnant and not even knowing about it until they give birth. Was I like these women—in such denial about my apparent weight gain that I had no concept of how grotesque I had become?

"Mabinty," I whispered to myself, "you are fucking fired."

Of course she couldn't hear me because she was all the way downstairs, but I said it again anyway. This time slightly louder, but still relatively hushed.

"Mabinty, gwann pack yuh bags 'cause mi dun wid yuh!"

Sometimes when I'm mad at Mabinty, I speak to her in Jamaican Patois (Patwa). It's a hybrid of English and West African dialects, and over the years I've picked up the basics.

"Mi a go fiyah yuh, Mabinty! Yuh gwann leave t'day! Yuh cyan neva come back!"

I grabbed my towel, threw it around my body, and started to search for Mabinty. We have a pretty big house, so I did the only sensible thing I could think of: start yelling.

"Where ina dis house ah yuh, Mabinty? Yuh cyan't go too far fi mi ta catch yuh! We need a talk! Yuh bettah start look fi a new job, Mabinty. Mi on di edge. Mi dun! Mi finish playin' wit yuh!"

I stormed down the front staircase and poked my head into ten rooms of the house before finding her in the laundry room. I was a complete and utter tornado of spite. I looked her straight in the eyes.

"Mabinty, Mi—"

"Babe, what mi do fi mek yuh fiyah mi? Huh? Dis 'cause mi told yuh daddy mi tink it's a bad idea fi yuh to go down a spring break to Cabo when yuh cyan't even drive yuh own cyar? He agree wid mi on dat, so yuh should nah be bahderin' mi wid dis right now," she said, folding a shirt without even looking at me.

"You have NO say anymore about Cabo, because you no longer work here! You're fired as my mother figure. Good-bye!" I began stomping out of the laundry room, then turned to Mabinty again. "And you know something else? Just stop folding those clothes. Throw them away. Burn them. They're not gonna fit me anyway. I'm fat now, nothing fits. Nothing fits anymore. I ate way too much. I'M FAT!!!!!"

With a screech, I ran out of the laundry room and straight to the kitchen, pulled anything edible out of the refrigerator, freezer, and pantry, and piled it high on the counter. With every calorie in the house laid out in front of me, I let out a deafening scream and started stuffing everything on the counter down the garbage disposal, trying to destroy it all as quickly as possible. After everything was gone, I grabbed the kitchen phone and collapsed into a pile of my own despair on the floor.

Then I did what I always do when I'm spinning out: call my therapist. She didn't pick up, but Susan never picks up when I call her. I left her the following message:

"Susan, I need need NEED to come in to see you ASAP! Mabinty said the most horrible thing about how I'm fat, and now I'm afraid I'm going to die from obesity or type II diabetes. I'm freaking out. I'm desperate. Please end the session that you're in right now and let the patient know that you have a medical emergency that you need to get to. If you could come to Bel Air, like to my house, that would be best. Also do you know where I can get a really good colonic?"

I was sobbing by the time I hung up the phone. I also realized that in all of the frenzy, I had lost my towel so I was naked. I lay there, crying, waiting for Susan to call me back. After a few minutes I decided that if I was going to conquer my disease (obesity), I would have to take matters into my own hands. If Susan wasn't going to come to me, then I would have to go to Susan.

I stood up, headed for my bedroom closet, put on a pair of shorts, sneakers, and a sports bra, then ran out the front door of my house. I felt like it made the most sense for me to run to Santa Monica, where Susan's office was. I'm not really a jogger by nature, but I didn't have my license (due to the fact that I'd failed my permit test three times), so I had no other way of getting there, and I don't do public transportation in LA.

When I finally got down to the bottom of the hill in Bel Air, I turned right and headed west on Sunset toward the 405. Taking the freeway was the only way I knew how to get to Susan's office. It was a long way, but I was on a mission, and my body was in such a state of panic that I was running on adrenaline. It became clear that I should have thought this plan through when I ran up the on-ramp to the freeway and was accosted by the fumes of all the cars flying past me. I could feel my pores clogging from all the smog and dust. It was hot, and I was a sweaty, disgusting mess, but I powered through.

It had always seemed like such a quick trip from my house to Susan's office when Mabinty would drive, but it felt like I had been running for hours and I wasn't even close to the exit for the 10 freeway. Cars began to honk, and I was sure the drivers were yelling fat slurs at me, but I was in too much of a haze to hear anything clearly.

I was about to collapse, when I turned to see a car slowly trailing behind me on the shoulder of the road. I thought for sure it was going to be a cop or a chubby-chasing rapist, but thankfully it turned out to be Mabinty. She'd seen me leave on the security monitor at our house and had been trailing me the whole time. Even though I was still mad at her, I was glad to be able to get into the car and off of my feet. She took the closest exit and parked on a side street.

"Yuh aright, gyal? Yuh look like shit and yuh smell like a gas station. What ina di world got yuh panties in a ruffle like dis?" she asked.

"*My* panties?! *My* panties?! What state would *your* panties be in if I burst into *your* bathroom and called *you* fat?"

"Excuse mi, little gyal. Yuh tink mi called yuh fatty? When did dis happen? Mi told yuh mi tink yuh look nice. Mi sey yuh look healthy."

"Well healthy in America means *fucking fat*."

"Yuh know yuh as skinny as di crack whores on di corner of Pico and Western."

"Thanks. I feel a lot better. Sorry I fired you. Just be more careful with your words next time. I'm as sensitive as a little Kapupal flower when I'm PMS-ing."

"Cyan yuh tell from mi face dat I'm not surprised to hear dat revelation?" she remarked, sarcastically. "Yuh actin a fool and yuh puttin yuh self ina harms way fi no reason atall. Yuh haffi be tough ina dis here crazy place dat yuh livin in.Yuh got plenty to be proud of when it come to yuh figure."

"Well today I'm looking puffy as shit, so what the fuck?"

"Yuh will be bloated in the tummy area from time to time. It someting all us females haffi deal wit. Yuh nah fat, Babe Walker." She comforted me.

"You know what I'm craving? A cheeseburger. Don't tell anyone."

"Fine wid me. Let's go get yuh one."

She started the car and drove us to the closest In-N-Out, where we ordered double cheeseburgers with grilled onions. We sat in the car and ate, not saying anything to each other. It was nice to have a quiet moment after a morning from hell. Plus the cheeseburger was delicious. On the ride home I farted and blamed it on Mabinty. Twice.

WHITE GIRL PROBLEM #4

You're my best friend, and I love you to death, but fuck you. Just kidding, I love you. Just kidding, I hate you. Call me.

A quick history lesson: When Babe Walker met Genevieve Larson on the first day of sixth grade at The Archer School for Girls, they had an automatic hatred toward each other. It was simply decided that these two girls were too pretty to be friends. However, over the years they bonded over a similar sense of humor and their understanding of the difference between cute and costumey. They eventually became each other's biggest fan.

In high school I had a very specific wake-up routine, so I was none too pleased when I was rudely awoken at the crack of dawn one morning when my best girlfriend, Genevieve, called me, hyperventilating. The ringtone she'd chosen for herself, "Gin and Juice," was blaring from somewhere deep in my down comforter, and I usually wouldn't have answered at 10 A.M. on a fucking

Sunday, but she kept calling and calling, and I hate that song, so I had to answer.

After ripping the sheets off my bed and soliciting the help of the closest cleaning person, I finally found my phone, set it on my nightstand, and put it on speaker in hopes that I might fall back asleep at some point during our conversation. I've found that falling asleep is the best way to politely excuse yourself from an unwanted interaction.

"Ugh, Genevieve. Why are you calling me at this ungodly hour?" My eyes closed, eye mask reapplied.

"Go fek yourself, Babe. I was at this after-after-after party with Roman last night, and I blacked out. Someone told me I was last seen doing a krump striptease. I'm in my bra, I don't know where my top is, and I've lost everything except for my wallet and cell phone! I don't know who these people are, but one of them has dreads—actually I stand corrected, it's just one big dread. You need to come get me. I think I'm in a warehouse somewhere downtown. I don't know how I got here, but I'm so hungover that I can barely move. Come pick me up and take me shopping. Bring coconut water."

The thing about Genevieve is she parties like a banshee, but she actually has her shit together. She's a total power bitch and has been selling real estate since she was fourteen, all the while maintaining a 4.0 GPA. She was the valedictorian of our graduating class, and *Seventeen* named her one of the "Cutest Brainiacs Under 18" (barf, but kudos to her). She's totally bossy, and totally hot, and sometimes I hate her but mostly I love her. She works hard and plays even harder. This is just one of the many times Genevieve's enlisted me to rescue her from this type of scenario. But what can I say? She's my best friend.

That being said, I fucking HATE shopping with other people. I insist on doing it alone because it's the only activity that truly centers me. It's meditative and personal. When I'm there, amongst the threads and colors that provide joy and confidence for thin women throughout the first world, I am the best version of myself. I am a woman of infinite possibility: Babe At Peace. I could leave the store as a statuesque neo-deco vixen in all black-and-white Lanvin, or as a bohemian vision of future chicness clad in Marni, Proenza Schouler, and Balenciaga. Do you know what I mean? So even if she had been roofied the night before, there was no way I was going to let Genevieve, who was clearly a mess this morning, into my serenity cave.

"Gen, you sound coked out. Do you want to just call a cab and go home and sleep it off?"

"I mean— What?! Babe, brush your hair, get in your car, go pick up some coconut water, and fucking come and get me. Bring me a blouse—or anything baggy by YSL."

I normally hang up on people who bark orders at me, but I needed to fuck with her just a little bit. "Can't you at least say please?"

"BABE! I'm not fucking kidding. I woke up facedown on a corduroy couch with Massive Attack blasting. I've lost my purse, my makeup, one of the diamond earrings that my mom gave me for graduation, my top is missing, my face is splotchy, I feel like Chlöe Sevigny in *Kids*, and it's freaking me out! GET THE FUCK OVER HERE."

"Where are you?"

"I told you. I don't know. I'm in a building surrounded by other buildings."

"What kind of buildings?"

"Fucking huge-ass fucking buildings, Babe!"

"Okay, shut up. Go outside, look at the street signs, and text me where you are. I'm out the door. Be there in ten minutes."

She let out a death squeal and hung up.

I pulled up three hours later, and the little damsel in a DVF skirt and a bra was sitting on the curb with an unlit cigarette hanging out of her mouth. I slowed my car down but didn't feel like fully stopping. I was super-annoyed because I had to drive all the way to downtown LA, which I file under "NEVER" and Genevieve knew that. As I rolled by, I told her to hop in. Genevieve smelled like she had mistaken toothpaste and mouthwash for Jameson and ice. She also looked like she'd punched someone, which she probably had. I handed her the blouse I'd brought for her (BCBG. My aunt sent it to me for Christmas that year, and it was bringing me down, so I needed to get rid of it).

"Hey bingey," I said, smiling.

"Hey purgey. What the hell took you so long? A blind person could have gotten here faster. I'm literally starving."

"Chillax, ecstasy-breath. I'm here now, so where do you want to go?"

"Wherever. I don't even care anymore. Thanks for the blouse, it's actually cute."

"Love that you think that. Keep it."

I made the executive decision to scrap the whole "us shopping together" idea. Instead, we'd go to Urth Caffé for lunch, I'd drop Gen off at home, and have the rest of the afternoon to myself.

By the time we got to lunch, Gen had sobered up a bit, and I was a little less annoyed. That was, until she got mad at me for only ordering an iced tea after she ordered an egg white omelet.

"Why are you eating less than me?"

One of her favorite questions. I could see a fiery little devil gaze lurking behind her contacts.

"Um, maybe because I already had a smoothie today, and I'm not drunk-binging at brunch. But that's just a guess." This sent Genevieve flying off the edge and spiraling through the turbulent skies of nasty girl realness.

"Wait a second. I had the worst fucking night of my life last night. Ryan Phillippe kept texting me to come meet him at Spider Club, and when I got there he was wasted, so I had to drink five vodka sodas and do a few bumps to catch up. Then I followed him to some godforsaken warehouse party in the middle of nowhere, and Ryan left to go home and told me I couldn't come with him because I'm 'not blond enough,' which obviously means he thinks I'm fat. Then, you show up three hours after I call you, and you trick me into eating brunch in front of you when you've already had a fucking smoothie?! What kind of friend are you?"

She had a point.

My gremlin of a brunch date didn't look at me or say anything for the rest of the meal—she just clinically deconstructed her egg white and veggie omelet, separating the vegetables by color and eating one slice of blackened zucchini with her hands. This was a new low for her, and frankly, I was embarrassed for the both of us.

"Look, I'm really sorry you're mad," I said, but didn't mean it.

"You don't even care."

"You know how I feel about you hanging out with douche bags at warehouse parties. It's not chic and it always ends in greasiness. What do you want from me?"

Genevieve cocked her head and squinted at me, the tiniest smirk playing on her lips.

"I want to shop. With you. Right now."

Oh God. I fucking knew it.

"On Melrose." She smiled, knowing full well what she was setting me up for.

"*Nunca.*"

"Please, Babe. I need summer looks. I need to feel free."

I knew exactly what she meant by this. I could tell Genevieve was being "wild" today, which meant she wanted to go East of Fairfax.

ON GOING SHOPPING ON MELROSE AVENUE: For those of you plebeians who have never had to navigate your way through the perils of LA shopping, be warned that Melrose Avenue is both a blessing and a curse. Melrose west of Fairfax is completely doable. I'm talking Fred Segal, Alexander McQueen, Maxfield, dogs on leashes, Olsen twins, even sidewalks, and potted plants. East of Fairfax is a cesspool of white people with dyed dreads and platformed, gothic extroverts trying to out-nasty Cali hooker types in plaids and cowboy boots. I don't even know what stores are over there, but they call themselves "vintage," which is code for "sick." It's disgusting. Especially on the weekend.

I had to take a stand. "Honestly, Genevieve, I can't go in any vintage stores, because I just had a facial yesterday, and the floating particles of cocaine residue will tarnish my shine. Plus you know I can't go shopping with you."

"Um, need I remind you of what the last fourteen hours of my life have been like?"

"What about my life, Genevieve? What about me? Have you stopped for a second to think about my needs in this scenario?"

Gen ate another slice of zucchini with her hands, chewed it up, and slowly spit it into her napkin. Staring at me the entire time.

"Okay fine!" I relented. "You win. But we're going to Barneys."

Some people (e.g.: Me) become empowered when they shop. Others (e.g.: Genevieve) want an opinion on every single article of clothing and accessory they try on. Genevieve also does this super-annoying thing where she shadows your every move and will try on the exact same stuff as you. I've of course only heard rumors about this, because I've never actually shopped with her, but I had no desire to find out if they were true. So the minute we walked into Barneys, I led Genevieve over to the sunglasses case.

"You should really look into Tom Ford's new eyewear collection. Great for those walk-of-shame dark circles!" Before Gen could respond, I walked briskly over to the shoe section, hoping she would be too mad to follow me.

I was trying on an insanely high pair of coral YSL tribute platforms when I heard Genevieve standing behind me, smugly tapping her foot on the marble floor.

"Thanks so much for the sunglasses tip, Babe. I ended up getting these supercute aviators that you actually had on hold. I feel like they'll really complement my bone structure. You're the best."

"No, Gen. You're the best. Excuse me?" I said to the shoe man. "I'll take these," pointing down to my feet. "And I'll take those," pointing to the Jil Sander gladiators Genevieve was eyeing. Her gaze shifted to a pair of Givenchy flats. "And those too. All in size eight. Thanks."

I was hoping that this would be the end of our trip, but Genevieve insisted on going to the third-floor women's CO-OP section, exclaiming she was looking for slutty sundresses to wear on the off chance that she might run into Ryan again in the near future. *Don't even.*

When I shop alone, I set aside a good three hours to put together looks and try them on. Today, I was too exhausted by Genevieve acting like a bitch to trust that I'd be able to accomplish anything further than buying those three pairs of shoes. So while Genevieve tried on all sorts of gross dresses that I couldn't support, I just sat on a couch in the dressing room, trying to imagine what my hair would look like if I cut half an inch off the bottom.

Then she came out in this dreadful body-con, bandage-y dress thing that I could practically see her nipples through. There's a painfully thin line between "I love my body and it's summer" slutty and "let's do street drugs together at your parents' Malibu house" slutty. I was doing my best to keep her in line with the former, without actually saying anything—just, like, using my eyes to display judgment. Gen kept asking me how she looked.

"You look really nice," I replied, scrolling through my phonebook and deleting numbers of girls I was over. "No, like, super-nice."

"Nice" is the worst review you can give a friend when they ask you how they look. It's a harsh, harsh word. That's why I was saying it, because I was really losing my patience. I could hear Genevieve huffing and puffing in her dressing room.

"I want to know if I look hot. You keep saying I look nice.

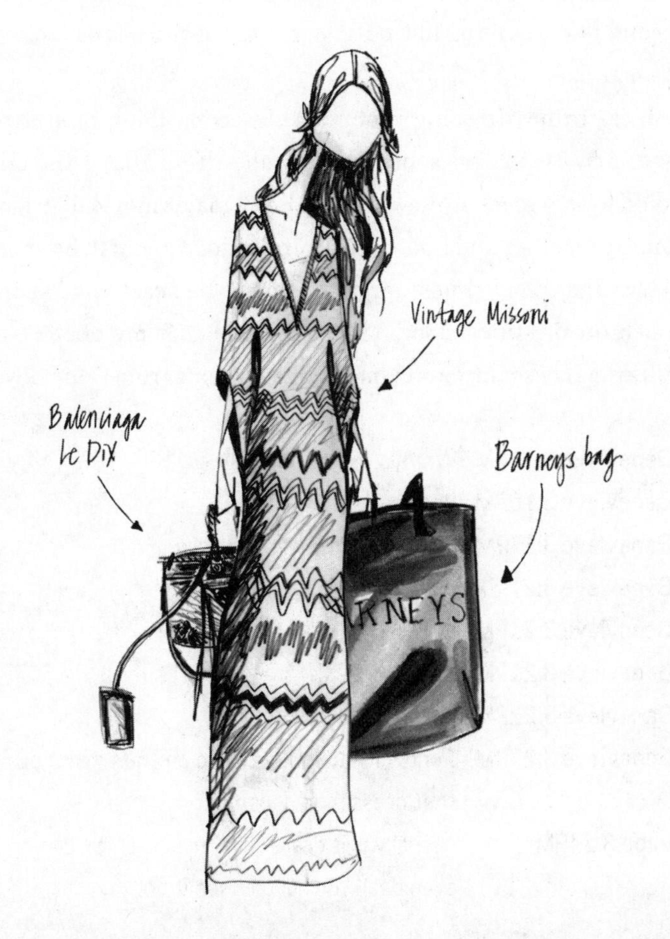

What the fuck does 'nice' even mean? Can't you put your phone down for six seconds and say I look pretty and thin and support me? You know what looks NICE, Barbara? Your eye makeup!" She slammed the dressing room door.

This seemed like lashing out. No one calls me Barbara. No. One. Why did I agree to go shopping with such a freak on a leash? I told her she looked nice again and then removed myself from the negativity by getting up and walking down to the second floor, praying to find solace in a sea of designer ready-to-wear.

I was in my dressing room on the second floor, humoring myself by trying on a Junya Watanabe dress that I thought would love to meet my new shoes. I had a major movie date look coming together and I was feeling pretty good about it. So good, in fact, that I had almost forgotten about the beast I had abandoned on the third floor. Then I noticed that my phone was blinking incessantly and I had eight new texts from Genevieve.

Genevieve 3:16PM What is your problem?
Genevieve 3:16PM Babe
Genevieve 3:17PM Stop it's not funny anymore
Genevieve 3:21PM Just say something
Genevieve 3:21PM Babe!!
Genevieve 3:21PM I miss you
Genevieve 3:22PM Whatever
Genevieve 3:23PM I know what you're trying on and trust me, that dress is heinous.
Babe 3:24PM Actually this dress is so fucking chic I can't even deal! You have to see it on!!

Genevieve 3:24PM	Actually I saw it on someone last night and it made them look 80lbs heavier than they actually are.
Genevieve 3:25PM	And actually it's actually really trendy. But whatever.
Babe 3:26PM	Actually that's what u think
Genevieve 3:26PM	That's annoying
Genevieve 3:27PM	You've actually been acting like a spoiled brat
Genevieve 3:27PM	Since yesterday and actually I'm so over it
Babe 3:28PM	That's what u think. Where are you? Are u almost ready to go?
Genevieve 3:28PM	I'm in the dressing room next to yours. Psycho
Babe 3:29PM	You're the psycho. I'm getting this dress and then I'm leaving
Babe 3:30PM	Don't be mad. I'm sure you actually look really pretty right now
Genevieve 3:34PM	Stop
Babe 3:34PM	I'm serious
Genevieve 3:35PM	So am I. Die.
Babe 3:35PM	You don't mean that. You'd feel so bad if I died in here
Babe 3:36PM	I'm sorry u think I'm being a bitch
Babe 3:36PM	I know ur just jealous I found the dress before you did
Babe 3:36PM	I still love u even though you're acting like Tara Reid today

Then a long and terrifying scream/howl emerged from Genevieve's dressing room.

Babe 3:37PM	Do u feel better now?
Genevieve 3:37PM	Yes. Sorry I've been so crazy today
Genevieve 3:37PM	And I'm sorry ur such a bitch to me when I'm being crazy
Genevieve 3:38PM	And I just needed to shop
Babe 3:39PM	I forgive you. Do you want half a Xanax?
Genevieve 3:40PM	☺

I stepped out of my dressing room and into Gen's. We hugged for .02 seconds and then I gave her half a Xanax.

"Let's get you home. If you ever make me shop with you again, I'll poison you. Just kidding."

I wasn't kidding. I'd totally murder her if we ever went shopping again. I paid for my new dress, then I drove Gen home, then I went back to Barneys to return those hideous gladiator sandals I'd bought as a joke.

My vagina is bullshit.

This is difficult to admit, because I've always taken pride in my body or whatever, but here's the truth: my vagina was forged in the depths of Hades and sent to me as a sick joke by Beelzebub himself. It wasn't a fair representation of who I was as a person, and I wasn't whole until I had it fixed when I was eighteen. The entire experience really grounded me—now I totally know what people go through when they feel like they were born with the wrong nose, or born obese, or born with a crippling birth defect. I empathize. I mean, my vagina looked like it had Down syndrome.

I was in middle school when, thanks to one of Genevieve's infamous slumber parties, I realized that my vagina was all sorts of wrong and had no business being on my body. Gen was feared and respected amongst the girls at Archer, due to the fact that she was really pretty and also a major bitch. Gen also had a killer pool/hot tub scenario as well as a miniature pony, so her house was the place to be, and her sleepovers were a *must* on the weekends. The problem was they all started and ended the same way: six girls ready to paint each other's nails and prank-call boys, and then six girls sobbing on the phone to their parents to come pick them up three hours later. It wasn't Gen's fault that she had a domineering personality and a penchant for tactical sleepover games, it was more every fifth-grade girl at our school's fault that they weren't emotionally equipped to handle these elements.

On the night of this particular sleepover, Gen and I were the only ones left at her house after she'd organized a Miss America pageant that really only consisted of a swimsuit competition. She'd enlisted me as the judge, and bribed me with Lip Smackers to crown her the winner. She'd gotten her boobs before everyone else in our group of friends, so the rigging of the swimsuit competition seemed totally fair to me, but Gen's also a lunatic when she doesn't get her way, so I was going with the flow. Anyways, the swimsuit competition caused a huge fight that ended with Gen calling all the other girls "jealous fat-asses" and telling them to leave. So there we were, in her bedroom, and she and I were changing out of our swimsuits, when she took off her bikini bottoms and I caught a glimpse of her girl parts.

Genevieve's vagina was streamlined and chic-looking, whereas mine was more . . . wild and free. I was instantly self-conscious, and really pissed. Up to that point, I'd thought my vagina was the norm. I had no idea that each one had a different tale to tell.

"Why is your vagina cuter than mine?" I demanded.

"Why are you looking at my vagina, lesbo?" Gen asked, putting on her pajama bottoms.

"Shut up, Gen. I'm not a lesbian. I have a boyfriend," I replied.

"Devon Sawa is not your boyfriend, Babe. You saw him at a Starbucks. Once. So stop with the lies."

"Um, Dev and I made eye contact, psycho. And I could tell he thought I was hot." I needed to get back on topic. "Your vagina looks different than mine. Why?"

"I don't know," she said. "I think there are three kinds of vaginas. One kind that's like this," she covered her face with her hands, "one kind that's like this," she opened her hands and peeked her head out a little, "and one kind that's like *this*," she poked her head out all the way between her hands and made a horrifying, wiggly face. She shrugged. "I guess my vagina's the first kind."

"Oh. What kind is mine?"

"Let me see it."

She got down on her knees in front of me, and I pulled my bathing suit bottoms off to show her.

"Definitely the third kind," Gen said. "Holy shit."

"Are you lying?"

"Yes. No. Yes. Maybe."

"That's it. I'm leaving."

Despite Gen's best efforts to say she was kidding, I knew the truth and I was furious. I pulled up my bikini bottoms and walked brusquely over to the bathroom, shut the door, and called Mabinty.

"Mabinty, I'm at Gen's and she said my vagina is the third kind and she's right and I know it's hideous and I just need to go home and please come get meeeeee," I wailed.

"Hold on, child. Mi be right dere."

"Thanks," I sniffed, and hung up.

Then I pulled a mirror out of Gen's drawer, pulled my swimsuit down, and put the mirror between my legs. There it was—a foreign, wildebeest monster, staring right back at me.

"Fuck you," I murmured. "How could you betray me like this? Enjoy your time flapping in the breezes of freedom, because one day it will all be over for you. I. Will. Win."

By the time I was eighteen, I had Googled "vagina" so many times that Mabinty felt it necessary to bring it to my dad's attention.

"Our gyal is a wild an outta-control lesbian," I overheard her telling him in his study one night.

"Mabinty, what in God's bloody name are you talking about?" he asked.

Mabinty went on, "Babe's curious about di pussy. She don Google it nine hundred and forty-four times ova di last month. She obsessin' ova it, and yuh know dat nah healthy. Mi try to talk wid her about it, but she nah listen."

She was right. I was obsessed—consumed by the idea of transforming my wanton vagina into a perfect beauty. Not a conversation I was entirely comfortable having with anyone.

"Babe, get your arse in here!" my dad hollered. "Why are you looking at minges on the web? Are you a lesbian? I thought you wanted me to call Heath Ledger and ask him to take you to prom. Do we need to talk about this? Are you bi-curious?"

"You guys need to stop freaking," I said. "I'm not a lesbian. Not at all. I just hate my vagina and I want a labiaplasty."

> **LABIAPLASTY** (lay-bee-uh-plaz-tee) 1) plastic surgery of either the labia majora or the labia minora or both (the external folds of skin surrounding the structures of the vulva) in order to reduce the size of elongated labia 2) salvation for those who are born with a vagina that looks like Fergie's face (Black Eyed Peas Fergie, not Duchess of York Fergie, but maybe both women now that I think about it).

My dad almost fell out of his chair. "What the motherfu—"

"Dad, stop," I continued. "Listen, I don't know what happened—my shaman, Steve, says it may be bad karma from a past life—but I was born with a Basquiat between my legs, and I need to have it fixed before I go out into the real world, aka immediately after I graduate high school. It's imperative that I have this surgery, Dad. I was going to wait until you asked me what I wanted for graduation, but seeing that *someone* has trouble keeping her thoughts to herself . . . ," I trailed off, glaring at Mabinty, "I had to go ahead and tell you now."

Mabinty threw her hands up. "Don't look at mi, child! It nah mi fault that yuh tink yuh gotta roast beef sanwich in yuh draws."

"Oh, that's just great," I muttered. "Mabinty, are you *stoned*?"

"Mmm hmm. So what? Check yuhself, Babe Walker." She turned and left the room.

I looked at my dad. "See how cruel people can be? I need this surgery, Dad. Please give me the vagina I was meant to have! *Please* give me this gift."

To say my dad was appalled by my request would be an understatement. He stammered a few versions of "No" and a few versions of "No bloody fucking way" and told me he was going to get me a car, then advised me to take my body issues up with my therapist, Susan.

Susan had been well aware of my situation for a few years now, and she'd been quick to diagnose me with vaginal dysmorphic disorder. Basically she spun some bullshit about how I perceived my vagina differently than how it actually appeared. Funny, because I had tried to show her my vagina once, but she refused to look at it. So technically she'd never even seen my fucking vagina, so how the fuck would she know? The nerve of some people.

I needed someone who was on my side. Someone who could vouch for me. I couldn't fight the battle alone any longer. Genevieve was out of the question—there was no way I was going to give her the satisfaction. Roman was the only other option, and besides, he'd already experienced my meow-meow when we'd had sex sophomore year, so I knew he'd have my back. We were shopping for graduation outfits at Burberry with my dad when I decided to broach the subject.

"Romeo, can we talk about my vagina for two seconds?" I asked.

"No fucking way."

"Okay, cool. Do you think I need a labiaplasty?"

Roman choked on his gum, "a labiawhat?" He looked worriedly at my dad, who was ten feet away browsing through some ties, and then back at me.

"A labiaplasty," I explained, raising my voice slightly, hoping my dad would hear. "Plastic surgery on my vagina to make it cuter and chic-er and more . . . me."

Out of the corner of my eye, I saw my dad glance over at us.

Roman started slowly backing away from me. "No, Babe. I don't think you need that."

I followed him into the menswear section, raising my voice even more. "Really? You've seen my vagina, though. It's out of control! It doesn't belong on my body. I think something went wrong in the womb, because I ended up with a devil where an angel should be. I've Googled it! It's a type three according to Genevieve."

"Babe, you're scaring me," Roman said, visibly sweating.

"Exactly!" I said, practically shouting now. "So you agree, my vagina is scary?"

"No! I never said that!" Roman was terrified. "Honestly, Babe," he said under his breath, "I never got a good look at it. I was wasted the night we had sex. I turned you over and fucked you like a dude, remember?"

"Just admit it, Roman!" I yelled. "My vagina is hideous. Be real with me! I can take it!!!"

"Barbara Walker! Stop carrying on with the vagina stuff for God's sake!" my dad shouted. "Nobody wants to hear about the problems you're having with your bloody axe wound! And stop picking at Roman. There's no way he's ever seen your vagina. Look at him. He's a poof!"

The entire store went silent. A saleslady stood next to my father, slack-jawed and horrified.

"I'll take these three ties," my dad said to her, composing

himself. "And a suit. 40R. You choose the color. And some shoes . . . doesn't matter which kind. Charge it all to this." He handed her his Amex Black Card. "Babe, you'll bring the stuff out? I'm going to get the car from the valet. Cheers."

With everyone in my life refusing to acknowledge my needs, I turned to the one person who I knew would never cast judgment on anyone's desire for plastic surgery: my grandmother, Rose, aka my Tai Tai.

TAI TAI *n* 1) term used in Eastern cultures for supreme wife (implying a situation where a man is wealthy enough to have several "wives") but no longer strictly interpreted; now applies to citizens of the world who are wealthy; a tai tai is a privileged lady of means 2) literal translation: Supreme of the Supreme; implies respect 3) replacement for the word "grandmother," as it does not imply old age.

I Skyped with her from LA, while she was vacationing on her yacht in the South of France.

"Tai Tai," I pleaded, "my vagina is ruining my life. Dad doesn't get it. Susan doesn't get it. Nobody gets it! Nobody gets *me*!"

"Darling girl, can you accept your flower for what it is and move on? Have you spoken to your shaman about this?"

"Yes. He tried to cleanse my aura but couldn't get all the orange out."

"Oh dear."

"I know. It's bad. He thinks I must have been a gargoyle in a past life. I have to get a labiaplasty. You need to help me."

"I don't know, darling. How does it work?" she asked.

"They laser off all the excess skin and sculpt your vagina into a masterpiece. Come ON! Tons of girls get nose jobs, and breast implants, and chin reductions, and their ears pinned back, and eyebrow lifts, nipple reductions and Botox. Unlike those idiots, I actually *need* this." I was on the verge of tears.

"What if I get you that crocodile Birkin you wanted instead?"

"No."

"You must be serious about this. The Birkin question was a test."

"I know. But I am serious."

"What if you wait until I get back from France and we get matching labiaplasties?"

"Tai Tai, don't," I sighed. "I seriously don't know how much longer I can walk the earth with the vagina I have now. Please. I'm begging you."

"Fine, my love. Let me make some calls and I'll get you a list of reputable surgeons. But don't tell your father. And stop frowning. It smushes your forehead. Love you."

"Thanksies. I love you too."

Tai Tai faxed me her list of references, and the next week, I scheduled a slew of appointments with various plastic surgeons around LA. These consultations were an essential part of my process of vaginal rebirth. My first appointment was with Dr. Larry Medford, a surgeon in Century City who closely resembled a garden gnome. Stature aside, I figured that his small hands would provide the necessary dexterity to get the job done.

I was nervous at first, but when he entered the room, I was instantly at ease.

"Miss Walker, what can I do for you today?" he asked.

"My vagina is a wild bird that must be tamed. I need a labiaplasty."

"Okay, let's have a look."

He examined me, and then much to my surprise said, "I'm a little unclear. Where is the problem area?"

"Are you blind?! It's a mess down there, and I'm trying to employ you to clean it up. I thought you were an f-ing doctor."

"I am a doctor, Miss Walker, and your vagina looks fine to me. I honestly can't see what needs to be fixed."

"I will NOT sit here while you stand there and lie to my face. Good-bye, sir!" I gathered my things and left his office in a huff.

I called my grandmother and left her a voice mail. "Nice try with Dr. Medford. I know you called ahead and told him to tell me my vag looks normal, but just so you know, your plan didn't work. Bye."

My next appointment was in Santa Monica with Dr. Penelope Wakefield, a surprisingly chic woman with an equally chic office and staff. Everything was going smoothly until she took a photo of my vagina and started altering it in Photoshop into her interpretation of what the "after" should look like post-surgery. Our aesthetics weren't gelling. She may have been chic as shit, but I wasn't about to walk around with some teeny little porn-star mini-vagina. It needed to be streamlined with a hint of character. Halfway through the consultation I gave up trying to communicate my vision and stared at her until she left the exam room. Then I hung out and read *People*, *Us Weekly*, and an issue of *Cosmo* to make sure I got my money's worth for the cost of the appointment.

My final appointment was with Dr. Hale Shaw, a Beverly Hills plastic surgeon who was kind of a hunk for being in his eighties. I got up on the exam table and hastily explained my situation:

"Look, I am literally at my wit's end and you have got to help me. This vagina is all wrong. It may be on my body, but it doesn't suit me. It's not working for me. We don't get along. Help me. I need this labiaplasty. I DESERVE THE GIFT OF CHANGE!"

"Okay, Miss Walker, calm down. Let's just see here . . ."

He took out a mini ruler and started to take some measurements. "I can see the problem very clearly. This vagina is too much of a free spirit, correct?"

"Yes . . . ," I said, somewhat suspiciously. "I mean, I'm a free spirit too, but I don't want my vagina to reflect that."

"You'd like it to be more of a natural beauty, am I right?"

"It's like you took the words right out of my vagina. Let's do this."

"Okay," he said. "We'll need to run some blood work and analyze the results, which will take about seventy-two hours. Then you'll come in for a pre-op appointment and medical counseling . . . so, why don't we schedule your surgery for next Tuesday?"

"I'll give you ten thousand dollars to do it now," I said.

"Barbara, these are the standard procedures you have to go through if you want the surgery."

"Fine. We can do it your way if that makes you happy. Just please, as soon as possible. I'm suffering. And don't call me Barbara."

"You're in good hands," he said.

The following Tuesday I experienced true redemption. Dr. Shaw and his nurse put me under, and eradicated that monstrosity of flesh that had lain beneath my La Perla undies all those years, and turned it into the Gisele of vaginas. All for the bargain price of $6,000.

After the stitches dissolved, it was clear that Dr. Shaw had worked his magic and liberated my body. Babe Walker: Reborn. I immediately e-mailed the before and after photos to Genevieve, who refused to admit that there was a difference. That was fine by me, because I knew she was just jealous. I win!

My major in college was picking my major, with a minor in being really bored.

My dad should have listened to me when I told him that college was not my thing. Instead, he insisted on learning a $200,000 lesson the hard way. That's the thing about college—you pay a ton of money just to realize that everyone is a fucking moron.

I always envisioned myself as a college dropout. Most creative types are. If you can get away with it, it's kind of chic. I just didn't think I would end up dropping out of college five times in three years. It's not like I'm proud of myself—far from it. Do you think I enjoyed going to five different universities and only earning one year's worth of credits? Absolutely not.

Not to brag or anything but I'm, like, *really* pretty. One of my first memories is someone asking me if I was a model. I think I was three . . . who knows? Point being, I am the kind of person that people respond to. I'm also a total free spirit, which means

I have difficulty with structure and discipline. All these elements of my personality, coupled with my bone structure, meant that I could only be one thing: an actress.

I realized my calling at the tender age of fourteen, but I put it on the back burner because I definitely didn't want to be a child star. I mean, do any of those people maintain relevance past their late twenties? Have you seen a recent photo of Amanda Bynes? I wanted career longevity, and I wanted to let myself grow up out of the public eye. By the time I was eighteen, I knew it was time to pursue my acting career. While all my friends were filling out their college apps, I was practicing my Academy Award acceptance speeches and performing scenes from *Girl, Interrupted* in my bathroom mirror.

I scheduled a meeting with my high school's college counselor, a round woman with a Pomeranian face and a banana smell, named Paula. I told her all about my plans, and instead of congratulating me on my career ambitions, Paula asked if I had told my father that I was planning on skipping the whole college thing for now.

"Why do I need to go to college? Lots of important celebrities never went to college. Angelina Jolie never went to college. Johnny Depp never went to college. Leo never went to college!"

"Leo who?"

"Leonardo DiCaprio, my fucking *soul mate*!!"

"Babe, you should consider your options. Lots of actresses pursue a college education as something to fall back on in case their career doesn't pan out."

"My face and body are both in a really good place right now, so that's virtually impossible. I'm out of here. See you at the Academy Awards, dream killer."

I realize now that I may have overreacted, but I can't deal with the jealousies of old people whose lives have passed them by. Not for me. That night, I decided to arrange a dinner with my dad and my Tai Tai to discuss my future. We were out to eat at Matsuhisa, enjoying wagyu tataki (Google it) and sipping on ice-cold sake when I decided to unveil my five-year plan.

"What college applications?" I said. "Just kidding, Dad. I'm totally planning on going to college once my acting career has taken off and the time comes to rehab my image as a smart and studious woman. Like Natalie Portman," I lied, studying my manicure. I had zero intention of going to college, but I figured that problem would solve itself once I was too famous to attend school. "I'm just holding off for now, you know?"

"Hold on a minute. You mean you haven't filled out a single fucking application?" asked my dad.

The thing about my dad is, he studied law at Oxford and started out representing musical acts like the Sex Pistols, the Clash, and Elton John. He was a very wild guy until he had me. Then he moved to America, settled down in LA, and joined one of the top entertainment law firms in Hollywood. Basically he's been really motivated his entire life and would not stand for his only child skipping college altogether.

"Dad. Dad. Dad. Dad. Dad. Dad. Dad—when you're an actor, every life experience is like filling out an application for your next job. So, yes. I have filled out my applications. And I got in, full ride, to Babe University. And, hello! Why do you think I spent twenty hours in the dry sauna last week? I'm eliminating toxins so I can glow in my headshots."

Needless to say, the rest of dinner didn't go too well. My dad immediately put down his chopsticks and started to go to town, lecturing me on the importance of an education, plus it was all said in his stupid British accent, so it was extra rude. When he brought up the fact that Genevieve was going to Stanford, I had to explain to him that she had to go to Stanford because she wasn't as pretty as me and therefore wouldn't have the same opportunities in the "industry." Then I reminded him that Roman was skipping out on college. (A lie—he was going to UCLA, but I was really losing this argument, so I had to do what I had to do. Sue me.) But he wouldn't budge, so I excused myself mid-sentence and went to wait in the car. I think Tai Tai was secretly on my side, because a few minutes later she came out to console me.

"Babe, darling, I get it. You and your father are butting heads because you're so similar. But this is a fight you're not going to win, isn't it?"

"Tai Tai, how the F am I going to be an actress if you and Dad force me to go to college? The best actresses are rebels who didn't go to school and were too poor to eat."

"Pussycat, you can be an educated woman *and* starve yourself and still be just as interesting and beautiful as all those white trash celebrities."

"Doubtful. You guys are really sucking right now. And also, if college is such a huge deal, then you're gonna have to figure out how I'm gonna get in, because it's way past the application deadline. And *also*, lest you forget, my grades are fecal. What idiotic school is going to accept me?"

University of Southern California

My dad made a call to his golf buddy, who happened to be the dean, and there I was—stuck going to USC. This was fine by me, because I figured I'd just live with my dad and commute to school. Also, let's face it—everyone knows USC is basically a rich-kid day care. I mean, a quarter of the kids in my high school's graduating class ended up there, including this one guy I thought was actually retarded, but as it turns out he was just stoned 24/7. So I figured I'd deal with going to classes until my big break, then abandon ship.

I enrolled in the Performing Arts program, and selected four classes for fall semester: Acting 1, Elements of Theater, Voice and Speech, and Chinese 1 (to fulfill my foreign language requirements). On my first day of school, I missed the first Chinese class entirely when it took me two hours to commute to campus. Turns out, USC is in a part of town reserved for drive-by shootings and Del Tacos. I didn't want to deal with explaining my absence to the professor, so I ended up dropping Chinese altogether. I figured it was best to have a light load, so three classes it was. Fine. I love odd numbers.

Side note: Did you know that performing arts majors are mental? They're all in a constant competition to out-loud each other. I have never met so many bright-eyed and bushy-tailed weirdos in my life. Where does their energy come from? Don't they realize that this is LA and the majority of them are on the path to permanent waiterdom? It's so depressing. For them, not for me. And you know what? Acting teachers weird me the fuck out. They're always talking about your craft, and using your body as an instrument, and living in the moment, and breathing, and feeling. This was supposed to be a college, not a yoga retreat.

I also made a huge mistake by showing up to the first day of classes sporting a really floral D&G dress/cardigan look. I must have looked like the kind of girl who wanted to braid other girls' hair and lend them tampons and make signs written in bubble letters for their birthdays, because I had never been approached by so many sorority girls in my life. Let me assure you—I'm nothing like that: (a) I don't touch strangers; (b) I don't want to hear about your period; and (c) I hate sorority girls and their fucking problems. After that fashion misstep, I changed my whole aesthetic to resemble Stevie Nicks meets Go Fuck Yourself by wearing layer upon layer of black. I also took up smoking Marlboro Reds and model-scowling at everyone to ensure that I would have no unwanted interactions. It worked, thank God.

Another annoying thing about USC is that it's full of dorky film guys. I thought this would be good, considering I needed to build some sort of acting reel, and who better to employ than nerdy, wannabe-Scorsese types who jizz their jeans when a girl gives them the time of day? Well, it turns out all these guys wanted to do was drench me in blood or make me the centerpiece of their horror fantasies. At the end of the semester my reel was more *Babe Walker: Saw Victim*, and less *Babe Walker: The Next Julia Roberts*. Not cute.

After one semester at USC, I was so over skipping class to practice monologues in the library bathroom, and so over smoking two packs of cigarettes a day, and so over being over it, that I dropped out of school altogether. Actually I didn't so much drop out as get suspended, for consistently parking wherever I wanted at all times. I didn't tell my dad or Tai Tai though. They would have flipped. Instead of going to school, I'd go over to Roman's condo in West Hollywood, lie out by the pool, and work on my tan. I also visited Gen every other weekend in Palo Alto (not that chic, but tons of smart Jewish guys). Then I started dating this annoying but muscly gorilla bro-man, Carter, so he took up a lot of my time as well, and when he cheated on me after a few months, getting revenge on him became a full-time job.

My dad was furious when he found out I wasn't in school anymore. When I tried to explain to him that the pressures of being a struggling actress, coupled with my boy troubles, were too overwhelming for me to handle, he was a little more understanding. However, he forced me to take general education community college courses over the summer so that I would at least have one semester of credits under my belt. I was so afraid of being seen on a community college campus that I went to all my classes in head-to-toe disguise. I'm talking oversized sunglasses, floppy hat, red wig. I even gave them a fake name, which it turns out you can't do, because then your credits don't get recorded. Oops. Dad's fault.

WHITE GIRL PROBLEM #7

I'm too pretty to be crying right now.

It was Saturday night, the summer after my first year of college. I had a birthday party to go to, and the guest list consisted of rappers, rappers' sons, rappers' sons' girlfriends and friends, video vixens, and old Jewish managers. It was going to be a huge party, and I was totally in the mood to grind like a snake and dance to some real hip-hop music. I had given some serious thought to how I could reconfigure my entire look for this party, because it wasn't in the right place to be going to this type of event. I was inhabiting the world of Chanel-at-the-turn-of-the-decade, when I needed to be on a private jet to Roberto Cavalli–land. It would not be okay for me to just roll up to Snoop Dogg's birthday party in my black Mercedes E350 Coupe wearing a blazer and skinny jeans. I needed to amp it up with a backless dress and an event-appropriate hairstyle, driving an enormous car. I had my concept for the night's look and I was married to it. The End.

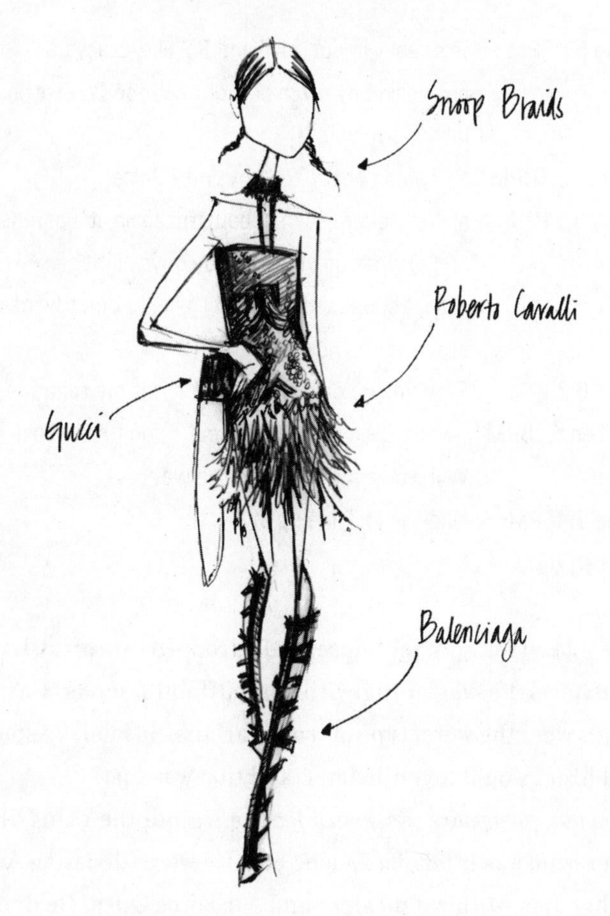

I texted Carter, my boyfriend at the time, to see if I could take his car because it was this monstrous Cadillac SUV thing that was so fucking big, oh my God you would die if you saw this car. So rude.

Babe 4:59PM Don't plan on using your car tonight. I need it for a meeting.

Babe 5:00PM	It's really important, and I'm like, crazy busy organizing everything right now, so I'll explain later. Love you.
Carter 5:10PM	No can do beautiful. boys nite 2nite
Babe 5:11PM	a) don't ever call me beautiful again, it's offensive and b) what do you mean by boys night? like what is that supposed to mean to me? I don't want to start a fight, just wondering
Babe 5:23PM	Fine. you go on boys night, but let me take the car
Carter 5:25PM	Sweet, I'll just drink more if I don't have to drive. Will u give me a beej on the way?
Babe 7:45PM	Unclear. Pick me up at 9.
Carter 7:46PM	k

He picked me up at my house, and I dropped him off at drinks or whatever he was doing with his buffoon friends. Carter's friends were the worst type of trustafarians. So loud. So smelly. I told him I would text him later, and that was that.

Rewind, backspace, flashback for one second: the thing about Carter is he was kind of a douche bag. He wore Christian Audigier hoodies, with wifebeaters and Air Force Ones. He'd make me eat at places like Ashton Kutcher's restaurant, and he'd force me to go to horrible, LA-based magazine parties and sit at corner tables with him and his friends, where there was always a reality TV camera crew around. You may be wondering why I would put up with all this nonsense—it was because Carter was amazing in bed. We would have sex for hours and hours, and he did this thing with his tongue that I will never tell you about because I'm a lady. On the surface, he left a lot to be desired, but there was something so appealing about his lack of interest in all things that I might find interesting. You know, when a guy is just dumb enough to make you feel smart, but not so dumb that he makes you feel dumb for dating him? That was Carter.

As soon as I pulled away from the joke of a bar where Carter was meeting his friends, I parked his SUV and did what any devoted girlfriend would do: I searched every inch of his car for evidence that Carter might be cheating on me. I thought he had passed the test until, just as I was about to accept that Carter was a trustworthy non-idiot, I noticed an unfamiliar lip gloss in one of the cup holders. It had been sitting there the whole time. Staring at me. Some kind of sick, strawberry, Bath & Body Works BULLSHIT LIP GLOSS WITH SHIMMER. I. Would. Never. Under. Any. Circumstance. Ever. Do. Anything. With. Shimmer. Ever. I was coming to the edge.

Babe 9:47PM	Are you having fun?
Carter 9:51PM	You just dropped me off. Jeff brought coke. Ima get hiiiiiiigh! Gonna miss you.
Babe 9:51PM	Awesome! I'm coming to pick you up. Emergency.
Babe 10:00PM	Carter
Babe 10:01PM	Carter.
Babe 10:04PM	Carter. Carter.
Babe 10:05PM	Carter.
Carter 10:15PM	are u ok??
Babe 10:16PM	I'm outside.

I pulled up to the bar, where Carter was outside with two of his friends having a cigarette. He looked surprised to see me.

"Carter, come here. I need to ask you something," I said flatly.

I heard his fat friends making fun of him, which I loved.

"I'm with the boys, beautiful. I'll text you later."

"Nope. Later doesn't work for me. Get in the car."

He was embarrassed, and started walking up the street with his friends, in an attempt to ignore me. Infuriating. I crept along next to them, continuing to yell, so pleased at how humiliating this was for him.

"Carter, I'm giving you ten seconds to get in the car."

"Dude."

"Get in the car, Car."

"No."

"GET IN THE CAR!"

People on the street were starting to stare.

"Why you acting so weird?!"

"GET IN THE FUCKING CAR!"

"No! Leave me alone."

"GET IN THE CAR!"

At this point, strangers were laughing, and yelling at Carter to get in the car. His face was bright red. It was amazing.

"FUCKING GET IN THE FUCKING CAR, CARTER!"

He hurriedly walked over and got in the car. People were clapping. He looked miserable. I was ecstatic, until I remembered why I had him get in the car in the first place. Then I was furious.

I hit the gas, speeding off in the direction of his house. I grabbed the lip gloss and screamed, "What is this?"

"Yo, Babe, you're acting crazy right now."

"WHO IS SHE?! WHO IS SHE! WHO IS SHE, CARTER? TELL

ME. WHO IS SHE? DO YOU LOVE HER? BECAUSE I FUCKING HATE YOU. WHO IS SHE?"

Carter was terrified and admitted that the lip gloss belonged to some girl he'd met at a club the weekend before, when I was "out of town" (chemical peel). Apparently, they'd fucked, but "she meant nothing to him," and he was "sorry." Bullshit.

As I pulled up to his driveway, I reached over Carter's lap, opened his door, shoved him out of the car, and threw that nasty lip gloss at his face.

"SEE YOU NEVER, BEAUTIFUL!!!" I screamed.

As I drove off, I could hear him yelling and asking stupid rhetorical questions like, "What the fuck?!" and, "Are you serious right now?" What a fool. I was so humiliated and angry. I parked his car in front of the nearest fire hydrant I could find, threw his keys in the bushes, and called Mabinty to come pick me up.

Sitting alone, on the curb, I broke down. How could a capital "S" *Shithead* like Carter think he could get away with this type of charade? Not only did he betray my trust, but he destroyed my chances of having an amazing evening at Snoop's party. I'd worn Cavalli for nothing. It was all so sad.

Of course, I spent the next twenty-four hours locked in my bathroom crying, moaning, and pushing things off the counter. I wouldn't even let Mabinty come in to console me. She was only allowed to pass kale smoothies through a crack in the door without looking at my face, which was a swollen mess of mascara and dried tears, as she tried to talk me down.

"Babe, yuh don't need to worry. Dat pretty boy jokestah won't be nuttin to yuh ina di long run. Be dun wit him. He nah mattah."

When I ran out of tissues, toilet paper, and tears, I pulled myself together, washed my face, and emerged from the bathroom with one purpose: to make Carter's life a living hell. It wasn't that I had any feelings for him, beyond having good sex and driving his massive car. It was that there was no way I could allow him to think that he'd gotten away with cheating on me. It was time for me to exact retribution. My revenge would need to be calculated and meticulous. Much like throwing a party, I was shooting for a harmonious cohesion between agenda and location, and all members involved had to be accounted for.

I decided to stage an intervention for Carter's obvious "sex addiction" at his parents' house. The guest list included: Carter's parents, his grandmother, his siblings, the priest that baptized him, and his ex-girlfriend. I had Mabinty pose as a professional interventionist and organize the whole thing for me. She's obsessed with the movie *Desperado*, so as you can imagine, she was on board with my total revenge story and wanted to be in on it. Plus, she owed me for a gram of pot I had spotted her from the week before.

Everyone Mabinty invited to the Cartervention agreed to attend. You'd have to be a real dick to blow off an invite to an intervention, but I won't say I've never done it. I mean, my cousin was addicted to gum. Not my issue.

I showed up to the intervention in a creamy, blousy, collared agnès b. top, black J Brand skinnies, and spiky Louboutin heels, with a big gray YSL Muse bag. The top of my body was reminding the world that my emotional state was fragile, even lost, while my bottom half was all about a strong sense of purpose. I named that look: The Dichotomy of Babe's Power.

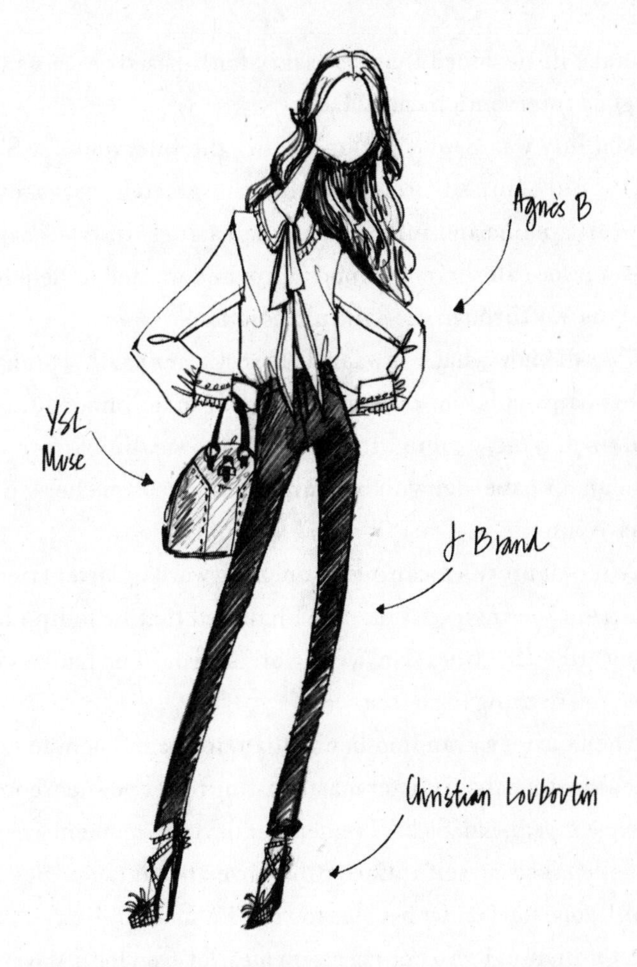

You could have cut the tension in Carter's family's living room with a dull knife. He looked pretty mad at me, but also kind of high and confused. His mom was sitting next to him, holding hands with his dad. Beneath her new face, you could see that her old face was sad, but you had to look deeply into her creases. I was happy to see that Father Andrews had been able to make it. He added that necessary faith-based realness that all good interventions must have.

Mabinty was a total pro at leading the intervention. She's always full of fun surprises like that. She greeted everybody by their first name and informed an increasingly frazzled Carter that we were all there to support him and wanted to help him find his way through his painful addiction.

"We all know what we gwaan do here. Carter havin' a prablem in his pants yuh know. We all cum today to tel'im we dun. We dun wit di lying, we dun wit di cheatin' and stealin'. Carter, yuh bahdah mi Babe, den yuh bahdah-rin mi. We came here to try to save yuh life."

After Mabinty's meaningful opening words, Carter tried to interrupt the intervention, but I handled that by telling him things like "It's fine, Car. We're here for you. The truth is out now. You're going to be free soon."

Then Carter's grandmother, Lillian, took a moment to tell a touching story about Carter masturbating in her powder room as an eleven-year-old. Sicko. I remember having a moment where I actually asked myself if Carter did have an addiction. Had my prank gone too far? Or become too real? Whatever. He deserved every minute of it. No one cheats on me. Not even John Mayer.

Everyone besides senile Lillian was pretty shocked. Carter's mother was sobbing, his father was shaking his head and had the most disappointed look on his face, his brothers looked terrified, and his ex looked like she was going to puke. The time had come for me to read the letter that I had written to Carter. I can't remember the whole thing, but it went a little something like this:

"Dear Carter—"

Carter's head was in his hands, and he was staring down at the floor.

"Dude, seriously. This is so fucking stup—"

"DEAR CARTER. I loved you. I can't go on living any longer knowing what I know and not doing anything about it. You mean too much to me, and frankly, I'm scared that your addiction will only get worse. Your addiction has affected me negatively in the following ways: Since we started dating last month, I feel like you've objectified me, and treated me like I'm just a hole. When you talk about other women, including your own mother, there's violence in your voice. Even when you *look* at other women, which is very often, I get scared that you're going to jump on them. You're addicted to sex, and you're addicted to your dick."

At this point I pulled up a slideshow containing every sext message and picture of Carter's dick/balls that he had sent me over the past month. I continued. "You're constantly masturbating. Your computer is full of porn. You need help. It's really sad."

Then I capped the moment by pulling out a folder of porn and a bag of dildos and pocket pussies that I accused him of making me hide in my car. Ta-dah!

I had the room in tears by the end of my monologue. Easily one of my best performances. Carter was slumped on the couch. He had learned his lesson, and honestly, his punishment thus far had been sufficient. I thought it was over, and we could all go home and take our respective showers, but I was wrong. Carter's parents took the intervention so seriously, and had clearly watched so many episodes of that TV show, that they decided their only choice was to send their son to true-blue rehab. So, just like that, he was whisked off to an exclusive rehabilitation facility in Malibu. Suck my dick, Carter.

I may have lit the match, but it was karma that kept the fire blazing. Sure, I went to extreme measures to get revenge, but my father always taught me to stand up for myself. There is nothing prettier than a woman with confidence. If you've ever been cheated on by someone who really should have been cheated on by you, then you know exactly what I went through, and you would totally agree that I did the right thing. So thank you for understanding.

My first trip to jail was not nearly as fun as I thought it would be. Supercute mug shot though.

I thought that my dad had relinquished the idea of me attending college, since I clearly hadn't taken to it, but he was insistent that I try again, this time suggesting that I attempt a more serious education at a more serious school. At the end of the summer, he called in a favor with one of his old college buddies from his Cambridge days and got me into some stupid school I'd never even heard of.

Brown University

The great thing about Brown is that tons of celebs' kids go there, and the awful thing about Brown is that tons of celebs' kids go there. What people don't get about most Ivy League schools is that at least 15 percent of the student body is there because someone called in a favor. I guess I should have felt bad to have taken a more deserving student's place, but I was actually glad to be leaving LA. My dreams of being the next Cate Blanchett weren't panning out, and my dad was dating a psycho gold-digger that I just couldn't deal with. I also wasn't going to be missing out on much socially. Gen was wrapped up in some sick relationship with one of the guys who invented Facebook, and Roman had left LA to do a study abroad program in Croatia. It was time for me to spread my wings and leave the nest. Providence, Rhode Island, was not really my East Coast destination of choice (I prefer NYC), but I felt like I could get behind a New England Colonial house moment. I mean, they're gorgeous. What's not to love?

I was entering as a freshman at age nineteen. This was only mildly embarrassing, because I arrived at Brown looking fifteen, thanks to having three microdermabrasion treatments and a tri-enzyme resurfacing facial the month before I left. I arrived in a collegiate ensemble of Louis Vuitton monogram everything, but had packed mostly Prada, Chanel, a couple Hermès pieces, and several furs in preparation for the cold weather and preppy student body. The campus was gorgeous and old, but I was expecting to be staying in my own place. I'd gotten a letter saying I'd be living in "Plantations House," which I interpreted as being a charming, Civil War–era estate, and I had already mapped out my decorating scheme. It wasn't until I arrived at registration that I discovered that "Plantations House" was in fact a "dorm" building, and that I was going to be living in a "dorm room" with a "roommate" named "Christine." Never. Upon hearing this information, I immediately turned and walked in the opposite

direction until I arrived at a chic little art school that was practically across the street.

Rhode Island School of Design

After escaping the stifling conformity of Brown, arriving at RISD was like returning to myself. I was at art school, surrounded by like-minded individuals. Finally! It's hard to explain, but it wasn't until I was truly immersed that I realized my calling was probably to be an artist. From the moment I stepped foot on campus at the Rhode Island School of Design, I felt artsy-er. There was a shift in how I saw the world and how the world saw me. I felt like I might finally be understood for who I was. I could be me—a bitch. A ponytailed art gay on a bike even flew past me and shouted, "Hey, hooker, nice bag!"

I was home.

Thankfully, RISD's classes started two weeks after Brown's, so I had time to find an apartment, rent a studio space, and text my dad the news that I had transferred. He called me to say that he wasn't pleased, but I'd already used his credit card to pay for fall tuition, so there was nothing he could do about it. Plus he was happy that I seemed to have found a passion for education, and impressed that I'd finagled my way into the most selective art school in the country, so he let me do my thing.

There are so many wonderful elements about art school . . . where do I begin? Art school gives you the opportunity to explore yourself and experiment with your boundaries. It's all about *you doing you* 24/7 and saying "fuck off" to anyone who tries to tell you that you can't. I hadn't fully dealt with being forced to give up my dreams of being an actress, so I used art school as a form of therapy to come to terms with myself. I majored in glass blowing, which was a really perfect metaphor for who I was as a person at that time: fragile, malleable when heated, beautiful, easily broken . . . you get the picture. My minor was "gender performance in non-Western documentary." The longer it takes to say your major/minor out loud, the less people will want to talk to you about school.

I never went to class, but I occasionally visited my glass-blowing seminar because the teacher, Kurt, was superhot and hairy in this weirdo hippie way. Normally I would never—but I was really drawn to his bun, beard, and clogs combination.

There are so many freaks at art school, and I loved it. Short freaks, medium-sized freaks, VHS freaks, and completely average freaks. They were everywhere, and I was into the feeling of living on another planet. I was soaking up the energy of being on that campus, around so many "creative" kids. I met a ton of super-amazing artists, and we all got really close. Even though we came from different backgrounds (some upper middle class and some upper class), we managed to bond over our mutual appreciation for carefree drug use, color wheels, and impromptu tattoos. (Mine have since been removed because my dad flipped.) I had my first group sex experience, which was not as weird as I hoped it would be, and I was even friends with a fat girl, which was totally out of character for me, but she was totally sweet and funny and really just GOT IT.

I knew a boy from Palm Beach who came to RISD wearing white linen shorts and a pastel yellow Vineyard Vines polo, with ambitions of being the next Alexander Calder (typical). Two months and an LSD addiction later, he was covered in tattoos and only wore eighties Adidas jumpsuits. He also made a lot of art out of cum. There was this other girl, Melody, who had totally beautiful hair and was totally my friend until one day she was dared to eat a live rat for $20. When her parents got wind that the dare could be seen on YouTube, they pulled her out of school. Poor girl. Maybe next time don't film it?

My best friend was this tiny creature of a girl named Aubrey, who thought it was appropriate to wear a Mao Zedong–inspired high-collared suit every day of the week. She was a print-making major who grew up somewhere in Northern California, and I don't mean Acceptable-Neo-Bohemian-San-Francisco Northern California, I mean Nothing-Up-Here-Besides-Meth-Matters-To-Anyone Northern California. We met in the seaweed section of the local grocery co-op when Aubrey asked me if I could reach the Dead Sea salts she was eyeing on the top shelf.

"Hey, skinny girl, can you grab me one of those blue jars off the top shelf?" I heard a raspy voice say. I turned around.

"Oh . . . um, yes. Sure. Sorry, I'm just a little taken aback by your whole look." I got the salt down and handed it to her. "Here ya go, less skinny girl. Or is it boy?"

"I'm Aubrey. Some people call me Audrey. Some people call me Jeff. I'm a girl, but not really a big fan of gender identification. Thanks for the hand, I'll see you around."

"No problem," I said, smiling. "By the way, chic flattop."

I knew from the second I saw her that she would be the perfect weird art friend, and she'd make me look super-tall and thin in pictures, so a strong bond was born.

I thought Aubrey was an amazing artist, and I loved all of her friends—or at least I thought I did at the time. I bought into everything they were about. I started using annoying words like "politicize," "subversion," and "sex-positive." My new friends convinced me to sleep with Kurt, but not for a better grade. It was all part of a group project that we were working on called *Daddy Tissues.*

Unbeknownst to me, art school was bringing out the worst version of myself. I got really into drinking and psychedelics while I was at RISD. I thought that if I constantly wrote down all of my feelings, then I could justify my drinking and write it off as artistic expression. So that's what I did. I became a raging alcoholic. I drank whiskey for breakfast, lunch, and dinner, which many people would have considered unhealthy, but I think I remember my nutritionist once saying something about fermented grain being coconut water before coconut water was coconut water.

I bleached my hair, grew a dreadlock, and never took off this very busy, very Helena Bonham Carter–y, Vivienne Westwood frock with layers and cutouts. I wore it every single day, without dry cleaning it once. Of course, I ripped the tag out in case any of my friends ever doubted that it was a vintage wedding dress dyed black (a lie I told them all). I started telling people shit like "I make all my clothes myself," and "Oh, I don't even know where I got this. It was three cents," and "I just found this in the dumpster yesterday."

My bullshit reached a fever pitch one night when Aubrey was over at my place. We had ingested enough mushrooms to kill a pug and were talking about nothing/Marxism.

"I'm so sick of feeling like it's my responsibility as a member of the proletariat to be happy," I complained to a very high Aubrey.

"Babe, I get it. NO, Babe! I totally get it. It's like my dad always says: money can't buy you happiness, only sappiness."

"What the fuck is that supposed to mean?" I said.

"I'm just like, talking about how I haven't trusted my father since he voted for Bush in the second election. It's like, what my installation at the dining hall was about. You were there, Babe.

You lit that plate of pasta on fire, remember? It was totally important."

"So important. I feel so like, weighed down by my possessions, you know? It's like, what do these clothes even mean?" I looked at myself in the mirror. "I keep telling people I make my own clothes, but I don't. I *buy* them. This kimono is Dior."

And that's when we came up with the brilliant idea for a performance art piece: I would make a bonfire, in the middle of the street, out of all the designer clothes in my closet. This is incredibly hard for me to describe, as I still have a realistic fear that I may go to hell after doing what I did with Aubrey that night, but I'll do my best to recall the events as they unfolded.

We were acting like total maniacs and cackling like Miranda when she thinks Carrie's made a really good pun about Samantha's vagina. We began by breaking the heels off of all my shoes. Then I think I squirted an entire tube of red acrylic paint at a hanging rack of Hermès scarves and ripped a fringed Prada skirt to pieces. Aubrey shredded a beautiful neon Christopher Kane raincoat with a pair of sewing scissors. I put my Fendi spy bag on my head like a cap and pulled out every article of clothing from my closet, tossing it to Aubrey, who tossed it out the window.

My entire wardrobe, all the contents of my closet, went out the window of my second-story artist's loft that my dad had rented for me and into an enormous pile in the middle of the street. We even threw a lamp and a chair out there. They were superexpensive so they had to go.

Aubrey and I ran downstairs like it was Christmas fucking morning and lit the whole pile on fire. This was the finale of our grand performance piece. At the time, we thought this was a transcendental, sacrificial moment. The last thing I remember doing was taking off my Westwood dress and throwing it in the blaze. I was screaming, dancing around, and crying too. Why was I crying? Couldn't tell you. Anyone who's ever blacked out while committing arson knows what I'm talking about.

I guess the cops arrived on the scene at some point, because I kind of got arrested that night. According to the police report, I bit an officer who tried to restrain me, then resisted arrest and ran around the block screaming the following things at the cops:

"I'm a monster baby, so don't YOU fuck with my face!"

"I want to be free like your daughters! My friends are prisoners!"

"Adopt me!"

"All hail Coco Chanel! The clown queen!"

They took me, kicking and squealing, to the station. I told the officer who took me in to "take me home, my maid is making dinner!" I had given up dinner for lent that year, so that was a complete and total lie. They made me blow into one thing and pee into a different thing and then they threw me in a group cell with three other jailed ladies, who probably thought I was a celebrity. I passed out when they took my mug shot, like fell right to the floor. I'd had my fun and was done with my night.

Twenty-four hours later, I woke up in a cab sitting next to Mabinty. If there is anyone in my life I can always count on besides my dad, it's her. She is my angel, if angels were more like maid/bff/potheads who fly in from LA to bail you out of jail in Rhode Island.

"Mabinty, I'm so glad you got my message."

I hadn't called her. I'd used my one phone call to call my psychic, who was not surprised. Clearly, I was still a fucking mess from the night before.

"I got arrested!" I laughed. "It was so dumb, ohmigod, Mabinty, NO, it was SO DUMB. What is this adorable beret you're wearing? It's giving your whole face a new shape. I miss you!"

"Babe Walker, yuh takin' mushrooms, yuh lightin' yuh clothes on fiyah, yuh ago get yuself killed one of dese days. Mi don' wan be around fi dat. Mi dun wid yuh wild ways." She was not amused.

"Mabs, I'm fiiiiiiiine. You don't need to worry about me. The mushrooms I took must've been laced. It's no biggie. Genevieve has been arrested like fifty times, and her record is still sparkly clean. I love you and I appreciate that you bailed me out, now please go back to LA and tell my dad that everything here is great. Everything will be fine," I said with a wink.

"Yuh say yuh fine, but dis be di last time I cum fi yuh. Next time mi no cum to yuh rescue. Trust what mi tell yuh." And with that she dropped me off at my apartment, and I went on with my heinous art school lifestyle . . . for a few more months.

I can laugh about that night now, but inside I'm still crying a little bit. The whole jail thing was a blip in the grand scheme of my artist moment, and I'll never get those clothes back no matter how many hours I spend on eBay. I was such a different girl then, and honestly, 2012 Babe needs to slap 2007 Babe across her smelly face because 2007 Babe was a fool.

A year after my installation/arrest, *Art Forum* ran an article about my couture-burning incident. They said I was some kind of rebellious "Hollywood Wunderkind" that was subverting her own privilege and lack of awareness through her art. Whatever the fuck that means. I was a little embarrassed by the attention, but it didn't piss me off too much because I had moved on by then. I'm not even sure what subversion is exactly.

I hate my horse.

After spring semester at RISD, I invited four of my closest friends to come back to California with me for the summer and live at my dad's Montecito ranch. I imagined it as being a very free-spirited, bonfire-y, Ryan McGinley-y, three-month festival of hallucinogens. I figured that the ranch would be the perfect venue for Aubrey, Ishi, Sasha, Harrison, and I to explore the subconscious, pseudo-political beasts within us all. We flew to California just days after our spring semester ended, and dove into a dope fest/art fest. The fun was fueled by a lot of whiskey from my dad's private collection and some peyote Ishi's parents sent over from Nevada.

The first few days were outrageous. Picture five naked hipsters laughing in a bathtub, five naked hipsters in a waterfall screaming, five naked hipsters on a sand dune jumping in the air, five naked hipsters killing a man in the woods, five naked hipsters climbing a tree in the middle of the night, high on salvia. All the typical shit. Gen and Roman came out to visit, but only stayed for a total of fifteen minutes because they said everyone seemed too homeless and too naked. Whatever. We were all so fucking hot, tan, and skandy (skinny/sandy)—it was heaven. We planned to document everything and turn it into a video installation, but our fun was cut short when I broke my back riding a horse over Memorial Day weekend.

I remember that night like it was yesterday: my hair was back to its natural color, I was wearing a pair of Emmanuelle Khanh sunglasses (it was midnight) and knee-high Hermès riding boots, and my nails were au naturel with one coat of clear on them. I had orchestrated a photo shoot featuring me on my favorite horse. I was in the barn with Aubrey and Ishi, and was posing naked while they took photos for their respective blogs. P.S. We were all on a ton of mushrooms, so everything we were doing seemed like a great idea at the time.

This particular horse was a Friesian, whom I'd named Mischa Barton as a fun joke. Mischa was a gift I'd received from Elton and David for my Sweet 16 and had been my confidant and spiritual guide since the day I laid eyes on his strong body. Side note: Mischa was named "Body of the Year" at the Santa Barbara National Amateur Horse Show in 2003.

I was on Mischa's back, trying to convey with my body that I was artsy and broken, when somebody snapped a photo of his eyeball. The flash must have terrified the horse, because he reared up and threw me off. The details are a bit fuzzy, but I remember landing on the ground and hearing a sickening crunch. I was flat on my back. Mischa cantered in circles around my

limp body, as if to say, "I'm kind of sorry," to which I replied, "You're a cunt." I was in the worst pain of my life and tripping pretty hard from the mushrooms. So, naturally, I started screaming like a banshee. Not cute.

The next thing I knew, I was being strapped down to a stretcher by three EMTs who I thought were trying to kidnap me. I was scared and furious, so I started flailing my arms wildly as I floated in and out of consciousness. I found out later that I broke one of the EMT's noses. Trust me when I tell you that he looks so much better now than he did then. He actually wrote me a thank-you note when his new nose healed. What a sweetheart.

Long story short, I woke up in the hospital faced with the cruel reality that I'd sustained a compression fracture of one of my lumbar vertabrae (L1). The doctors explained that I'd undergone major surgery and that, while I would definitely make a full recovery, I'd have to spend the rest of the summer in bed. I had Aubrey, Ishi, Sasha, and Harrison sent back to their respective towns of origin so I could heal in a pure, lonely, depressed, dark environment. (The only silver lining was that I lost six pounds during my hospital stay.)

I was released a week later. Mabinty came to get me, and we went straight back to the Montecito house so I could spend the rest of my recovery in peace and quiet. I would've rather gone back home to Bel Air, but Mabinty informed me that my dad had dropped the psycho gold-digger and acquired some new side-piece girlfriend thing, and I just couldn't deal. The Montecito house would have to do. When I was wheeled into my bedroom, I was assaulted by hundreds of hideous bouquets. They were everywhere. Sunflowers, daisies, carnations, and BALLOONS?! Who the fuck were these well-wishers and had they even met me?

The shock of the accident snapped me out of the weird, artsy mind frame I had been brainwashed into at RISD. Getting severely injured during a bullshit photo shoot for someone's bullshit blog made me realize how silly and fake I'd been acting all this time. That just wasn't me. It would never be me. I'm not the girl who spray paints her teal snakeskin Fendi leather jacket black because she wants to impress some smelly sickos. I'm not the girl who doesn't wash her hair for five days. I'm not the girl who wears Chuck Taylors. I was grateful for the opportunity to be purged of the dirty, tattooey thing that had become my life, but I was pissed that I had to break my back to get there.

Mabinty gave me a little pep talk one night. She could see I wasn't going to get through this experience without some extra love.

"Yuh down on yuh self deary. Mabinty cyan see dat in yuh eyes. But dis, dis yuh time to pull it together. Nobody on dis god damned eart cyan save yuh besides yuhself, yuh know dat. Mi wan yuh do sumting fi Mabinty. Mi wan yuh to repeat afta Mabinty." She placed her hand on my forehead. "Mi dun. Mi dun. Just sey dat ova and ova to yuhself, Babe. Mi promise yuh go feel betta by sunrise, yuh hear mi now."

Mabinty was right, I was down on myself. My four-poster bed had become my personal Alcatraz. I was a prisoner in my own skin. The pain was borderline unbearable. My back brace made me look fat. I lost the very little muscle tone I had in my legs, my roots were obscene, and I was wearing sweats, exclusively. I couldn't move. I couldn't sleep. I missed Barneys. Even though my dad had all the best doctors and physical therapists working with me, my soul was unwilling to let my body heal. I turned into a gremlin. I hated everyone, and they hated me. I spent my days ignoring my physical therapist and my nights crying, alone. Mabinty even tried to perform a voodoo exorcism on my demons, but all the eggs broke, and all the goats died.

The morning after my failed exorcism, something extraordinary happened that changed my whole perspective. I got a package from Tai Tai that contained some items intended to cheer me up. Included in the package was a letter.

My Dearest Barbara,

I am so very sorry to hear about your accident. In Asia right now, and there's no cell phone service at the monastery, so please accept this care package along with my condolences. I remember being bitten by a black mamba in Uganda. I was paralyzed for a week. I used a piece of charcoal and my mouth to write down all of my thoughts. To this day I believe that the power of the written word is what helped me to heal. That and the anti-venom.

Love,

Your Tai Tai

In addition to the letter, Tai Tai had sent me a book about hormones written by Suzanne Somers, and a Smythson notebook. A diary of sorts, with lizard-skin binding. It had been personalized with my initials on the front cover, and the color was the most tranquil of jades. The gift really perked me up, and I knew it was just the dose of sophistication I needed in order to recover. I decided to write poetry.

Thus began a renewing period of my life that I now refer to as my "Babe emerging from the darkness of unremitting suffering" phase. I really focused my efforts on creating the most powerful poems that have ever been written. I'm convinced that without the poems and that chic little notebook, I would have never fully recovered.

Every day I wrote, I got better. I had a purpose again. I wasn't just a worthless blob who barked orders at people that worked for me, I was a creative blob. The notebook was what I really needed to give myself the permission to heal. It took the whole summer and four more of the lizard-skin notebooks, but I made a full recovery.

Here is a sampling of some of my strongest works:

Dream Lover

You lay me down in the grass.

It's wet.

I'm wet.

Your name is Josh.

Hartnett.

Sonnet #17

I will not be confined to my own bed
For I have lost touch with the me in me
So much of life has gone with things unsaid
I'm past the point where life is what I see.
Oh stop, it is a never ending dark
It looks as though there's dust upon my heart,
I am the star to no one but Mabinty,
My Worth's unclear although I'm at the start.
My back won't bend, though glossy lips appear
Upon my face so I must take some rest.
Will I embrace the space and have no fear
For what is clear is I have tried my best.
If what I find is at the end I'm wrong,
Then I will spare you more sad sullen songs.

*I only wrote one sonnet, because sonnets are really fucking hard and long, but I called it Sonnet #17 because I like the number 17

My Hands

My hands are perfect

i have

Perfect

hands

A Babe Haiku

A fallen dress is green.

Couture at rest.

The cold breeds the cold. I die.

Getting There

I'm like a prisoner.

I'm like a prison.

I'm like a total freak.

I'm like getting better.

I'm like positive that Tom Cruise is not gay.

I'm like a moment.

I'm like a song about a song.

I'm like a bird.

I'm like freezing right now.

I'm like me, again.

*This is tattooed on my side, in French

I AM

Je suis.

Sorry for texting you ninety-three times last night.

I was ready to go back to school, but I had no idea what to study next. Hollywood wasn't ready for me yet, and the art world was clearly too dangerous. Thankfully, I'd cut ties with my RISD friends and was back on good terms with Roman and Gen after my accident. At the tail end of my healing process, I had an epiphany that I needed to devote my life to something that would merge my love of art and my love of myself. That's when it hit me—I would be a fashion designer.

Parsons School of Design

I enrolled at Parsons as a freshman, because they wouldn't accept my previous total of six credit hours from my time at USC, Brown, and RISD. I'm not good at grades, get off me. I was back on the East Coast, but this time I was in the right city, the only real American city, New York. My dad and I had a serious heart-to-heart while I was in recovery from my accident, and he'd decided to let me have a clean slate and start over. Mabinty and I flew to New York and picked out an apartment for me to rent in Nolita. Once I was settled in, I fully committed myself to becoming a slave to fashion.

The secret to excelling at fashion school is 90 percent looking the part and 10 percent actual schoolwork. I spent most of the semester meticulously curating my outfits and being at the right parties at the right time. Also, due to my extensive hallucinogen use, it was super-easy to come up with concepts and mood boards. Like, for a capsule collection of jumpsuits I dreamed up this whole under-the-sea-on-the-moon vibe that earned me stellar grades during finals, and one of my professors even asked if he could use some of my fashion illustrations in a textbook he was writing. I came out of my first semester at Parsons with a 4.0 GPA and a mission to be the next Diane von Furstenberg. Instead of going home for Christmas break, my dad and Tai Tai came to New York to toast to my success. It seemed I had finally found my calling.

Because I'd done so well my first semester, I decided it would be okay to skip the first day of my second semester, so I went to Barneys to pick up a very important Celine bag that no one had bought me for Christmas. The first day of class is always the same anyways. Teachers, books, students, turn your cell phone off, raise your hand. I get it.

The weather was insane. A perfect wintry day. It was cold, but not too cold, and snowy but not slushy. My Celine purse and

I went to the top of the Empire State Building, which I know is the cheesiest, but she'd never been there before and I thought it would be a really cute *Sleepless in Seattle* moment for both of us to treasure and remember forever. Then we grabbed a light lunch of mixed greens and Diet Coke and headed uptown to Central Park.

I was sitting on a park bench, texting Genevieve about my new purchase.

Babe 2:35PM	Guess what I got.
Genevieve 2:36PM	Your HPV vaccination? Finally?
Babe 2:36PM	No. You are beyond rude. Hang on let me text you a pic.

Celine was sitting on my lap because there was no fucking way I was going to let her touch a filthy New York bench, and I could not get a flattering picture of us together. I felt someone tap me on the shoulder. Irritated that my moment was being interrupted, I whipped around and came face-to-face with a man's chiseled visage, complete with chocolatey eyes and shaggy brown hair. Supercute, super-straight, and super-fuckable.

"Hi," he said. "I'm Robert."

"Hi, Robert."

"Were you in Barneys earlier?" he asked, smiling.

"Um, who wants to know?"

"I thought I saw you in there earlier, buying that bag." He pointed to Celine.

"Maybe I was, maybe I wasn't. You tell me, stalker."

I turned around and went back to trying to take a picture,

which may have been kind of cold/bitchy, but guys love bitches. And I didn't want to make it too easy for this sexy "Robert" person. He was wearing a suit, and was so tousled and cute, and muscular but not too muscular.

He sat down next to me.

"You're never going to get a good angle sitting like that," he said. "Here, let me see your phone."

"Excuse me?"

"Your phone," he repeated, taking my phone out of my hand and pointing it at me. "Now, smile."

I was beyond shocked, but I pulled myself together and flashed my pearly whites.

"Beautiful." He handed my phone back to me. I looked at the picture. Celine and I looked GORGEOUS.

"Wow," I said. "Thanks. Sometimes I'm not as photogenic as you'd think I'd be, but this turned out perfectly."

"I'll say."

"I'm Babe Walker."

"Nice to meet you, Babe Walker. Can I take you to dinner tonight?"

"Well, Robert, I normally only do liquids after six-fifteen."

"Would you make an exception for a sushi restaurant that serves really small portions?"

"Did you just ask me to marry you?"

"Not yet."

Over dinner I found out that Robert was a sports agent, with a great sense of humor, who loved his job and had season tickets to the Knicks. He also had a passion for shopping at Barneys and was there getting fitted for a suit for his friend's wedding when he saw me picking up Celine Deneuve Jezebel Walker (I'd given her a full name), and then took spotting me in the park after his lunch meeting as "a sign that he had to ask me out." In addition to being six-foot-four and handsome, Robert also had a huge dick. I knew this because waist size + neck girth ÷ length of ring finger = dick size. I also knew this because we fucked on the couch, and on the bed, and in the kitchen of his incredible Tribeca loft. Normally I don't give it up on the first date, but Robert and I obviously had an intense connection.

After four more dates, we were officially boyfriend and girlfriend, and it was incredible. He was the Francisco Costa to my Calvin Klein: a complete rejuvenation of my brand. His laid-back approach to life was the perfect complement to my passionate nature. He loved my love for fashion and really supported my dreams of being a designer, which inspired me to work a lot harder in school. He was also really funny. I mean, I consider myself the most hilarious person I know, but Robert was a close second. Plus he was super-athletic, and because of this, I even started running a couple miles a week (which was disgusting and slobbery at first but became really chic once I bit the bullet and bought the entire Stella McCartney for Adidas line).

A few months into dating, everything was going spectacularly. Until the transition happened. It was a Saturday. We'd spent the day sleeping in and walking around the city being cuddly, then had plans to go to a Knicks game that night. Even though I don't give a shit about sports, I'll always give a shit about courtside seats. It's just who I am. After the game, Robert took me to his favorite Italian restaurant, where I actually ate pasta (whole wheat) for the first time in four years. It was so romantic. It was unnerving. I could feel myself falling in love with him, so I ordered a few glasses of white wine to take the edge off. I was a little drunk after dinner, and when we got back to my apartment, I felt like being naughty so I pulled a joint out of my bedside drawer.

Pot has a tricky way of making me want to fuck like I'm sixteen and the world is ending. So there we were: stoned, making out, ripping each other's clothes off, and then having The. Best. Sex. Of. My. Life. He was on top, then I was on top, then we were side by side, then we were scissoring, then I was riding him reverse cowgirl, then we were on this rocking chair I have that turned out to be amazing to fuck on, and I was looking into his eyes and I didn't know whether I was going to come or die. I started screaming.

"I fucking love youuuuuuuuuu!"

Immediately after saying that, I regretted it. Too soon? No. Robert was into it. Really into it.

"I fucking love you too! I fucking love you, Babe!"

"No I love you. I love you!" I panted, fucking his brains out.

"I LOVE YOU, BABE WALKER!" he roared. "Oh my God!"

"AGHHHHHHHHROBERRRRRTTTTTTT!!!"

We must have both passed out after that, because the next morning I woke up and Robert was gone. Fuck. I knew it—I'd freaked him out. He was gone forever, and I was about to be that crazy chick who dropped the "I love you" way too soon in the relationship. I choked back a scream-cry, rolled over, grabbed my phone, and sent a text to Robert.

Babe 9:27AM Where are you?

I was about to speed-dial my therapist when all of a sudden I heard a toilet flush and Robert walked out of the bathroom.

"Where the hell were you!?" I demanded. *Whoa*, I thought to myself, *where did that come from?* I hadn't meant to sound so harsh. "Sorry," I said. "I got scared that you left and you were never coming back."

"I was just in the bathroom, Babe. Are you okay? Come here." Robert got in bed and leaned toward me for a kiss.

I pushed him away.

"No way, Jose. I don't like kissing you first thing in the morning. Especially when you've brushed your teeth more recently than I have. It's just one of my insecurities, so next time just tell me when you're going to brush your teeth, okay? Is that so hard?"

"Um, will do, Boss," Robert said, laughing.

"So you're mocking me now?" I didn't know what was happening, but I couldn't stop the words from coming out of my mouth.

"What?"

"First you abandon me, then you won't kiss me because I have morning breath—were you texting someone in the bathroom?" He *definitely* hadn't been texting anyone—his phone had been charging on the nightstand the entire time.

"Babe—what's going on?"

"I don't know. You tell me, cheater. Let me see your phone."

"Wha—"

"PHONE!"

"Here!" he yelled, grabbing his phone off the nightstand

and handing it to me. "What is up with you right now? You're acting crazy."

"I'm fine," I said. "I just want to see who you're sexting with. Okay, here it is. One text, two minutes ago, from me. 'Where are you?' . . ." I trailed off.

Something was wrong. Really fucking wrong. I mean, I definitely wouldn't classify myself as a low-maintenance dish, but psycho is never on the menu when it comes to my dating style. What in the world was happening to me?! I loved this guy, so why was I acting so mental? Then it hit me: Babette was back.

BABETTE (2 *syll.* ba-bette, bab-ette) [the girl's name Babette is pronounced as BahB-Et (French origin)] : stranger; traveler from a foreign land; foreign woman

You know that feeling when you're in a relationship with someone and you know you're acting totally irrational and weird but you just can't stop? Babette is that version of me. She does whatever she wants, whenever she wants. Babette is hyperemotional, needy, sensitive, erratic, and tacky—you name a negative quality and Babette's got it. She completely takes over my entire personality when I'm legit in love with someone, and there's nothing I can do about it.

Babette had been in hibernation until this moment. From this point on, I feel it necessary to refer to Babette in the third person, as none of the following actions are a true representation of who I am as a human being.

Robert hustled out the door shortly after my interrogation that morning, running off to a business brunch. The rest of the day went by and I didn't hear from him at all. Didn't he even care? Babette decided to call Robert and check in a few times. The phone went straight to voice mail, so she left messages.

8:00PM: *"Hola Roberto. Just checking in on you. Give me a call when you get this. I miss you. What are you up to? How was brunch? My day was pretty good. Where are you? Okay, well hopefully you get this and call me soon. I love you!"*

8:30PM: *"Honey where are you? This is so unlike you—should I be worried? Do I need to call the police? Just text me and let me know you're okay."*

9:00PM: *"Okay mister, now I'm pissed."*

9:30PM: *"I'm pregnant. I hope you're having fun. P.S. We're broken up now, so don't you dare call me back."*

I wasn't pregnant, and I'd had no intention of telling Robert a lie of such epic proportions, but Babette was in control, and that bitch does whatever she wants. She even called him one last time at 10 P.M. and left one final voice mail consisting of sniffles and whimpers for two minutes and forty-nine seconds.

Robert was at the door of my apartment the next morning. Babette answered, wearing a tank top and underwear.

"Hey you," she said to Robert. "What a surprise! You look really tired and cute. I have a great idea—let's go get a Jamba!" Babette loves Jamba Juice.

"No, Babe. I don't want a Jamba. Are you really pregnant?" Robert asked.

"What are you talking about?"

"You left me a voice mail last night saying you were pregnant."

"Oh, that? False alarm. I got my period this morning. Such a good thing too, because being a single mom is hard, and I don't think I could trust you enough to marry you right now. Where have you been? Why are you wearing those shoes? You know I hate them. You need a Jamba."

"Babe," Robert said, looking concerned, "I don't know what's up with you, but I think we should take some time and not talk for a few days, and then touch base when you're feeling more like yourself."

"We're not even together anymore, Robert, so do me a favor and stop acting like my dad. God, you're so possessive," Babette said, shutting the door in his face. "Byeeeeeee."

That night, Babette thought it would be a great idea to surprise Robert at a Knicks game. She got all dolled up in thigh-high boots and a Knicks jersey that she belted and wore as a dress. She told her cabdriver to "take her to the basketball place." Babette got to Madison Square Garden and finagled her way into the locker room, where she found Robert hanging out with some of the players.

"Hey, Eight-Incher," Babette said in a low, sultry voice.

Needless to say, Robert was pretty surprised to see Babette.

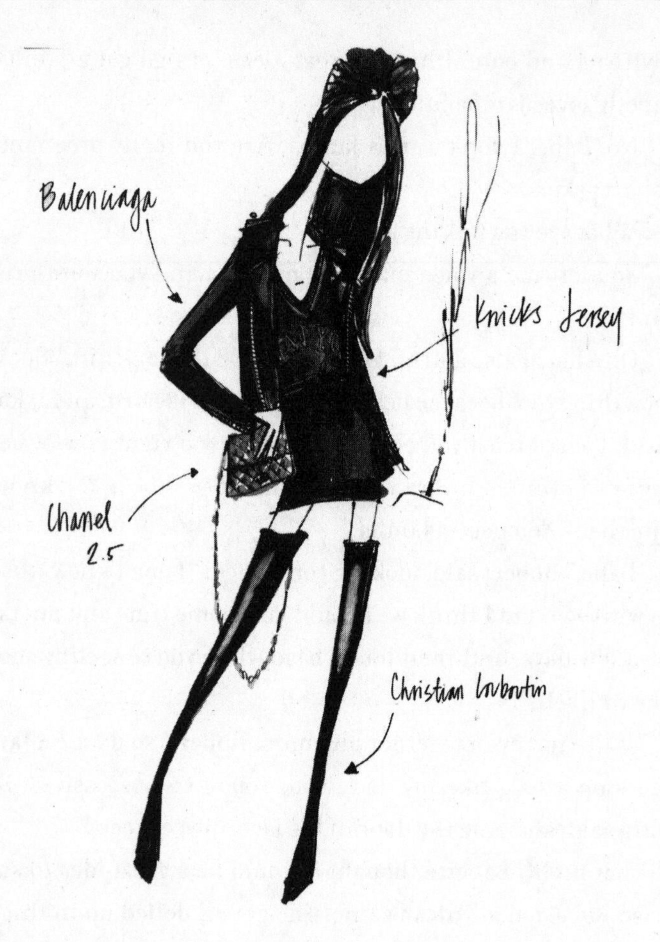

Especially when she threw her arms around him and kissed him on the lips.

"How did you get in here?" he asked, forcing an uncomfortable smile.

"Aren't you going to introduce me to your really tall, really nice-looking friends?" Babette asked, looking around suggestively. She nodded and winked at one of the players. "Robert talks shit about you all the time, don't you, honey?" Babette laughed a little too loud. "Just kidding. You're huge. Do you play football?"

So embarrassing. Normally I'm great at talking to pro athletes. Robert pulled me gently into the hall.

"Look," he said, "I don't know who you are right now, or what you think you're doing here, but you are literally scaring the shit out of me. I miss the Babe Walker I knew and was in love with a couple days ago. That girl was so beautiful, so sure of herself, and had such an amazing sense of humor—what happened to her?"

That was so sweet, and I wanted to hug him and start over, putting Babette's reign of terror behind us both. But Babette had a different idea.

"Oh, okay. Well next time, why don't you just tell me I look fat to my FUCKING FACE!" she screamed. "I'm over it. Bye."

Babette stormed out of MSG and decided to take advantage of being near Times Square and go out for the night. She loves chain restaurants, so she found the nearest Hooters and ordered herself a pitcher of sangria. Then she found some out-of-towner-bro–types and made them buy her shots and Hooterstizers and take pictures with her. She immediately uploaded the photos to a Facebook album entitled, *Single and the City*. Around 1:30 A.M., Babette started drunk-texting Robert:

1:28AM: I love you.

1:28AM: I'm sorry.

1:33AM: Do you hate me?

1:39AM: Fuck uuuuuuuuuuuuuuuuu.

1:45AM: I didn't mean that. I'm sorry.

1:51AM: Actally I dod mean that. FUK. YOU.

1:51AM: Fick you

1:52AM: Where aret u?

1:52AM: Send me bavk those Loubs u borowed or I'm goig to rip your eybals out next time I c u [meant for Genevieve, sent to Robert by mistake]

1:53AM: Sorry. That text wasnt 4 u.

1:59AM: Do u even care?

2:12AM: Over it.

2:13AM: Over it.

2:14AM: Over it.

2:15AM: Over it.

2:16AM: Over it.

2:17AM: OVERIT.

2:18AM: OVerit.

2:20AM: Over. It.

2:25AM: O

2:26AM: V

2:27AM: E

2:28AM: R

3:00AM: it.

3:27AM: I'm os sorry. I love you.

3:30AM: Going home w Mitch frm Arizona hes fuckng hot and Im so horny.

3:32AM: What are you doing? You should com here.

4:14AM: Where am I?

4:15AM: Are u ok? I'm alittl worried.

4:19AM: Did u get my text. I calld the police.

4:20AM: woooo 4 20 wooooooo! I'm with all these guys and Im os stoned right now.

4:30AM: Want 2 hang out? All my friends want to meet uu

4:32AM: Fine dont text me. 2 can ply that game mister.

4:33AM: ok

This chain of texts was the last straw for my poor, beloved Robert. He called me the next morning and broke things off completely, telling me to lose his number. Somewhere during Robert's breakup speech, I came out of my Babette haze long enough to explain that I had freaked out because I loved him, but he didn't care. He was done, which meant I was left alone with Babette, again.

Being the *Fatal Attraction* BITCH that she is, Babette couldn't accept that it was over. She texted Robert incessantly until he changed his phone number, then she stalked him until he moved to an unlisted address. I, on the other hand, threw myself into finishing my spring semester, enrolled promptly in an anger management course, and started focusing heavily on my long-distance video-chat therapy with Susan. Despite these positive measures, I ultimately spiraled into a nervous breakdown that sent me fleeing to London to be with my Tai Tai once the school year had ended.

My grandmother is milking the shit out of this one.

I had to get out of New York.

Central Saint Martins College of Art and Design

Thanks to my above average grades at Parsons, and thanks to my grandmother being one of the most connected women in the London fashion scene since the sixties (she was Twiggy before Twiggy was Twiggy), I was allowed to transfer to Central Saint Martins for an independent study program. I threw myself headfirst into my work and designed a line of ethni-chic turbans that Tai Tai started wearing to society events all over London. Harrods even ordered fifty of them for fall. Tai Tai had always flitted in and out of my life, so it was nice to spend some quality time with her. We were really bonding, and things were kind of on the up and up, but all of that changed when tragedy struck.

I woke up one morning to find a note from Tai Tai in the refrigerator, saying that she'd left the country to go on a safari vision quest in Namibia. She'd taped it to the hemp milk, where she knew I'd find it. Tai Tai was the bald eagle of uncaged free spirits, so I didn't think twice about her sudden disappearance. A week later, I found out that she'd been mauled by a lion.

When the Namibian police officer told us that Tai Tai was wearing her favorite zebra-skin trench coat at the time of her death, I knew it wasn't an accident. After an autopsy, it was discovered that Tai Tai had a rare bone cancer and hadn't had very long to live. She was not the kind of person to let anyone—or anything for that matter—rule her destiny, so she had chosen to cut her losses, keep her hair, and take matters into her own hands. She had planned the whole thing. The lion that killed her sits, stuffed, in my dad's study and scares the shit out of me every time I see it.

My grandmother's last will and testament requested that her circle of friends and family come to Africa to spread her ashes on the dunes of Namibia, which meant I was going to need a lot more print-heavy, shapeless, smock-type garments. I partook in a mini shopping spree on the way to Heathrow Airport. Every cloud.

Tai Tai's death had really affected me deeply, especially after we'd had such an amazing time living together and drinking together in London. My grandmother was an amazing human being. She was unlike anyone I'd ever met and I respected her for it. She knew what she wanted, got what she wanted, and did so with a measure of grace that made you realize that she operated on another level.

Even though her façade always seemed inviting, Tai Tai was trained in the art of cuntyness. For example, if offered a basket of bread before a meal, she would invariably administer a freezing-cold death stare, leaving the waiter with no choice but to scurry away, bread basket in hand. The night I got my first period, we were having dinner at the Polo Lounge and she stood up and made a celebratory toast to the entire restaurant, including my father, his girlfriend, and the headmaster at my school, who happened to be at the restaurant with her husband celebrating their wedding anniversary. Tai Tai was an incredibly generous tipper, both with cash and advice, which usually came in the form of a backhanded remark. "Next week, when you hand me my check, please try and look a little less Spanish," she'd say, smiling and pressing a $100 bill into the waiter's palm. Tai Tai's absolute favorite game was to tell people we were sisters.

I met my dad at the Johannesburg airport, where we took a private plane to Namibia. I sobbed on his shoulder during the whole flight.

"Who am I going to get facials with now?" I cried.

"This must be hard as hell, darling," he said, comforting me. "I know how much she meant to you, and you should know that you were always her gem. You were her bloody gem."

"Thanks, Dad."

"And, sweetie, she was effing proud of the person that you're becoming."

"I get it. But like, I don't get it. It seems kinda rude that she made us all come to Namibia. She can be the biggest attention whore." I wept on my dad's shoulder. "I'm sorry. I shouldn't have said that."

"Trust me, if anyone knows that woman, it's me. I'm not the least bit surprised that even from the afterlife, she's managed to make it all about her. All of this drama is a bit self-involved, isn't it?"

On the day of the ceremony, it was literally nine thousand degrees. In a cruel twist of fate, I was in Africa for a funeral, so I had no choice but to dress in all black. So it was a Dolce & Gabbana dress with a long-sleeved sheer floral overlay and knee-high Jil Sander gladiators. I did the best I could with what I had, but I was still super-sweaty.

The funeral itself was really chic. A shitload of African dignitaries showed up, and their looks (costumes?) were major. We all cried when Ladysmith Black Mambazo performed "Send in the Clowns." At the end of the ceremony, we released Tai Tai's ashes over the dunes. It wasn't until I saw them floating through the African atmosphere that I realized I would never again see my grandmother smack a tailor, or throw her keys at a valet, or give a waitress the silent treatment. My eyes welled with tears. No one would ever replace Tai Tai and I missed the fuck out of her.

The after party took place on the beach in Windhoek (birthplace of Shiloh Jolie-Pitt). It was tented and featured fire pits, traditional cuisine, and an elephant. I had to give it up to my grandmother and her party planner, they knew how to put an event together. Apparently they'd been planning her funeral

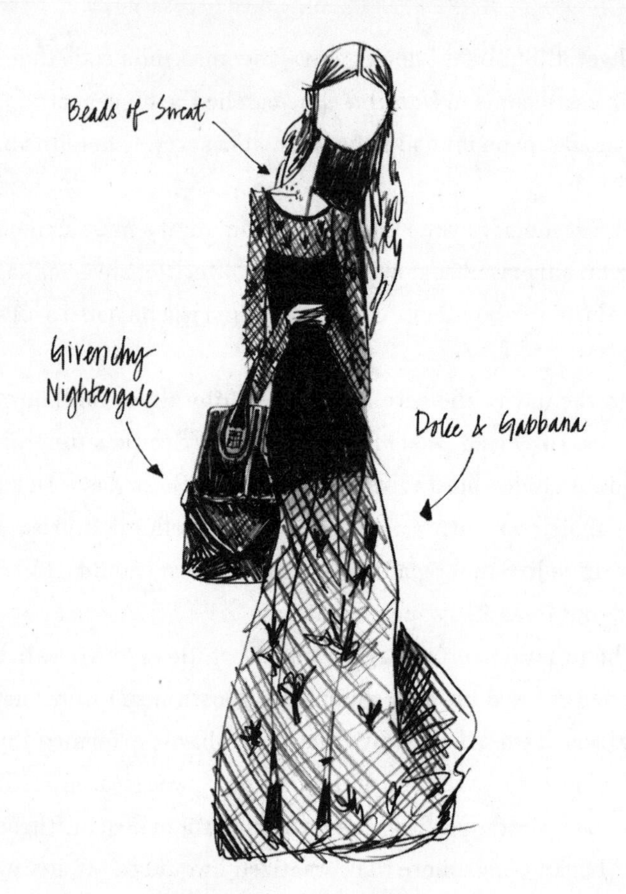

for almost two months. She was always so good at surprises. One time she threw a surprise party in my backyard for my eighth birthday that would have been flawless if the fireworks hadn't been so loud and scary. I peed through my skort.

My dad and I (and some cousins who don't live in LA or London, so . . . unclear) and some other funeral guests sat around a huge bonfire, poured bottles of French rosé, and shared our favorite memories about Tai Tai. Most of the speeches were snoozeworthy, and I got progressively less sober as the night went on, but I do remember some of the good ones.

My dad talked about how, when he was a kid growing up in London, Tai Tai would take him to the movies every Wednesday after school. Without fail, she'd finish a bottle of champagne during the film and be asleep by the time the credits rolled. My dad would have to drive them home, so he basically learned to drive when he was seven. Also, they drive on the wrong side of the road in Britain, so in American years he was like three. He got really choked up talking about how Tai Tai helped raise me. She'd dropped everything and moved in with us from the time I was born until I was four. He told everyone about how I'd had a minor lisp when I first started talking, but Tai Tai corrected it by soaking my bottom lip in gin every night before I went to bed. I never knew that story, and I was touched to learn how selfless my grandmother had been with her time when my dad needed her most.

"My mother might've looked like a tightly wound broad, but those of us who knew her well can attest to the fact that she was a scrappy one." My dad continued, "There wasn't a problem she couldn't fix—or rather, a fuckup she couldn't gracefully get herself, or her loved ones, out of." He found me in the group and looked right into my eyes, and I knew he was about to say something emo. "Babe, you remind me of Tai Tai every day. Your laugh, your twisted sense of humor, your passion, and I know that she's sitting up there, or down there, with a cigarette slowly burning in her pretty little fingers, smiling at you. She was fucking proud of you, Babe." And he sat back down on the bench between two half-naked tribeswomen. I would've cried if there weren't strangers around, I swear.

Her plastic surgeon praised her for having "the hair of Grace Kelly, the boobs of Helen Mirren, the attitude of Cher, and the wit of Blanche Devereaux." He also claimed that she had some of the finest bone structure he had ever come across. She was his favorite patient because her taste in facial adjustments was refined and classic. It was always a collaborative effort with Tai Tai. Also, his date may have been Joceyln Wildenstein (Google her).

Tai Tai's gardener, Daniel, told a weird story about the time that he and my grandmother were arrested for having ten kilos of marijuana growing under hyroponic lamps in a shed on her property. He went on to say that he wasn't mad at her anymore for making him take the blame, and that serving fourteen months in a correctional facility in San Quentin was the best thing that had ever happened to him. So supersweet.

To conclude the long evening of drunken memories (it was 3 A.M.), I gave an impromptu speech about what my Tai Tai meant to me. I told everyone that she taught me how to dress, and how to eat, etc., blah blah blah. I'm normally terrible at public speaking because, as a former actress, I respect and rely on other people's words. When I don't have a script, I get flustered and usually end up ruining my speeches. This time was different. I was so present that night on the beach, I could feel the sand on my skin and taste the ocean in the air. At the end of my monologue, I facilitated a silent prayer that brought everyone to tears. It was beyond. I may have even levitated for a sec.

After twenty hours on a plane, seven Xanax, thirteen Bloody Marys, six hundred Diet Cokes, and zero cigarettes, I was back in LA. My dad and I went to Tai Tai's lawyer's office for the reading of her will. I'd never been to a will reading before, and besides being slightly morose, the whole event was very chic. We weren't there long, but the gist was this: my dad got most of her fortune, she gave a crazy amount of money to charity, she gave me her furs and a very sizeable trust, she gave Daniel the gardens he had been taking care of for the past thirty years and the guesthouse on her estate, and she gave Mabinty her Rolls-Royce. I think we all fared well, but I would've loved some jewelry. Just saying.

As we were leaving the lawyer's office, he handed me a small envelope with my name written in Tai Tai's florid cursive on the front. There was a letter inside:

Dearest Babe,

Shut up and listen to me, darling, because I'm only going to say this once. I know my death may seem sudden, and I know you may hate me for making you wear all black to an outdoor wedding in Namibia, but this is the way it was meant to be. From dust to dust.

I love you very much and I have all the faith in the world that one day you will get your shit together. I've left you my furs and I expect that you will care for them like the beautiful pets that they are. I needn't remind you that they'll require their own temperature-controlled storage unit. I've also left you a bit of cash, which is to be released to you in increments. Don't spend it all in one day. However, the most important thing I can leave you is the following wisdom:

Never accept a marriage proposal from a man in open toed shoes. He's either gay or a gypsy.

Never cry. It causes swelling.

Doctors, lawyers, and princes come and go. Oil money lasts forever.

Get your first face-lift by the time you're forty-two, after that it's too late.

Don't go to bed with a full face of makeup on, unless you think you may die in your sleep.

You should never have to work to make a living. You're smarter than that.

I miss you already, my love, and I'll be watching over you. So spend my money with good taste. I deserve that.

Love,

Your Tai Tai

WHITE GIRL PROBLEM

#12

My waxer knows me better than I know myself.

The best thing you can do for your social life is to leave home for a long period of time and then come back unexpectedly. I try to do this as often as possible.

I had just gotten back home to LA after five brief stints at five universities and an uncomfortably hot funeral in Namibia. My return home was the beginning of a new chapter in my life, so I chose to be in a place of renewal and receive the positivity that the world had to offer. The first few weeks back in town were amazing. The trust my grandmother had set up for me kicked in, and my dad threw me a huge welcome home party and let me redecorate my room. I decided on a marriage of two motifs: Zen garden meets Brazilian jungle. I was super-focused and ready to take on the rest of my life, or whatevs.

I also reconnected with Roman and Genevieve. Gen had graduated with honors from Stanford and was selling real estate.

She was the youngest broker at the hottest firm in town, which was especially impressive because she was also doing enough coke to blow up the sun.

Roman had gotten into the business of promoting nightclubs and had just opened a new hot spot the week before I got back. I wish I could say more about it, but it was a members only thing. Sorry. So fucking chic though. Just like . . . the kind of place where everyone can relax while dressed in head-to-toe Celine and lounge, and no one cares who anyone is because everyone is somebody. Very easy and real.

In Los Angeles, twenty is the new fifty. So once I was home it became my full-time job to make myself look ten. I didn't realize how far I'd gone down this dark path until one day it occurred to me that I was e-mailing my waxer more than anyone else in my life. Let me break it down:

CUT/COLOR/BLOWOUT

I pride myself on being a daredevil when it comes to my hair. I have the face for it. I've tried it all. Shapes, lengths, extensions, colors. You probably think that having a team of seven (stylist, backup stylist, colorist, roots specialist, extensionist, hairspirationist, hair director/archivist) makes it easy to keep my mane in flawless shape, but you also probably think that getting your hair cut and colored every three months is sufficient upkeep.

The cut is the most important story your hair will ever tell. It's all about shape and movement coming together to create a perfect synergy. I've worked with an array of haircuts. My hair is constantly evolving, and I don't let myself get stuck in one look. When I was in grade school, I was all about how I accessorized my haircut. From a crimp, to a full head of beads (to let everyone know that I'd been to Cabo over Christmas break), to baby barrettes, to bejeweled headbands and oversized bows. Then I turned ten, calmed the fuck down, and realized that the haircut itself is the perfect accessory.

I became obsessed with celebrity hairstyles. I tried everything. I started with The Rachel, then The Gwyneth (circa Brad), then The Meg Ryan (circa *City of Angels*), The Leo (circa *What's Eating Gilbert Grape?*), and then the Slim Shady (a huge mistake but I was young, so I totally got away with it). Obviously, this was a huge learning period for me.

When I was fourteen, my hairstylist, Tommy, came into my life. He taught me how to streamline my look and base my haircut on my bone structure. He's a genius, and has been my stylist and confidant ever since. He collects all things leopard print, which makes it super-fun and easy to shop for his Hanukkah gift every year. Our relationship is like a marriage. We don't always see eye to eye, but at the end of the day the most important thing is our child, aka my hair.

I've used a long layered cut as a canvas for the last eight years or so. It's the style that best suits me, and it's easy to build off of. Since returning home from college, I've been getting my hair cut every six weeks to maintain my trusted look and ward off split ends (death). As far as color goes, I took my time to experiment when I was young. Now I stick to enhancing my natural hair color, which is a rich brunette, with highlights or lowlights, or ombre highlights. Sometimes I need to go blond for a few weeks here and there, but I generally end up coming back to my signature look.

Blowouts are a tricky necessity that I require twice weekly, otherwise I feel like I'm living a flat half-life. Also (and this is major), my stylist should always be the one to do my blowout. It's not just about my hair, it's about follow-through and professionalism.

I need to be dealing with one person per appointment because, otherwise, the orders regarding my hair have to be passed from the stylist to the colorist to the assistant, or the fucking assistant's assistant, or the *intern*. Interns always, and I mean *always*, have a blank stare on their face, and the only thing they seem to do right is bring bottles of sparkling water from point A (somewhere) to point B (me). This is going to sound horrible, but if the person handling your blowout looks dumb, then they are dumb. If you suspect that they might be the type to leave the faucet running while they brush their teeth, or talk with their mouth full, then you should just grab your bag and leave the salon.

On the rare occasion that I'm stuck with one of these ex–American Apparel employees, I always end up having to painstakingly explain what I expect from them. If it's been a long day, this can bring me close to my breaking point. I'll tell them:

"My hair looks healthy, thick, and full, but it is extremely delicate, so I'm going to need lots of volume. Not some va-va-voom, hairsprayed bullshit—real volume that's going to last. I need you to pin up the hair that's already been dried, so that it's not just hanging there, all weighted down, while you're finishing the rest. If you think you can just use a curly brush, blow my hair dry, and let it go, I'm going to end up raising my voice at someone who was involved in hiring you. Also, I hate it when my hair feels too clean and shiny. It should feel textured and authentic, so use whatever product it takes to make that happen. If my hair is smooth and clean feeling when I walk out the door, it'll be flat in two hours, and tomorrow it'll be a greasy mess, and the next day I'll be on the floor of my therapist's office feeling very overwhelmed. I need this blowout to last three full days. So, that's about it. I just don't want to have to get mad at you."

P.S. I'm still on the fence about these new "Blowout Bars" that only offer blowouts. It's a cute idea, I guess, but I get a little freaked out that one of the employees might snap and shoot someone after doing six thousand blowouts in one day. I don't want to be around for that.

Manicure/Pedicure

Hands are beautiful creatures, while feet are gremlins that live on the bottom of the sea. No one said it's easy to have model-quality hands and feet, but I strive.

I take incredible care of my hands. The last thing I need is to wake up one morning having a midlife crisis, saying to myself, *Babe, you're twenty-seven, you're a has-been, and you have the wrinkly hands of a pottery teacher.* This fear causes me to keep my hands excessively moisturized at all times. I typically moisturize between 100 and 110 times a day. Nothing sloppy, just a little squeeze of a non-FDA approved French cream that is intended to treat third degree burns. When I'm in cold climates, I sleep with an alarm set on my BlackBerry to go off once a night, so I can wake up and moisturize my hands.

My first manicurist taught me that hands are a representation of where you've been in your life, which I interpreted to mean that a woman's hands, like her shoes, are the window to her soul. The lines in her hands tell an intricate story, while her nails provide the soundtrack. OMG that's fucking brilliant. I just came up with that last part myself.

My choice of nail color represents three things: my mood color at the time, an interpretation of Nature's seasonal color of the moment, and finally, a touch of influence from the week's racks at Barneys. With all of this in mind, I allow my trustworthy aura to pick the color. Sometimes my nails want to be fire engine red, and sometimes they want to be minty green, or airbrushed, or buffed with clear polish, or black, or white, or khaki or pastel or whatever, I'm bored of listing colors. I try to get my nails done twice a week, always by the same woman, who executes a consistently clean and bubble-free manicure.

Pedicures freak me out. I get them because I'm a human being and have no choice, but all things involving feet are touchy with me. You know how your yoga instructor is always talking about the edge of comfort? Well, feet take me to that edge, push me off, and laugh as my body smashes against the rocks. Sorry if that image offends you, it's all the Björk I've been listening to recently. She gets me. Deal with it.

It's not that I don't like a professional's small and able hands getting in there and releasing the tension from my exhausted body—I love that. What I don't enjoy is the idea that someone's whole job, their whole world, is about feet. I always imagine other people's foot energy all over the pedicurist's hands, seeping into their fingers and fingernails, and I just can't. Our feet hold so much life force, you know? The quicker the pedicure the better, if you ask me. Also, taking half a Klonopin with a Diet Coke always helps to ease my nerves.

The best option I've found is to go to Japan, or somewhere closer if you can find it, and treat yourself to a Doctor Fish pedicure. All you have to do is dip your feet in a little tub and a hundred tiny carp fish go to town, nibbling off all the dead skin. It tickles a little bit, and then it feels like your foot is asleep, and then you think you have no feet. I prefer this to someone's feety little hands all over my sub-ankle region.

EYEBROWS

Eyebrows are super-important to me because they're the accessory that you wear every day of your life. I always keep my eyebrow shape the same, which means they must be waxed at least once every two weeks. My eyebrows tell you that I'm listening to you, but I'm not like, crazy into what you're saying. Or, wait. Maybe they say that I'm *not* listening to you, but I'm thinking about something important that you should probably want to know. I can't remember, but it's one of those.

TEETH WHITENING

White teeth are an absolute must. No fucking around. No matter how many cigarettes I smoke, or how much coffee/red wine/Red Bull/Diet Coke/kombucha I drink, or how many ice cubes I eat as snacks, I am INSISTENT on my teeth glistening. My father has shit teeth (British), and I refuse to fall into that unfair lineage just because I was born into it. Absolutely no way.

Not with today's medical advances. Genevieve thinks I'm crazy to spend so much money on my teeth, but Genevieve doesn't know what my nightmares look like.

To achieve a glaring white smile, I have them acid washed, bleached, and lasered. Three different dentists, obviously. If they knew I was getting all three treatments simultaneously, they'd lose their licenses. Whoops.

Massage

I find it much more relaxing to have a massage in my own home than to go out into the busy, crazy, sick world and find a spa that can accommodate my body's hushed needs. (If your house doesn't have a massage room, then you can repurpose your photo darkroom or home gym into a temporary massage environment.) I get a massage once a week by my masseuse, Aurelia. It's ninety minutes, usually on Sunday, and it is the cornerstone of my week. Aurelia studied massage technique under the tutelage of Muhammad Ali's massage therapist, so she knows how to use her body weight to get the job done. I transcend time and space every time Aurelia touches my body. I have her use olive oil as a lubricant because I prefer a toxin-free massage. All in all, it's a three-hour process that includes my pre-massage dip in the Jacuzzi, actual massage, and post-massage steam/nap.

Laser Hair Removal

There is no such thing as acceptable body hair. The end. Therefore, I have taken it upon myself to systematically get rid of 100 percent of my body hair, because I don't see the point of having hair anywhere besides on the top of my head, my eyelashes, and eyebrows. I totally get that if you work outside, and you live on a farm in Michigan, or wherever, and you have a penis, you're going to need a little extra warmth in the winter, so a light fuzz might come in handy. But that is so not me.

waxing

While laser hair removal is great and everything, it's not foolproof. The hair does grow back, and when that happens, I run to my waxer, Marcia. I can't stand by while a crop of lone rangers pop up one by one, because eventually it will be a hostile takeover. A little bit of warm wax, and your jungle turns into an opera house.

peach smoothie (the vagacial)

Since I wax, I have to do this. The Peach Smoothie is a facial for your area down there. It feels like your basic facial, if your face was between your legs. You know, the aesthetician gets rid of ingrown hairs, she dabs your vag with exfoliants; there are moments of dread, hints of shame, but ultimately you leave feeling renewed.

anal bleaching

I know most girls don't like to talk about this, but some guys really love an anal moment. My ex-boyfriend Carter happened to be one of those guys, and he was great in bed, so I was able to get on that train. Anal bleaching isn't something I've always done. In fact, I used to think that only porn stars bleached their brown eyes, but bleaching your back door is one of those things that's *SO LA, OMG* that I actually love it. So what? Get off me.

Facials

When I feel an emptiness in my soul, I'll usually get a facial. It's a necessary cleansing ritual that also fulfills my need to glow. When I'm a little greasy, or can't think of anything to do with my afternoon, a facial is the perfect pick-me-up. Guys are obsessed with their cars being fast, stage moms are obsessed with their kids being famous, and I'm obsessed with my face looking approximately three years younger than the rest of my body. *Capiche?*

I'm always trying new facial treatments. Last summer was all about stem cells taken from Norwegian pears; this summer it was all about an exfoliant made from peanut shells harvested in the Ivory Coast. Trying to keep up is not an easy task. Also, not all treatments are a good fit for my delicate face. It's a gamble. Sometimes I win and sometimes I lose.

Voodoo Skin Ritual

Okay, this is going to sound kind of funny, but I *swear* by this ancient Jamaican voodoo skin regression ritual that tightens and rejuvenates your facial skin by tricking your subconscious into believing that you're younger than you actually are. Mabinty learned this ritual from her grandmother, growing up in Kingston, Jamaica. She does the whole thing while I'm asleep, so I'm not sure exactly what goes down, but I will say that I once woke up in the middle of it and there were three newborn babies on my bed. The babies were not mine, or Mabinty's, but the next day I felt like I had a brand-new T-zone.

TATTOO REMOVAL

At a certain point in my relationship with Robert, Babette, my cunt of an alter ego, thought it would be a good idea to have another guy's name tattooed on herself. The name Babette chose was *Stewart*, which, not coincidentally, was Robert's dad's name. Needless to say, this was a misstep, and I've been in the process of getting this tattoo removed for two years now. Every four to six weeks I take three Valiums, drink at least one vodka OJ, and have Mabinty drive me to the doctor's office to continue the painful removal process.

I have other tattoos that I will eventually get over and they will eventually need to be removed, but for now, *Stewart* is the extent of pain that I can deal with.

AROMATHERAPY

Every other weekday morning, I like to wake up inhaling essential oils that have been set out the night before. My aromatherapist, Jules (who is a total doll), prescribed a fantastic and simple lemon juice/fresh lavender/ginger liqueur/bat urine concoction. When it's been vaporized at the right temperature, inhaling this mixture allows me to wake up feeling mega-refreshed. It also gives me vivid sex dreams starring Jordan Catalano. A must-do for a productive day.

Airbrush Tanning

I hate admitting this, but coming clean is a part of my process. I get spray tans with Roman when we're completely, unbearably, deafeningly depressed. Totally works.

Eyelash Extensions

For events with Persian men in attendance, I get eyelash extensions.

WHITE GIRL PROBLEM #13

It's 5:15. How much weight can I lose by 8:00?

Genevieve and I were having lunch one day in Beverly Hills, and she was going on and on about her personal trainer and I was ignoring her because I hate it when people brag.

"I mean, Babe, I have never felt better, slash, looked better in my life," she was saying. "Look at my arms. No, seriously—look! They're like, half Pilates arms and half Madonna arms, without being too muscly. I'm telling you, Tony is amazing. Look at my legs. They are starting to look like they did when I was nine. I've never been so happy."

Blah, blah, blah. I was annoyed, so I started deconstructing my chopped salad into color categories, which is not easy, but beautiful once you've done it.

"And the thing is, he's *so* unconventional. He developed his own method of training called The Tony Method." Gen smiled. "Don't you want to know what The Tony Method is?"

I glared at her. "Not really," I said, pouring a ton of pepper on the rest of my salad, rendering it inedible.

"Sex, Babe. He literally fucks you into the body of your dreams."

"Give me his number."

"No way! He's my trainer and he's super-exclusive and never takes on new clients. Why don't you Ask Jeeves?"

"Give me his number, Gen."

"Babe, come on. You're not even into working out," she protested.

"Exactly. I've been feeling depressed lately, and I think having a trainer will lift my spirits. Number."

"Ugh, fine, I'll text it to you. I'm seriously hating you right now."

The following Tuesday I set up my first appointment with Anthony, aka Tony of The Tony Method, to train me at my home gym. When I got to my gym, he was pissed because I was literally two minutes late. He gave me some big speech that involved me not taking my fitness seriously, him threatening to leave, and something else but I was really over being lectured so I can't remember what it was. I apologized profusely and told Tony that I was ready to take my body to the next level and that I would do my best to arrive to our sessions on time, and he agreed to train me.

Tony's method was as follows: Phase I (Muscle Strengthening), Phase II (Conditioning for Lean Muscle), and Phase III (Total Transformation). All exercises in The Tony Method were performed while being fucked by Tony. He developed this method to build clients' self-esteem and allow them to hone breathing skills and total body awareness. He believed that, in order to achieve maximum results, a trainer should know his client's body inside and out. Tony personalized a plan for me based on my request that my body be "Gwyneth meets Gisele meets sample-sized."

The Tony Method

Sample Workout

CARDIO - BICYCLE

- Tony positions himself on the stationary bicycle seat, facing forward.
- Mount Tony, facing forward as well.
- Cycle for 20 minutes while working your body up and down on his dick.

ASS BLASTER

- Lie on your back with your hands to your sides and your knees bent and legs spread shoulder-width apart.
- Begin by tightening your core and ass, and lifting your hips to meet Tony's dick, achieving full penetration for 1 set of 50 reps.
- Repeat in double time 1 set of 25 reps.

(*continued*)

- Repeat in triple time 1 set of 25 reps.
- Slow back down to original pace and complete a final set of 50 reps.
- Repeat entire workout 2 more times, one time while keeping the right leg lifted vertically and the next time keeping the left leg lifted vertically.

THE PUSH-UP PUSSY POP

- Roll onto your stomach and lift your body into plank position, keeping your feet wider than shoulder-width apart, and positioning your chest directly over your elbows.
- Tighten your core and kegel muscles, holding this position for 30 seconds while Tony drills you from behind.
- Lower yourself, and repeat for two more sets, extending to 60 seconds, then 90 seconds. Repeat all three sets twice.

KICKBOXING BONER SQUATS

- Stand over Tony with your feet shoulder-width apart. Tighten your core.
- Squat all the way down onto Tony's dick, keeping your feet firmly grounded with your weight in your heels.
- As you lift back up, karate kick your right leg out to the side, keeping your core engaged.
- Return to starting position, repeat with the left leg.
- Do 3 sets of 20 reps.

THE ABDOMEN SKEET BLAST

- ❍ Tony sits on an exercise ball.
- ❍ Mount him, facing each other.
- ❍ Engage your core and rock back and forth for 50 reps.
- ❍ Repeat 5 times.

THE WET WILLY

- ❍ Tony stands in a dry sauna with both legs firmly planted on the ground and his arms at his sides.
- ❍ Climb onto Tony, wrapping both legs around his waist, and fuck him for as long as you can before sliding off.

ANAL

- ❍ Anal sex, 20 minutes.

STRETCHING

- ❍ 10 minutes of stretching, no penetration.

After the first Tony Method workout, I was so exhausted I could barely stand up, let alone lift my post-workout smoothie to my lips. Phase I was the hardest phase of The Tony Method. My body had to get used to doing lots of strenuous physical activity, and up until that point in my life, the most physical I'd ever been was my daily, seven-minute treadmill walks, thirty-minute sauna naps, and the four miles total that I ran when I lived in New York. I also had to overcome my fear of sweating in front of another human being, which was at first terrifying then liberating. That was the great thing about The Tony Method. It showed you how strong you really could be.

Tony and I continued our workouts, substituting lunge fucks and my personal favorite, the bridge position, on days when I needed to feel that extra burn. He was the best. And it wasn't about the sex—yes, Tony had a great dick, GREAT dick, but he also pushed me to work really hard and wouldn't let me give up when I was tired, which was always. One time he actually came into my room and pulled me out of bed to go work out after I'd tried to text him and cancel all our sessions for the week. I'm pretty sure in most cultures that would be considered rape, but I let it slide. That's just the kind of guy Tony was—really attentive to my needs and fitness goals. For example:

FROM **Babe Walker** <BDubs@gmail.com>
TO Anthony Chasen <Tony@thetonymethod.com>
DATE Wed, May 4, 2010 at 11:39pm
SUBJECT Legs

My thighs are getting way too muscly. WTF.

FROM **Anthony Chasen** <Tony@thetonymethod.com>
TO Babe Walker <BDubs@gmail.com>
DATE Wed, May 4, 2010 at 11:45pm
SUBJECT Re: Legs

Babe,

Don't worry. We'll start incorporating more muscle lengthening exercises and cut down on squats in Phase II.

FROM **Babe Walker** <BDubs@gmail.com>
TO Anthony Chasen <Tony@thetonymethod.com>
DATE Wed, May 4, 2010 at 11:47pm
SUBJECT Re: re: Legs

Okay. I would totally not be worrying but I was measuring my thighs and calves earlier, and the ratios were off by approx 0.42 inches. Not okay. Like, please no more squats. I'm not a bodybuilder Tony. Also, I'm looking in the mirror, and I'm thinking that when I turn to the side, I want my torso width to be exactly 2x my arm width. Doable?

FROM **Anthony Chasen** <Tony@thetonymethod.com>
TO Babe Walker <BDubs@gmail.com>
DATE Wed, May 4, 2010 at 11:50pm
SUBJECT Re: re: re: Legs

Yes. We're switching gears entirely in Phase II. Phase I was all about building up your muscles and getting your body used to rigorous aerobic activity. Phase II is all about lengthening your proportions with Pilates and ballet inspired movement. Trust in the method, Babe. You'll see results.

FROM **Babe Walker** <BDubs@gmail.com>
TO Anthony Chasen <Tony@thetonymethod.com>
DATE Wed, May 4, 2010 at 11:51pm
SUBJECT Re: re: re: re: Legs

It's hard for me to trust the method when I look in the mirror and see The Hulk staring back at me. It's hard for me to trust you.

FROM **Anthony Chasen** <Tony@thetonymethod.com>
TO Babe Walker <BDubs@gmail.com>
DATE Wed, May 4, 2010 at 11:55pm
SUBJECT Re: re: re: re: re: Legs

Have faith, Babe. You better get some sleep. We're on at 7am tomorrow.

The next day we got into Phase II of The Tony Method, and Tony was totally right—we switched gears entirely. Gone were the boner squats. Phase II was all about barre stretching, barre fucking, and Pilates exercises. All the strength-building work we'd done came in really handy when I had to keep my core tight while Tony plowed me on the Pilates reformer. Side note: The reformer is the best invention ever, after the blender. Who knew it was possible to lengthen my leg muscles and have incredible sex at the same time?! I was well on my way to the body of my dreams, and feeling really confident about myself. All my measurements were falling into place. My hip bones were protruding at just the right longitude past my abs, which were less six-packy and more one smooth packy. They were, like, really toned. And Tony was right, my legs lost that bulky muscle I'd been worried about. Before I knew it, it was time for Phase III, where Tony had promised I would achieve maximum results. I was so excited the night before our first Phase III workout that I could barely sleep.

FROM **Babe Walker** <BDubs@gmail.com>
TO Anthony Chasen <Tony@thetonymethod.com>
DATE Wed, Jun 15, 2010 at 3:15am
SUBJECT Phase III

PHASE III TONY!!!! I AM BABE WALKER: INVINCIBLE.

Tony and I were on minute six of our warm-up (holding various stretches for thirty minutes in relevé while getting pounded) when suddenly, some random stranger of a man burst into my home gym, followed by Mabinty.

"I couldn't stop him, Babe. He gon and bust in the fron door, screemin like a banshee, sayin he mister Tony's husband."

"What the fuck is going on here, Tony?!" screamed the stranger man.

Both Tony and I were too surprised to try and cover ourselves up, so there I was, standing in nothing but a sports bra and sneakers, with my leg raised at the barre, with Tony behind me and still inside of me. Super-awkward. For everyone else but Tony and me, that is. We were working out.

"Um, can't you see we're in the middle of a warm-up here?" I asked. "Kindly escort yourself out of the gym. I don't like exercising in front of strangers."

"I'm not going to escort myself anywhere!" the hysterical man screamed. "What do you mean by a warm-up? A warm-up to what? You guys are fucking! Tony, what the hell is going on?"

"Exactly. It's The Tony Method. Hello!!" I said. I looked at Tony for support, but he was clearly scared speechless.

"Look, dude," I continued, "there's nothing sketchy going on here. This is a completely professional relationship, and I resent you operating under the assumption that it is anything but. I have literally worked my ass off and I'm in Phase III now, so please let me continue my workout! Plus, we're wearing two condoms, so it doesn't even technically count as sex."

"Tony is di real ting," Mabinty chimed in. "Mi know dat for di fact. Mi been tryin' di moves wid mi man. Look at mi arms. Like Gwyneth."

Throughout all this, Tony was still standing behind me, inside me, dumbfounded.

"Thanks, Mabinty." I smiled.

Apparently Tony was as gay as the day is long, and he'd forgotten to explain his famous workout method to his husband, Sean. He'd caught Tony after stumbling across a batch of e-mails from his clients, and decided to investigate further. I guess Sean had stopped by Genevieve's house first, because when I checked my phone later that morning, I had a missed call and an urgent voice mail from Gen warning me about the situation. Needless to say, Tony's husband's discovery brought his career as a personal trainer to an abrupt halt. I never got to experience Phase III because Tony had to leave. Immediately. He was busted and there was nothing I could do about it. Last I heard he was working at the Yogurtland at Universal Citywalk. Tony, if you're reading this and you're divorced by now, e-mail me, k?

I miss you, unless you miss me, in which case I'm over you and into me being me.

Even though my training had come to a screeching halt due to Tony's infidelities, my body was in a really good place, and my beauty appointments were going well (no chemical burns). But while everything seemed to be going swimmingly, beneath the surface, my heart was in the depths of despair. I missed Robert. I couldn't stop thinking about him—his eyes, his laugh, his smile, his perfect penis. I knew I'd messed everything up by acting like a psychopath and there was no way I could get him back, because of the restraining order. Living in London and my Tai Tai's death and my homecoming were all great distractions, but once the dust settled, reality seeped in and I started feeling kind of miserable and alone.

My depression came to a head one afternoon while I was lying out by my pool with Roman and Genevieve. We were drinking vodka lemonades, sunning, and discussing the pros and cons of anal sex when "Islands in the Stream" by Dolly Parton and Kenny Rogers came on the outdoor surround sound speaker system and I lost it. I tried to tell them to turn off the song, but my cry-perventilating was making it hard to get any words out.

"You . . . Guys. I can't . . . with this . . . song. Robert . . . I . . . Please . . . Please . . . *please* . . . OFF!!!!"

"Oh my God, Babe. Reel it in. I'll put on some JLo or something," said Roman, getting up to go change the playlist to something more gay/Spanish.

"I cannot believe that you're still hung up on a *sports agent*," said Genevieve, walking over to the pool bar, pouring me a glass of straight vodka, and grabbing me a tissue. "Here. You need to get over it. I'll let you sleep with my brother if you think that'll help you move on."

"I fucked your brother over Christmas break two years ago, so thanks but no thanks," I sobbed. "And I don't want to have *sex*. I want to make love. With Robert. He was my everything and now it's over. My life sucks."

Roman sat back down and started spraying his ridiculously sculpted chest with tanning oil. "Gen's right, Babe. The only way you're going to get over Roberto is to find someone new."

"How the *fuck* am I ever going to meet someone new in LA?" I asked. "Guys here are either heinous on the inside and beautiful on the outside, or heinous on the outside and beautiful on the inside. There's no hope for me."

"Maybe the man of your dreams is waiting for you to find him on OkCupid," said Roman.

"Is that some kind of sick joke?" I responded, unamused.

"I mean, I can't say I've never fucked around with guys that

I've met online. But I also can't say that it's necessarily my thing. And I also can't say that I won't do it again. Tomorrow night," said Roman.

"Yeah, Babe, you should *totally* go on a dating website," agreed Gen.

"That is disgusting!"

"Um, no it's not," argued Gen. "It's a great self-esteem pick-me-up. Whenever I feel depressed, I do a trial week on Match.com. I post like two pictures, then a million guys message me, and it makes me feel so much better."

"Whatever. Gross, Gen."

"It's totally not. Do you think you're actually gonna meet someone in *person*? At a *bar*? That's primitive."

"No, you're primitive."

"You're primitive."

"You are literally so primitive."

"Fuck off, Babe! You and Robert broke up, like, over a year ago, and I'm done listening to you bitch about missing him. I'm trying to help, but clearly you don't want any of my advice because you'd rather be a psycho for the rest of your life. God! I'm out of here," she yelled, packing up her things. "I need to pick up an eight ball for . . . a friend. Roman, do you want a ride to somewhere in the direction of Encino?"

"Yeah, I guess so," said Roman.

"Good. I'll be in the car." Gen turned and stormed off up to the house.

"Ugh, sorry, Babe. She's so moody these days. It's the cocaine talking. Anyways, you should think about online dating. It's only gross if you make it gross."

"Bye, traitor."

"Don't be mad. Come out tonight! Have a drink. I'll be at the club around eleven. Loves you, even when you're sad and lonely."

Thirty minutes later, I'd polished off the rest of the pitcher of vodka lemonade and was feeling sad, tan, and drunk. I stumbled up to the house and into my room, put "Islands in the Stream" on repeat, and threw myself on my bed, weeping. At some point during the eleventh time through the song, I did something really stupid. I pulled out my "Robert + Babe = 4 Ever Box of Memories" from under my bed and started looking through it.

If you are a girl, and you've had a significant relationship with someone, chances are you've saved all the pictures/letters/supercute little notes from that relationship in a box that is somewhere in your room or apartment or mansion. Smart people discard this box after a relationship is over. Dumb people hold on to this box and torture themselves by looking through it every once in a while when they are drunk and slightly sun poisoned. This is always a huge mistake.

Tears were streaming down my face as I rummaged through photos of Robert and me from happier times, mixed CDs, matchboxes from dinners we'd had together, ticket stubs from movies we'd seen, old photo booth strips, a swimsuit calendar I'd made for him for Valentine's Day. It was too much for me. All the memories of our relationship flooded my brain and I couldn't take it. A postcard Robert had sent me from Florida with a kitten sunbathing on it that read, "Miss you! Whisker you were here!" was the last straw. I ran into my closet and collapsed, sobbing into a nest of clothes.

I don't know exactly what happened next, but before I knew

it, I was wearing a tube top and reeking of some awful scent from the Victoria's Secret "loose slut" collection. I walked over to the mirror and saw that my hair was in . . . braided pigtails. I looked down at my hands and decided I was over my mint green polish and was craving a French tip scenario for my nails. What the fuck was happening to me? Then I realized that there was only one person I knew who thrived on drama and bad taste: Babette. It was uncharacteristic of her to appear like this, but my trip down memory lane must have triggered her. I was still so hung up on Robert that she'd decided to make a surprise guest appearance for old times' sake.

Babette immediately sat down in front of my MacBook Air and started filling out a profile for an Internet dating website.

Name: *Babette*

Relationships: *Tons. I am a lover and a fighter! JK, I'm just looking for The One.*

Have Kids: *Not yet!!!!!!!!!!!!!!!!!!!!!!!!!!!!!!!!!!*

Want Kids: *Duh.*

Ethnicity: *What does "ethnicity" even mean? I love Indian food!*

Body Type: *Not fat.*

Height: *Let's just say I don't date guys under 6'4". Sorry! Don't hate me! LOL.*

Religion: *Christian/Atheist/Democrat. I'm not religious, just spiritual.*

Smoke: *Only when I drink. ☺ Get over it.*

Drink: *Only when I smoke. ☺*

I'm most passionate about: *I am so sick of rumors that my favorite actors are gay. Let it go, people. Tom Cruise, John*

Travolta, and Will Smith have WIVES and KIDS. OPEN YOUR EYES YOU FUCKING MORONS!!

Three things I'm thankful for: *Jamba Juice, miniskirts, animals*

When are you happiest?: *When I'm head over heels for a guy! Come over!*

What is your motto?: *Live, laugh, love, and never use a condom.*

What is the most important quality you are looking for in another person?: *My heart's been broken and I want to find someone who can help me pick up the pieces and put my soul back together. My dream man is tall, has brown eyes/brown hair, and is my ex-boyfriend Robert. Robert, if you're on here, message me!!!!!!!!!! If you're not Robert, but you think you have what it takes to make me fall in love, don't be scared, message me!!!!!!!!!!*

Within minutes of creating a profile (and uploading multiple photos of her posing in a bikini), Babette was delighted to see that she had messages from several interested suitors. She took particular interest in a guy named Robby, aka "TaeKwon-DoRob," and after they'd sent a few messages back and forth, she'd arranged for them to meet at California Pizza Kitchen in the Hollywood and Highland mall at 10:30 P.M. Robby seemed to be really excited.

Robby 9:30PM: Hey beautiful. Can't w8 to c ur sexy bod in person. C u @ CPK in an hour.

Babette 9:49PM: U got it. XOXO!

Babette 10:00PM: I may be a little late to keep you on your toes. Hehehe :)

Babette 10:15PM: But I'm worth the wait LOL.

Babette 10:20PM: U there? I hate it when guys don't respond to my texts.

Babette 10:21PM: It's my #1 pet peeve.

Babette 10:25PM: ????????????????????????

Robby 10:26PM: Sorry hon. parking now! See you soon. I'm wearing a red hat. ;)

In preparation for her date with Robby, Babette decided to throw on a denim miniskirt and pink tube top with matching pink Candie's heels and a pink Chanel 2.5 bag.

Babette met Robby in front of CPK at 11:00 P.M. From the looks of it, he could have been anywhere from twenty-five to thirty-five. He was also about six-four, wearing pointy-toed loafers, True Religion jeans, and an Affliction T-shirt. Robby also must have been at least three hundred pounds of pure muscle. Like, his biceps were bigger than his face, which was actually kind of handsome.

Babette loves roided-out muscular guys, so, naturally, she thought Robby was the cutest. She started the date off with a bang, greeting him by pinching his nipple, and telling him how glad she was to finally be dating an older man who could provide for her financially. Robby was a little taken aback but did a good job of hiding it while Babette ordered two Long Island iced teas and three pizzas, because she wanted the white pizza with shrimp *and* the BBQ chicken pizza but wanted just a taste of the sausage pizza. She also ordered two appetizers, which she didn't touch.

Babette took one bite of each pizza, and drank both Long Island iced teas, while explaining to Robby that her last serious boyfriend never let her be herself and stressing that she was "so glad to have found a father figure and a boyfriend in one."

After the meal, Babette wanted to go out, so she asked Robby to drive her to Roman's club. Since Robby wasn't a member, he couldn't go in, so Babette made him wait for her in the car while she went in, had a couple drinks, and paid with his credit card. Once she was inside the club, she started dancing with her own reflection in the mirrored ceilings and texted Robby a series of pictures of her getting motorboated by a couple different guys and one woman.

At some point in the evening, Roman came up to Babette mid-text and pulled her into the men's bathroom.

"You're soooo sunburnt! What in God's name are you wearing? Are those Candie's? Oh fuck, you've turned. Hi, Babette."

"Hey, hon! Do you love my shoes? They're totally fierce."

"Um, no. Your outfit is death. I get that the nineties are back, but for God's sake, get a grip."

"What are you talking about? I'm just in a really good mood, *capiche*? I have a secret."

"What?"

"I'm in love. With Robby."

"I know, and it's sick."

"Not Robert. Robby! My new boyfriend that I met online. He's so sweet. You have to meet him. You're gonna love him!"

"Where is he?"

"He's not on the list, so he's waiting outside for me in his new Nissan Juke."

"What? I can get him in if you want him in here."

"Nooooo. No. It's better this way."

"Who is he?"

"Some big, muscleman guy. Such a cutie."

"I know it's unholy, but I kind of love this side of you. Call me tomorrow, okay? I need to check on Bono's bottle service. People love him, but I just don't get it. He's so cranky."

Babette spun off into the crowd, dancing with her hands above her head. She made Robby wait outside until the club closed and then had him drive her home. Needless to say, their first date was also their last.

Babette spent the following week going on multiple dates a day with random dudes she met on Match.com, eHarmony .com, OkCupid.com, and some app on her iPhone. The menfolk were really responding to her online presence. Turned out, the cyber-dating community was the perfect place for Babette to thrive. She could act as crazy as she wanted and still get asked out left and right. And even though every guy ran for the hills after each first date, Babette always managed to have a guy around to pay for multiple trips to the Cheesecake Factory, Red Lobster, and all CPK locations within a five-mile radius of Bel Air.

Dating became Babette's full-time job. She had breakfast, lunch, and dinner accounted for, and had activity dates scheduled to cover every minute in between meals. Sometimes Babette would flit between dates and sometimes Babette would stick with one guy the whole day.

One of her many victims was named Jarrod. Jarrod and Babette met up at a Jamba Juice, then they walked over to a pottery class, where Babette reenacted her favorite scene from *Ghost* with the instructor while Jarrod watched. Then she made Jarrod take her to a pet store and buy her a puppy. After spending the day in the park with their new love animal, Babette wanted to "put the baby to sleep and go on a double dinner date with her bestie Gen."

Gen and I hadn't spoken to each other during the time that I'd become possessed by Babette. That was, until Babs dialed up Genevieve and left her the following apologetic voice mail:

> **3:45PM:** *Gensies. I took your advice and started online dating and I love it. Come to dinner with me and um . . . Jarrod tonight? We're going to The Melting Pot at seven-thirty. The one in the valley. Love youuuuu. P.S. Did you get my "I'm sorry for being a cunt" edible arrangement? Okay, talk to you later!*

Genevieve must have gotten the edible arrangement and been curious as to why the fuck I would be calling her and asking her to go to dinner at a fondue restaurant in the middle of nowhere, because she actually showed up to The Melting Pot, with her boyfriend Clark, at 7:25 P.M. Clark happened to be a really hot eighteen-year-old boy that Genevieve met when he and his parents came to an open house she was showing in Malibu. Genevieve prefers not to date people her own age, so her boyfriends are always either much younger or much older than she is.

The double date started off all right, despite the fact that

Jarrod had ditched Babette and the dog sometime in the afternoon, claiming that he needed to go visit his "grandma in the hospital." It hadn't deterred her from securing another date for the evening, and showing up to dinner drunk, with some biker dude named Lonnie in tow. Babette had poured herself into a sequined romper from bebe, which she'd accessorized with a really tacky vintage Chanel chain belt (let's face it, even Karl makes mistakes). She was also wearing sky high black patent leather Loubs, making it really hard for her to walk.

Lonnie sat down in the booth, and Babette sat on his lap, introducing him to the table as her "new bad-boy boyfriend, Lon Lon." When the waitress arrived, Lonnie ordered two shots of whiskey and a beer, Genevieve ordered a water, Babette ordered a Long Island iced tea, and Clark ordered a rum and Coke (then he was ID'd, so he ordered a Sprite). Babette drained her Long Island in four seconds and immediately ordered another. She then waved down the waitress and ordered a different kind of fondue for each person at the table, turned her attention to Clark, and began asking him all sorts of questions, like: "Do you like my hair?" "Do you think I need a boob job?" "How did you and Gen meet?" "Where are you from?" "Do you mind if I call you Robert?" etc. etc.

As Babette got friendlier with Clark, Genevieve looked pissed, and Lonnie looked like he was going to stab someone.

"Babe, let's go to the bathroom," said Genevieve, flatly.

"Um sure! BRB, guys. Don't start fighting over me. Or do. Whatever," Babette said, winking at Lonnie and Clark.

Once we were in the bathroom, Genevieve confronted me.

"Edible arrangements? The Melting Pot? Lonnie? You did

happen to realize that he's, like, a Hell's Angel, right? Where's that Jarrod guy you were talking about? You've transitioned into Babette again, and you know I love a train wreck just as much as the next person, but this is disgusting. Snap the fuck out of it and stop flirting with Clark."

"Sorry, but Clark and I are just vibing on each other's vibes right now," said Babette. "No need to be jealous."

"Well, please stop vibing on my boyfriend. You smell like a hooker."

"No I don't. It's Victoria's Secret. It's sexy. Clark likes it."

Gen slapped me across the face, instantly jarring me out of my Babette haze.

"Ow! Genevieve, what the fuck is your problem?! Why is everyone trying to hurt me? Why do I smell like ass?"

"Get your shit together, Babette or Babe or whoever the fuck you are. I'm out of here. Fondue is sick. Stay away from Clark."

Genevieve left the bathroom, and I collected myself as best I could, taking into account the fact that I was wearing a sequined strapless romper from bebe and a pound of makeup. What had become of me? My obsession with Robert had driven me to madness once again, and I wasn't going to be able to get over him by dating random weirdos.

By the time I got back to the table, Gen and Clark had left the restaurant, leaving Lonnie alone to wait for me. He gave me a ride home on his motorcycle, which I thought was pretty sweet of him. I guess it is totally possible to meet nice guys online.

When I got back home, I knew what I had to do. I ran up to my room and poured my emotions into the following letter:

Dear Robert,

When we first met, I thought you were really cute. I still liked you even after I found out you were a sports agent, and I fucking hate sports. I think that's when I realized that we could have something special. (You also gave me multiple orgasms and had an amazing apartment, so that helped.) When we fell in love, I couldn't handle all the emotions I was feeling so I went a little crazy. I wanted to be able to control myself, but I've never been in love with anyone before—unless you count Roman, but he's gay and even though we did fuck once, it doesn't matter because we're just friends now. And I guess I kind of love this one guy who works at my favorite macrobiotic restaurant, but he has dreadlocks, so it would never work out. But when I told you I loved you, I really meant it. I didn't know how to cope with my feelings/how to trust you, so I messed everything up. For that, I'm truly sorry. I'm also sorry for repeatedly telling you I thought your dad was hot. That must have been super-awkward for you to hear. He was hot though. Sorry again. Mostly, I'm sorry that I lost you. I miss you. Do you ever miss me? Well I guess it doesn't matter, because this is good-bye. It's over, and I know that. I hope you have a good life. I hope you miss me.

Love,
Babe

Then I grabbed the box of Robert + Babe stuff from under my bed and headed out to the backyard. I spent the next two hours sitting by the fire pit next to the pool and burning every last shred of evidence of Robert's and my relationship. It was difficult, but ultimately cathartic. As all our memories burned to a crisp, I could feel Babette loosening her grip on my psyche.

I ended the night by reading the letter aloud, then throwing it into the flames, along with the robe I was wearing (I just needed to cleanse myself of *everything*, you know?). It took another few months, one public hysterical crying fit at Fred Segal after seeing a Robert look-alike, and a couple random make-out sessions with complete strangers, but eventually Babette left my body and I began to move on. To clear up any concern about the puppy that Jarrod got Babette, he's fine. She named him Moses Martin, wrapped him in a blanket, put him in a wicker basket, and set him afloat in our pool. Mabinty found him and has been taking care of him ever since.

I'll eat anything, as long as it's gluten-free, dairy-free, low-carb, low-fat, low-calorie, sugar-free, and organic.

In order for you to understand how I became so in-tune with eating properly, I need to tell you about my "chubby" phase. When I was thirteen, my dad sent me to a culinary summer camp in Napa Valley for eight weeks. I had been warned about the dangers of puff pastry and handmade ravioli by my eighth-grade nutritionist, but I went anyway. I don't know what to say, except I was young, it was summer, and I thought that my skinny little nine-year-old legs would last forever. Reality is life's cruelest mistress. Needless to say, I came back home looking as oversized as my Louis Vuitton speedy, albeit a Michelin-level chef. It wasn't until I noticed a muffin top peering over my Abercrombie & Fitch miniskirt that I realized things had gotten completely out of control.

What weighed heavier on my soul than the extra poundage

was the fact that the world would see me as a "fat girl." I could feel society's disdain for my lack of self-control. I had nightmares about being the kind of person who would be forever described as "having a great face." I wanted to love myself, but self-acceptance and unwanted body puff don't mesh well. I had to take control of my physique and get back in shape.

I went into hiding for the last four weeks of summer. I made my dad fire our live-in chef and appointed myself master of the kitchen. I started with a three-day liquid cleanse detox and developed a diet plan for myself that utilized elements of the Zone, Atkins, and Grapefruit Diets, combined with Eastern fasting traditions. It took three weeks to lose the weight, and one additional week for me to learn to love myself again. I mean, what the fuck was I supposed to do? Enter my freshman year of high school looking like a total heifer? Do you know how damaging that would have been to my psyche? Not to mention the cruel judgment I would have received from Gen. She has such high standards for me, and I love her for that. Thank God sack dresses were in style, because I practically lived in them during those difficult times.

I've since gone to great lengths to destroy all photo evidence of this period of my life and have had countless hypnotherapy sessions with my psychic, Myrta, to try and erase all memories of being overweight. Myrta thinks that I gained weight due to my aura somehow getting crossed with Kirstie Alley's while Saturn entered my fifth house of fame and fortune. I think Myrta is a genius.

Now I'm obsessed with what goes in my body. Some people

(doctors, nutritionists, therapists) have criticized my eating habits, throwing around words like "eating disorder," "orthorexic," and "self-flagellation." Such bullshit. When I say, "No thanks, I'm full," I truly mean it. I don't deprive myself—I have an equally healthy relationship with the food I eat and the food I don't eat. Plus, look around: *everyone* in America is fat. So sue me for loving vegetables, sparkling water, and half portions of soup.

Every single thing I put in my mouth must serve a nutritional purpose and also enhance my beauty. That being said, there are some things that I won't budge on—e.g., dark chocolate. No matter how many health nuts rave about its nutritional qualities, I won't allow myself to be led right into that trap. First you're eating one ounce of dark chocolate once a week, and the next thing you know, you're shoving fistfuls of donut holes down your throat and crying about how you'll never be as strong or thin as Gwyneth.

I've been in charge of the hiring and firing of chefs since becoming a culinary authority at a young age. Due to my ever-changing diet needs and my mercurial palate, the turnover rate for chefs in the Walker household is above average. I am highly selective, and every applicant undergoes a rigorous interview process complete with an extensive background check. Whenever a new person is hired, I always take it upon myself to have Mabinty issue them the list of what foods I will and will not allow to be brought into my home.

Eating at restaurants is something I end up having to do a lot. What? Did you think I stayed home and drank smoothies all day? This is real life, and I have friends and family who like to go to restaurants for meals. For me, dining out is all about dressing for the occasion, experiencing the ambiance, and looking at/smelling the food. I enjoy going out to eat, and I manage to let myself relax my rules here and there when I venture outside of my house. My life is all about balance—yin and yang, etc.—so I like to keep it über health conscious inside the house and then let myself splurge a little when dining out. It's just the way I live my life. I deserve it.

I've found Los Angeles to be the perfect place to dine out while remaining hyper-conscious of your eating habits. There are plenty of raw/macrobiotic/vegan options to choose from. Also, LA has a salad game unlike any city I've ever lived in, so no matter where I end up, if worse comes to worst, I can at least get a plate of lettuce with lemon juice on the side.

I like to get very up close and personal with the waitstaff when I dine out. Like all important relationships in my life, it's all about intimacy and understanding. Whenever a waiter asks to take my order, I'll take his or her hand in mine and stroke it while softly whispering my order so they're forced to listen to my requests carefully. This makes them feel special, like we have a deep connection because I'm telling them a secret. Then they do whatever I say. For example:

"Let's do the Caesar salad, but let's go with organic butter lettuce instead of the romaine, ahi tuna instead of the grilled chicken, and cherry tomatoes instead of the croutons. Also, balsamic vinegar on the side instead of the Caesar dressing. Oh, and hold the parmesan. Thank you so much."

"I'll have six ounces of the grilled chicken breast. It's not on the menu but trust me, it's delicious. I'll make sure to recommend it to all my friends."

"Can I get the scallion and egg white omelet, and mixed greens with just a hint of truffle oil on the side? And can the omelet be prepared table-side so I can oversee the process? I'm allergic to egg yolk."

If I'm at a party, I'm there to socialize and have people ask me about the amazing jacket/top/dress/necklace/pants/skirt/shoes/cape/smock/romper/fur I'm wearing. Or I'm there to drink and do coke with famous people. Or I'm there because Brett Ratner invited me. Any way you cut it, I'm not there to eat. Nothing makes people want to talk to you less than if you're standing by the hors d'oeuvres table scarfing down every bit of food you can get your hands on like some kind of wildebeest.

On the other hand, if it's an intimate affair, like a dinner party, it's rude to avoid eating the food, so I utilize this go-to device: I keep a mental tab of every dish that comes out of the kitchen and make sure to put a little on my plate. Then I push it around, eat whatever is on my "Yes" list, and rave to anyone within earshot about how amazing the food is. Nine times out of ten this works like a charm. No one ever remembers what you actually ate at a dinner party. I can get through the meal without breaking my diet, and the host thinks I am an amazing guest.

I also consider myself a smoothie connoisseur. They're my culinary calling, if you will, and a great way to pack a shitload of nutrients into an eight-ounce glass. Over the years I've perfected my favorite smoothie recipes, and now I'm ready to share them with the world.

Smoothies: The Answer to All Life's Questions

RAW CELEBRATION OF LIFE SMOOTHIE

This smoothie is a super-delish way to nourish your body and soul through raw ingredients and the magic of nature.

SERVES: 1
TOTAL PREP TIME: 7 days

½ cup raw almonds, sprouted and peeled
½ large aloe leaf (gutted)
1 young tai coconut
1 large organic strawberry
4 organic blueberries
1 tablespoon fresh carrot juice
4 tablespoons fresh lemon juice
4 tablespoons fresh lime juice
1 star fruit
3 tablespoons fresh kiwi juice
1 whole orange
¼ cup fresh mango juice
1 teaspoon raw honey
1 teaspoon fresh bee pollen
1 cactus flower
¼ cup Babe's Cactus Flower Tea (Bring ½ cup water to boil, add one drop of rosewater and a cactus flower from the Mojave Desert that has been given a "purpose

and joy" blessing from your shaman. Place in refrigerator to chill for exactly twelve hours before using.)
Handful of ice cubes made from alkaline charged water
Pellegrino to taste

Soak the almonds in a covered Pyrex pan of alkaline-charged water for 3 days. Pat dry and peel off almond skins. Place peeled almonds back into uncovered Pyrex pan and allow to sprout for four more days. Place all ingredients in power blender and blend on HIGH for 3 rounds of 109 seconds. Add tablespoons of Pellegrino to taste while pulse blending for an additional minute. ■

OMEGA 3 HAIR AND SKIN REJUVENATION SMOOTHIE

You will literally glow after drinking this. Not for smoothie beginners—it's taken me nine years to be able to drink an eight-ounce glass.

Serves: 1
Total Prep Time: 10 minutes

8 ounces fresh salmon sashimi
1 teaspoon organic, cold-pressed, extra virgin olive oil
1 pinch Himalaya salt
Juice of 2 lemons
2 tablespoons Greek yogurt
2 tablespoons ground flaxseeds
½ cup tomato juice
Handful of spinach
3 oysters

Combine all ingredients in power blender and blend on HIGH for 2 minutes, or until frothy. Serve immediately. ■

TOOTHPASTE SMOOTHIE

This is a great way to combat cravings for solid food. It leaves your mouth with a minty, fresh, come-hither taste that you won't want to ruin with a messy bowl of pommes frites! And it's calorie-free! Enjoy!

SERVES: 1
TOTAL PREP TIME: 5 minutes

1 tablespoon Toms of Maine organic toothpaste
1 tablespoon fresh chopped organic mint leaves
5 tablespoons Pellegrino

Mix ingredients in food processor for 30 seconds. Pour into shot glass. Swish in mouth for 1 ½ minutes. Spit mixture into nearby sink. ■

¡ARRIBA! COFFEE SMOOTHIE

Whenever I'm feeling like my metabolism needs a little jump start, I make this smoothie and it totally does the trick.

SERVES: 1
TOTAL PREP TIME: 5 minutes, with a possible 8-hour elimination period.

¼ cup raw cacao
4 shots of espresso
1 tablespoon ground cayenne
1 cup brewed kopi luwak

3 tablespoons hemp milk
Splenda to taste

Place all ingredients in high-powered blender, except for hemp milk and Splenda. Blend on HIGH for 2 minutes. Pour in hemp milk. Blend on pulse for 1 minute while adding Splenda to taste. Don't leave the house for the next 6–8 hours. Stay close by a toilet if you can. Good luck! ■

LEMON SMOOTHIE

This is a refreshing, super-low-cal treat. Using a whole lemon, including the skin, maximizes nutrient absorption. Also this smoothie is the perfect silent companion for lying out by the pool and reading magazines.

SERVES: 1
TOTAL PREP TIME: 10 minutes

1 cup crushed ice made from alkaline-charged water
2 whole lemons, halved
4 packets of Splenda
1 egg white

Blend ingredients together for 5 minutes. Yum. ■

WHITE GIRL PROBLEM

#16

He's not a doctor, a lawyer, or a prince.

My dad was battling a terrible epidemic that must be brought to our attention: stubborn belly fat. Tummy weight leads to heart disease, which leads to orphaned me. I couldn't just stand by and watch the most important person in my life accept this cruel fate, so I fired our longtime chef, Frederic, and started a search for some new blood in the kitchen. I tried to steal the chefs at a few hot restaurants in town, but none of them could work around my diet restrictions: no white ingredients, no grains, and if my poop sinks, you're fired. Then there was an exhaustive but fruitless screening process that included two trips to the South of France and my dad's guest appearance as a judge on *Top Chef*. I was desperate. Was there no one who could make my dad thin again?

And then, fate intervened. My dad was at a small dinner party at a really big client's house and was so blown away by the meal that was served that he hired the chef, Jean-Raphael Guillaume Louis, on the spot. I'm normally the one making these types of major decisions, but I trusted my dad's opinion—especially after hearing that Jean-Raphael's meals were typically five bites or less and never took more than two minutes to eat. JR began working for us the following week.

Side note: Hiring a chef is never as easy as it sounds. Most people think that you just decide on someone, hire them, and then live the rest of your life in healthy, delicious bliss. The truth is, training and consulting your chef is a grueling, time-consuming process. Much like training a full-bred German shepherd. They're great listeners, but at the end of the day, discipline is the key to a successful relationship.

On JR's first day of work, I came downstairs to the kitchen and opened the fridge to find a frothy glass of some green, smoothie-like substance sitting on my designated shelf. I was pleased to see that JR had done his research and knew that I started weekdays with a kale smoothie. But we hadn't even had our first one-on-one consultation, so I wondered how he could have known what ingredients I considered acceptable. The texture and color looked promising, so I was encouraged. I positioned myself in the doorway of the fridge, facing in. This is how I take most of my meals, so that nobody sees me eat. I cautiously reached for the glass and took a tiny sip of my first Jean-Raphael smoothie.

It was so next-level. The splash of kale, swishing around harmoniously with the quiet and controlled robustness of the agave, all dancing on a pond of finely crushed organic ice, dripping down my esophagus like a cool rain. I do my best never to associate food with pleasure, but my senses overwhelmed me and I couldn't help myself. I became aroused and began to moan and writhe in ecstasy. I was uninhibited.

My moaning was getting louder and the intensity of my pleasure was deepening. In all of my personal commotion I failed to realize that I was no longer alone in the kitchen. Jean-Raphael had apparently returned from our garden sometime between my first sip and me practically climaxing in front of the fridge. I turned around and was mortified to see a gorgeous stranger staring at me. This was supposed to be my private moment, but it was very clear that Jean-Raphael had seen the whole thing. Um,

1. Why is Olivier Martinez in my kitchen?
2. Did my father really think it was okay to hire someone who looks like this?
3. Would I sleep with someone who works for me?
4. Did I really just have a foodgasm in front of a man I don't know?
5. Did I really just have a foodgasm, period?
6. Why me?

I was face-to-face with the most beautiful chef that ever walked the face of this earth. He was so French, so masculine, and so perfectly unkempt. I said something that I have never said before and have never said since. "Is there any more of this smoothie laying around?" Jean-Raphael, who had been staring at me blankly, shook his head no and grabbed the small towel that was draped over his shoulder, approached the slack-jawed smoothie whore that was me, and very gently wiped my face of the excess smoothie.

"*Je m'appelle Jean-Raphael*," he said with a grin.

"*Je m'appelle Babe.*"

There was no denying the chemistry between us. My feet were glued to the imported Brazilian tiles. JR and I were staring each other up and down.

"That was one of the best smoothies I've ever tasted. Let me guess, organic kale, oxygen-infused ice, one strawberry, a handful of blueberries, half teaspoon of agave nectar, spirulina, coconut oil, coconut meat, coconut hair and . . . an egg white?"

"*Oui.* Impressive."

"Delish. Next time, lose the agave. It's as bad for you as corn syrup. You should use raw honey instead. I just read that on GOOP. I apologize for that ghastly display just a second ago. I'm not a whore, I swear."

"There is no problem with enjoying something I prepared for you."

Sometimes when I meet a guy I like, I start lying uncontrollably right off the bat. "Well, I have a super-busy day ahead, so I better get started on all of my . . . work—charity, e-mails, voice lessons, Pilates, and everything else. So maybe I'll see you around, but probably not, because as I said, I'm swamped right now. With e-mails and voice mails and brushing my teeth and hair and just work in general. Biiiiyeee."

Smiling, I slowly backed away until I was sure I was out of his eyeline, then I ran up to my bathroom. I placed my hands on the marble countertop surrounding my sink and slowly looked up into the mirror, emitting a horrific and deafening silent scream. I was in love with my chef, Jean-Raphael. This was a major problem. Not only was it going to limit my ability to walk around my house in sweatpants, but I'm also not comfortable with a man I'm sexually attracted to knowing every single piece of food I eat. It's creepy.

For three weeks, I avoided the kitchen at all costs. It seemed to be working really well, plus I was definitely eating a lot less, but I knew it couldn't last. One night, I was suffering from designer's block. I had spent hours sketching on my iPad, but I couldn't come up with any designs for my leather scarf line that felt natural. I needed to clear my head and unwind, so I went down to the kitchen to meditate and give myself a little treat. My favorite indulgence late at night is one of my own creations. I call them: Splenda Bites. They're perfect for a 4th of July party or anytime you're feeling a little naughty and need something sweet to reward yourself. My secret is that I make thirty at the beginning of every month so I can eat one per day. During the holidays I make sixty.

Here's the recipe:

SPLENDA BITES®

SERVING SIZE: 1 bite

AMOUNT PER SERVING: Calories: 0, Total Fat: 0g, Sodium: 0mg, Protein: 0g

SERVES: 30

TOTAL PREP TIME: 10 minutes

FREEZE TIME: 5 hours

Approx. 5 cups filtered, organic, antibiotic-free water (If you can't find this, then bottled water will have to do.)
30 packets of Splenda

Combine the water and the Splenda in a large mixing bowl. Stir. Pour mixture into 3 standard-sized ice cube trays. Place on level surface in Sub-Zero freezer for 5 hours. This is a great opportunity to take a quick nap or catch up on current events. Remove ice trays from freezer and enjoy.

**Note:* You can always add a garnish to enhance your experience. For example, if your chef is doing Mexican night, garnish your Splenda Bites with lime. Then fire your chef. Mexican night? Are you kidding me? ■

So there I was, standing over an open freezer, a Splenda Bite melting in my mouth, examining the protrusion level of my hip bones, when I realized I wasn't breathing. The ice was lodged in my throat, choking me. Unable to move or scream for help, I accepted my fate and closed my eyes, praying that my death would be quick and painless.

Suddenly, there was a presence behind me. I knew it was a man, because I could smell his skin. I felt his hands wrap around my waist, gripping me tightly. They were big hands and they were caressing my frozen body. At first I was startled, but something was happening. I was so lost in the rush of heat that I almost forgot I was seconds away from expiring. I had never been touched like this before. He was squeezing me, over and

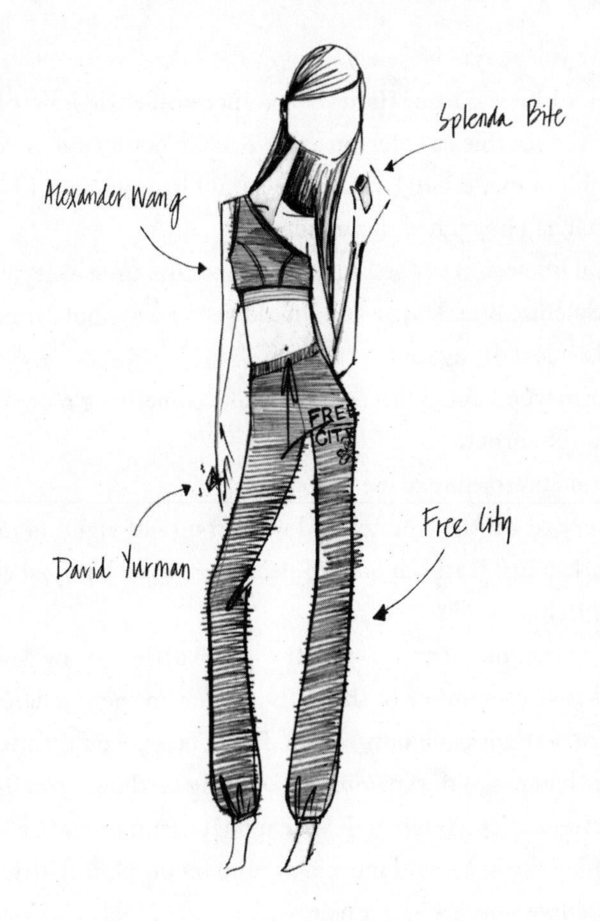

over with force. Then, like a bullet from a loaded gun, the Splenda Bite shot straight out of my mouth.

I turned to see who had saved my life, only to be met with Jean-Raphael's handsome face. He looked so chiseled in the uplighting of the Sub-Zero freezer drawer. That body! He reached out and tucked a loose wisp of hair behind my ear and rested his hand on my shoulder.

"Are you okay?" he asked.

Then I kissed him. Hard. It was incredible. He hoisted me up on the marble countertop and we made out for I don't even know how long. Finally, we stopped and I had a chance to realize what had happened. I wanted more.

"You know, I'm in the kitchen around this time every night for a Splenda Bite. Maybe you should keep an eye out for me in case I almost die again."

"Or maybe I could teach you to make something more delicious, like sorbet."

"Don't try to change me."

I hopped off the counter and walked myself right up to my room, leaving Jean-Raphael to deal with what had just happened in his own French way.

From that moment on, everything was different. By day, we would pass each other in the hallways and in the kitchen like nothing was going on between us. By night, we would embrace in the shadows of the "moonlight" setting on the Lutron lighting system in our kitchen. Jean-Raphael would prepare something delicious, I would move it around on my plate a little bit, and then we would fuck for hours.

Divided by class, united by the cosmos, our forbidden love was elevated with every encounter that we shared. A shoulder graze as we passed each other in the hallway felt like a long, passionate embrace. A stolen kiss in the pantry felt as if it were as powerful as an hour in bed together. We were falling for each other, and I loved how wrong it felt. I mean, this was my fucking chef we're talking about! It doesn't get more Romeo and Juliet than that.

For a brief moment, Jean-Raphael was my everything. I convinced myself that it could work, but it truly wasn't meant to be. There was no way we would be able to pull off this relationship long-term. He was my family's employee and he wore Crocs. I was so afraid of being found out by the other staff members or my father that I would go out of my way to treat JR like shit in front of them. So I decided to end it. I did my best to let him down gently one morning over coffee.

"JR, I love that you have a huge dick, but this isn't working. You're my family's employee, and you wear Crocs. We're over. Don't blame yourself. It's not in the stars."

He actually took it really well, which was annoying. Who knows? Had JR not been my chef, we might have had something solid. But in the end I couldn't justify a relationship with someone who gets off on the smell of bread. I am Babe, and I have my rules. Although I may not always stick to them, I always end up on the right side of them. JR and I still fuck on occasion when I'm bored (and once when I was stoned), but he knows it's never going to be more than that.

I need a therapist to talk about the problems I'm having with my therapist.

By the way, I've been seeing my therapist, Susan, since I was seven. She's my only friend who lets me talk about myself without making me feel guilty, so I can forgive her penchant for gray skirt suits. I can also forgive her retro-thick-rimmed-glasses situation, and I want to be cool with her tendency to take off one shoe mid-session, but honestly, and I've said this before, feet sick me the fuck out. But what can I do? Her feet, her life. I have to accept her just as much as she accepts me. So, in a lot of ways, I guess I'm her therapist.

I used to think everyone should be in therapy, until a few months ago, when I had a really bad session with Susan that led to us breaking up. I haven't seen her since that fateful Tuesday afternoon. I was at Susan's safari-chic office in Santa Monica, lounging on her Ralph Lauren Home distressed leather couch, and having what I believed was a major breakthrough. I remember this because I was wearing a new Dries Van Noten skirt that I was obsessed with.

"I don't know, Sue, I'm on the verge of something. It's like, I'm tired of always having to be the strong one in my relationships with men. When do I get to break down? When do I get to

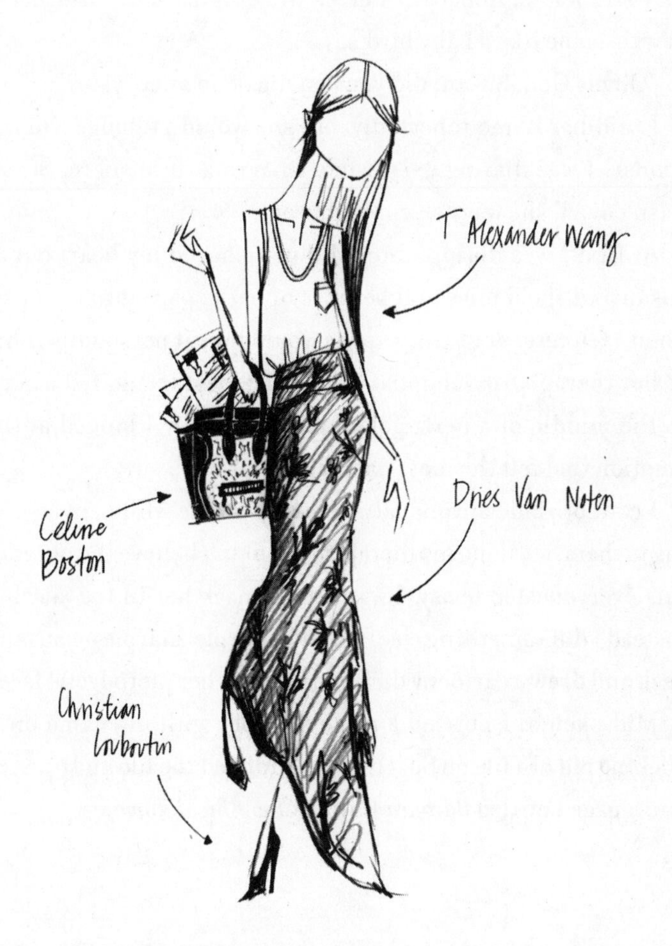

have a soft side, or be vulnerable? I'm done picking up the pieces of other people's broken lives. I think I need to start smoking more weed, don't you think?"

Susan said nothing, which I interpreted to mean, "Go on," so I continued to delve into my revelations until our time was up. I grabbed my bag and turned to smile at Susan, and noticed that she was slumped in her chair, eyes closed, head back, mouth agape like a baby bird's.

"Oh my God, Susan, did you just die of an aneurysm?"

I said her name repeatedly, but she wouldn't budge. No response. I was dialing 9-1-1 when I heard a little snore. Susan wasn't dead, she was asleep. Lights out.

At first I was disappointed. I'd just poured my heart out to Susan and she'd missed it because of her apparent narcolepsy. Then I felt hurt—I mean, anyone would take it personally if his or her therapist/psychopharmacologist/best friend fell asleep in the middle of a personal epiphany. Finally I landed at the emotion that felt the most natural: ANGER.

I cannot abide anyone falling asleep on me while I'm speaking to them, let alone my therapist. I couldn't believe the nerve of this overeducated hussy. I wanted to smack her in the jaw, but instead I did something else. I found a purple Sharpie on Susan's desk and drew a cartoony dick and balls on her pterodactyl face.

Mid-sketch, I noticed a piece of paper with my name on it sticking out of a file on Susan's lap. I grabbed the file and opened it to a page entitled *Barbara Walker: Client Breakdown.*

Susan F. Newman
11312 15th Street #103
Santa Monica, CA 90404
CA LIC # 10208-1224

CLIENT BREAKDOWN

PATIENT: *Barbara Walker*

DIAGNOSIS: *Narcissistic Personality Disorder*

CRITERIA:

Barbara Walker exhibits an unrealistic sense of self-importance as evidenced by her admitted dynamics with friends and house staff. She is convinced that she is "special" and feels more comfortable associating with other "special" individuals or groups. She exhibits a strong sense that she is entitled to more than she has earned or deserves. She has delusions of success, intellect, and physical beauty that are not based in reality, but based on a false notion that she is a hardworking individual. Barbara wavers on the ability to empathize with, or recognize, the feelings of others. She is sometimes unwilling to accept responsibility for her actions when their outcome is negative. Due to her underlying insecurities and doubts about herself, she is constantly seeking admiration and praise from those around her.

TREATMENT DURATION: *15 years*

MEDICATIONS PRESCRIBED OVER COURSE OF TREATMENT:

Adderall, Xanax, Ativan, Klonopin, Valium, Ambien, Sonesta, Lunesta, Paxil.

Who the fuck did this bitch think she was? Clearly she had no idea what she was talking about. I left her office with a slam of the door, taking my file with me.

Sue—

Had to run. Borrowed the book you're writing about me, but will return it next week with comments.

xo, B

P.S. Fuck you. Falling asleep?! Really??

When I got to my car I began to devour my file. It included notes from most of our sessions. Here are the highlights:

June 6, 1994

First session: Barbara Walker (7 years old) arrived in a suit and tie, briefcase, and glasses. Inspired by her love for the NBC sitcom Frasier, *she said she had come here because of her interest in becoming a therapist. She sat down on the couch and said, "Shoot." I informed BW that I was in fact the therapist and she was the client. Once she understood our roles, she had no interest in talking about anything other than the "to-scale" dollhouse of her Montecito home. She wanted my professional opinion on window coverings for her bedroom. She was concerned that her fabric guy wouldn't be able to match the patterns for the valances on such a small scale. She appears to need to control every little aspect of her life, and at such a young age it is concerning.*

August 15, 1995

Barbara came to our session today accompanied by her

nanny, Mabinty, and requested that I mediate some issues that they were having. BW explained that Mabinty refused to acknowledge the fact that BW is not a child, but an autonomous young woman, and shouldn't be grounded for surfing pro-anorexia chat rooms on AOL. BW doesn't have a very firm grasp of her social status in her home, and she is exhibiting signs of NPD at very early age (8 years old). The environment in which BW lives exacerbates her predisposition towards narcissism. Mabinty was highly verbal during the session and the three of us came to a civil agreement that allowed BW one hour of AOL time per week, with a block on any adult content.

December 14, 1998

BW arrived with a gift for me, which seemed to be an olive branch of sorts, after a string of particularly tumultuous sessions. But further discussion revealed that what she had purchased for me (a Hermès Scarf) was actually more of a message than an act of kindness. BW revealed that she felt it was important for me to start taking pride in the way that I looked, and that a pop of color wouldn't kill me. She also explained the importance of everyone on her "Team" being on the same page in terms of aesthetic. She assured me that I was not the only person with whom she felt the need to have this conversation. She gave me her cell phone number and told me to call her at any time with questions about current fashions. Although I have been dealing with BW's NPD for the past few years, I have found it a challenge to discuss some of her personality issues openly with her as she is only 11.

October 31, 2000

As it is Halloween, BW came in full costume to her session today. She was dressed as NEO (sp?) from a film called The Matrix. *All black, sunglasses and a trench coat. BW was in character for the entire hour-long session. She barely spoke, but when she did she referred to herself as The One, and addressed me as The Oracle. Throughout the session she referenced issues that she was having with Agent Smith and Trinity, who I later figured out were actually BW's father and BW's best friend Genevieve, respectively. Her commitment to her false reality was unwavering and actually quite impressive. Towards the end of the session BW informed me that she needed to leave through the back door of my office because Morpheus had set the rendezvous point with the Nebuchadnezzar in my office's back parking lot. As I watched BW get into her car from my office window I saw Mabinty waiting outside of the vehicle dressed in the exact same outfit that BW was wearing.*

March 11, 2002

Today Babe informed me about an elaborate scheme to lose her virginity to her best friend, Roman, who happens to be openly gay. When I advised her that this may not be the best plan of action, she covered her ears and started loudly reciting the names of her favorite designers in alphabetical order. Once she finished her list, she explained that losing her virginity would have to be on her terms, and her friend's orientation had nothing to do with it. She then changed the subject entirely and began talking about her upcoming driver's test, and what make of car would best suit the image she's curating for her formative years. She weighed the pros and cons of SUVs versus sedans until the last 30 seconds of our session when she mentioned that her father's girlfriend had died in a Botox-related chocking incident, yet she had no feeling either way about it.

January 26, 2004

BW is convinced that she was born with the wrong vagina, and has been trying to get me to weigh in on its appearance. I have repeatedly refused to do so and it is becoming a point of contention. I spent most of today's session explaining to BW why this was a matter that she should take up with a gynecologist or plastic surgeon. Our session was cut short when BW became too frustrated to communicate and stormed out of the room screaming. She returned seconds later, completely nude and I had no choice but to politely push her out of the room with my eyes closed. Another example of BW's problems with boundaries.

August 15, 2005

Today BW arrived 10 minutes early to her session and sat in the waiting room until it was her scheduled appointment time. When she came into my office she looked at me, said, "I can't with you today," and left.

June 9, 2006

A girl named Genevieve Larson arrived at my office this morning dressed as BW. GL explained that BW couldn't come to the session due to a double booking but GL had, with her, a list of things that BW wanted to go over with me during today's session. I explained that I do not conduct treatment of my clients in that manner and sent GL on her way. As I am writing this, I have received a text message from BW that says, "Why did you reject me like that? I needed you today."

July 21, 2006

10 minutes after our session was scheduled to begin, a cell phone came crashing through my office window. I was shocked and frightened and there was broken glass everywhere. The cell phone was ringing, so I picked it up and answered it. It was BW and she very calmly stated, "Sorry I'm Late." I was speechless so she continued. "I just can't be confined by the walls of an office today. I need to be out in the open, and I need you to be indoors, so I figured this is the best way to accommodate my needs." I very angrily explained that this behavior was completely inappropriate, but BW couldn't seem to grasp the severity of her actions. She had already scheduled for a new window to be installed in my office.

December 30, 2007 (Phone session, BW is away at Parsons)

BW lost control. She has become obsessed with a particular handbag that has apparently "sold out at every store in the world." Her unhealthy relationship with something as materialistic as a purse is severely interfering with her ability to function. She claims to be suffering withdrawal-like symptoms, and is having severe difficulty eating and sleeping. She refuses to discuss anything but the handbag. It is possible that this is the first time in her life that she has been unable to get something that she really wanted.

March 5, 2008

When treatment began with BW 14 years ago, I was asked by her father to tread lightly on the subject of BW's mother. I have tried on numerous occasions to initiate a discussion pertaining to this matter, but have been met with severe noncompliance. Today I asked BW what she would say to her mother if she were to walk through the door. She spent 45 minutes sitting in silence on the couch, refusing to speak on the subject. She has a tendency to shut down completely when I ask her about her relationship with her mother.

May 30, 2010

BW arrived 25 minutes late, only to tell me that she had to leave 10 or 15 minutes early to get to her blowout on time. She is posing for a friend's photo shoot and spent the 10 minutes that she was actually on the couch talking about the one cellulite dimple on her left thigh. Wanted to know if I thought that was grounds enough to cancel on her friend.

After reading through Susan's file of lies, I realized that she didn't even know who I was. *Narcissistic Personality Disorder.* Is that even real? I'd thought our friendship was a bond that couldn't be broken, but obviously she was jealous and felt the need to attack me. I don't do toxic relationships, so I decided that Susan and I were officially done. Falling asleep was one thing, but slandering my name behind my back was the last straw.

I was mad, but I was also confused. The unsettling notion that I didn't have a therapist anymore was weighing on me, and I could feel a panic attack coming on. I took two Xanax and got in the bath to think through what my next move would be. Four hours later, the water in the tub was freezing and my hands and feet were ridiculously pruney (great for the skin FYI).

I couldn't just cut Susan out of my life. I had to find a way back to the way we were. I wanted to make an effort to rebuild trust and mend our relationship, so I texted her.

Babe 7:24PM: Heyyyy. So sorry for drawing on your face.

Babe 7:24PM: Look, everyone makes mistakes. I want to forgive you.

Babe 7:25PM: I read about an amazing couples therapist in O Magazine, we have an appointment with him tomorrow at 5.

Babe 7:25PM: Cool?

Susan didn't text me back. The next morning, I got an e-mail from her explaining that she couldn't work with me again until I figured out what it was that I wanted from treatment. She asked me to write her a list of specific reasons why I'm in therapy and how it could help me. I didn't do it, and I never wrote her back because I was super-busy that week. I did, however, think a lot about her question. I'd never considered my reasons for going to therapy. I used to think what I wanted was a best friend who would listen to me and a chic office to hang out in for two hours every week, but after all this rehab bullshit, I'm starting to think otherwise.

My dad's girlfriends are the best. Without them I'd have no one to scream at and blame everything on.

So I've covered the fact that my real mom wasn't really around (at all), but in a weird way, her nonexistence was a non-issue. She was MIA and I was tot-tal-ly fine with it. Seriously. I had my dad, I had Tai Tai, and I had Mabinty, and all three of them loved me to death. They showered me with affection and attention and I loved them right back, so we were all good, but I never understood why my dad kept trying to introduce our family to his ridiculous girlfriends.

Natalia

I was the only child my family needed, so you can imagine how strange it was when I was ten years old and my dad started dating a model who was twenty. Natalia is the first girlfriend I remember my dad having. She was six-foot-one, stick-thin, and Romanian. I spent the majority of their two-year relationship thinking Natalia was just a gorgeous, but somewhat retarded, foreign exchange student. It wasn't until I caught her and my dad naked in the wine cellar one night that I realized she was definitely not retarded and definitely not an exchange student.

When I noticed Natalia's affinity for hideously cheesy Louis Vuitton jewelry, I realized she was a gold-digging skank who, despite having the face of a Victoria's Secret Angel, was not to be trusted. Even at the young age of eleven, I couldn't stand by and watch my dad be used that way. Could she not have at least bought some elegant vintage Van Cleef instead? I had to get rid of her ass, which was surprisingly easy. Tai Tai and Mabinty both hated her from the start, so all I had to do was tell my dad how scary and confusing it was when Natalia asked me if I "knew anyone that sold heroin" and poof! Just like that, she was gone.

Jasmine

I guess my dad was into dating models, because there was an unfortunate string of them that followed in Natalia's precarious footsteps. At the time it was fine with me, because they were all psychos, so nothing ever got too serious between him and any of the girls he brought home. Plus I loved stealing their makeup when they'd sleep over, so I was cool with his whole "I need to date young to feel young" M.O. Then all of a sudden, he was off models and on to Dr. Jasmine Bleeth (such a sick coincidence, I know), a Beverly Hills plastic surgeon responsible for the unnatural-looking faces of just about every A-List actress in Hollywood in the early 2000s (see: *Hanging Up, Dr. T and the Women*).

Unfortunately, Jasmine suffered from a pretty intense addiction to her *own* face. She over-injected her chin with Botox one morning, rendering her lower jaw immovable. This made her look like the cover of one of my *Goosebumps* books, so I politely requested that my dad not bring her around the house anymore. He totally understood. Jasmine's accident, which you'd think a plastic surgeon could overcome, was actually detrimental to her health and ended up killing her. Like, she died trying to chew a rare piece of filet mignon at Mastro's during a business dinner. She should have stuck to smoothies, but the Beverly Hills lifestyle can make some people so greedy. It's dark. It's all very dark. And not my problem, so that's all I really want to say about Jasmine.

O

Jasmine's death really threw my father for a loop. I think it made him realize how fleeting life can be, and yearn for a woman with substance as opposed to a woman with substance abuse issues. This was when he started dating a celebrity—I'm talking major celebrity—so major, in fact, that I can't say who it was. Though I will say she was super-fucking-wise, super-fucking-influential, and super-motherfucking rich. I was obsessed with her. Mabinty and I watched her talk show religiously until it went off the air last year. Long story short, she was based in Chicago and my dad was based in LA, the long distance thing didn't seem to work out for them, and they eventually broke up. O, if you're reading this,

I'd like to make amends. I should never have sent that text message to you, and I am so, SO sorry.

Lizbeth

Aside from the psycho who tried to strangle me once (can't go there right now), that pretty much sums up my dad's romantic entanglements and brings me to his current girlfriend, Lizbeth.

Lizbeth met my dad when she was seeking legal representation. She was writing a soon-to-be-best-selling workout book and negotiating the release of her own line of reasonably priced, kind of cute (for her) fitness DVDs. She and my dad must have really hit it off, because two years later, they're still going strong.

I first met Lizbeth in London, when my dad brought her with him to visit me while I was in school at Central Saint Martins. I was annoyed, to say the least, and didn't really have much to say to her, so I spent their entire trip pretending she didn't exist, which is super-fun to do to people. I'd written Lizbeth off as just another piece of the month, until I arrived back home from my college tour to find that she and my dad were still *very* much together. Um, okay? I wasn't happy, and may have broken a few Hermès serving platters when my dad told me that he "loved" her, but that was to be expected. Not only was I going to have to deal with a woman who was super into yoga, juicing, and talking about her feelings, but I was going to have to *vacation* with her. Don't get me wrong, I love healthy lifestyles, but I wasn't down with some perky gym-body constantly hanging around the Walker family household.

Lizbeth sensed my resentment toward her and, in an attempt to make nice, scheduled a yoga/spa retreat for the two of us under the guise that we would "have a really fun girls trip, get to know each other better, and learn our mantras!" How fun and intimate and original you are, you clever little ladyboy you! I tried to explain to Lizbeth that biceps, breathing, and silence were not my thing, and that I didn't give a shit about my mantra. She responded by telling me that without a mantra, one is lost and wandering the earth aimlessly. For my dad's sake, I restrained myself from slapping her perfect tits off, and immediately took my frustrations to lululemon, where I poured my heart into crafting the perfect yoga retreat wardrobe. We were off to Ojai that weekend.

What I thought might be a really disturbing trip turned out to be a really great exercise in patience. Upon arriving at the retreat, Lizbeth and I were greeted by our personal yogi, Baba. Baba was a limber and sinewy man, with huge, I mean *huge*, hands. He was sporting a major yoga body, and I was sporting a vision of him naked on top of me in crow pose. I was convinced he could give me the most intense and tantric of orgasms, but Baba and I weren't exactly on the same page. Not even my best smizing efforts during our first session together could crack his placid and concentrated visage. Lizbeth, on the other hand, was relishing the seriousness of Baba's practice and quizzing him on his methods. They seemed to really be stroking each other's yoga dicks, and I cannot take it when yoga people talk to each other about yoga, so I excused myself and went in search of an herb salad.

I came back to the room and announced to Lizbeth that I was taking a vow of silence for the rest of the day. She was super-excited by my sudden commitment to my practice and said she would do the same, joining me in lying out by the infinity pool, reading magazines, and roasting in the sunshine. And smiling. That's one thing I can give Lizbeth credit for. She met all of my attempts at rudeness with a really good attitude, never once acting like a bitch and always insisting on doing everything together.

The truth is, you can really only sit silently through eighteen hours of meditation, sweat lodge sessions, salt showers, and body wraps with someone until you have to say something to them. So I eventually broke my vow of silence, and found out that Lizbeth had an irritatingly friendly response to just about every single thing I said to her.

In the middle of deep breathing exercises in a meditation cave:

Me: I had a labiaplasty when I was eighteen. My dad doesn't know though. Don't tell him.

Lizbeth: Oh that is *so* cool. So many women benefit from having that surgery. You know what, my best friend in the world just had a vaginoplasty last week and she is *loving* the results. I won't tell your dad. Sometimes guys just don't get it. I'm gonna go grab a wheatgrass shot. Want one?

Over lunch after a yoga session:

Me: I really want to fuck that Baba guy.

Lizbeth: He is so cute! I could totally see you guys together.

Keep wearing those yoga outfits you brought with you and it's on. Want a coconut smoothie? They're delicious.

During an almond sprouting seminar:

Me: Are you trying to destroy my life?
Lizbeth: No way! I'd like to be friends. I don't even think I could destroy you if I tried! From what your dad's told me you're a really strong and vivacious woman, which is so inspiring. *Namaste.*

I eventually got around to hooking up with Baba, and Lizbeth was even cool about walking in on him opening up my sacral chakra with his tongue:

Me: Lizbeth, get the fuck out of here!
Lizbeth: Oops! My bad. You go, girl!

All in all, the trip was fine. Annoying but fine. I lost ten pounds from eating mostly herbs and was given the most beautiful mantra by my Vipassana guide. It's a secret, but if you've seen me naked and can read Sanskrit, you know what it is. Though it pains me to say this, Lizbeth is actually very sweet and I'm sure she'll be good for my dad. Either that or they'll get married and divorced within six months. They're basically polar opposites, so we'll see. I guess it's okay for him to find love and happiness. Personally, I think he'll always have commitment issues because he's still hung up on my mom, but what do *I* know?

When you say, "Get a job," I hear, "I hate you."

I got home from a particularly stressful yoga retreat to find out that the boss at my dad's law practice had finally decided that he was rich/old enough to retire/die, and the board of the firm had decided my father should take over as the new senior partner. My dad had pretty much been running that place since the day he started working there, so it was exciting for him to be recognized for all of his hard work. It's pretty clear that I got my incredible work ethic from my dad, and I'm so proud/lucky to be his daughter.

As soon as I got news of my dad's promotion, I began planning a surprise dinner party in his honor. It was going to be everything that he looked for in a great dinner party: good friends, lots of wine, and British food (almost impossible to do with my calorie restrictions, but I was up for the challenge). I got to work curating a guest list and menu that would suit the occasion.

I kept the guest list small: me, my dad, Mabinty, Roman, Genevieve, and a few other partners from my dad's firm. I hired Jamie Oliver (a client of my dad's) to prepare dinner for us, and spent days figuring out the lighting scheme, tablecloth, place mats, napkin color story, and the perfect playlist. I was in the zone—not unlike when I'm creating a new smoothie and every new ingredient I think of only serves to enhance the overall flavor-to-calorie ratio. The icing on the cake was that I'd confirmed Elton to come by and play my dad's favorite song ("Straight to Hell" by the Clash) at the end of the night. It was shaping up to be a perfect evening, and I knew that my father was going to be so thrilled by all of the love and time that I had poured into this celebratory dinner.

This was my dad's night, which really meant that it was my night, which really meant that Lizbeth was NOT invited. I wanted to spend time with my dad, and I didn't want to deal with him sticking his tongue down his girlfriend's throat, so I told her that the dinner party was on Thursday night. It was on Wednesday. Not my problem. I figured I was killing two birds with one stone: Liz wouldn't be there (point for me) and my dad would be annoyed with her for not showing up (point for me). We would have our dinner, drink our wine, make our toasts, and send him on his way to being head honcho at the biggest shop in town.

I was beaming with pride on the morning of the dinner. Mabinty and I started editing the looks that I'd put together the night before. Sometimes her taste is a little off for me, but I always value her input on my sartorial choices—Jamaican culture really embraces a bold color palette, and I can always get behind that. I stood in front of two hanging racks in my room and explained my approach to her.

I pointed to some busy/bright dresses. "Okay—so this rack is all about celebration and joy—hence the patterns and bolds," then I motioned to a bunch of earth-toned pantsuits and long skirts, "and these looks are more of a subtle and civilized nod to Dad's accomplishments, without taking away from his moment. I know you lean toward patterns, so you're probably the worst person to ask for help with this, but which vibe do you think is the right vibe? I'm kind of stumped."

"Yuh know mi like di bright ones," she said, glancing at the racks.

"Okay, knew you were gonna say that. Which dress?"

"Yuh cyan't ago wrong wid di Missoni. Yuh look damn good ina print."

"Yeah, but I can't show up to this dinner looking like a gypsy."

Mabinty held up a blue sequined Dior. "Dis shiny one might be real nice fi yuh."

"Really? I don't know, I wore that to a rave once, so I can never look at it the same way. And it's so loud."

"Why don't yuh go and try it on, and Mabinty cyan go down to mi room to take a teeny little nap."

"Not funny."

"Okay, okay. Yuh need to go wid sumtin' fun and fancy, yuh know?"

"Mmm hmm . . ."

"Get yuh hair real big. Yuh father loves di rock and roll and he will most definitely be ina good party mood tonight."

"Okay, I like where this is going."

"And Sir Elton is comin' tonight too, so yuh wanna look like a drag queen for him. He loves a good show. Go wid di Dior. Yuh cyan't go wrong wid Dior."

"You're absolutely fucking right. Sometimes you just get me."

As soon as I tried it on, I realized Mabinty was wrong about the dress. It could not have been less event-appropriate—this was my dad's dinner party, not a disco. But Mabs was right about going with blue, so I ended up resurrecting a cerulean Chloé dress from 2007. It was perfectly daughterish.

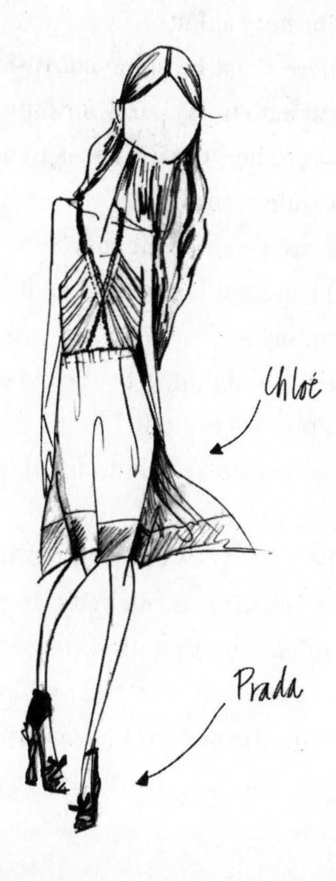

As the day progressed, I was so preoccupied with last-minute details that, when 6:45 P.M. rolled around, it dawned on me that no one from Jamie Oliver's team had shown up yet. Not a sous chef, nothing. They were supposed to be in the kitchen, prepping soufflés at 4:00. *Fuck*. I was panicking and my stomach started to turn. And it wasn't a hunger pang, because I'd had a huge cucumber salad for brunch at eleven.

I immediately got Jamie's assistant, Sara, on the phone.

"Hi, Sare Bear, Babe Walker here. Where is J.O.? His team was supposed to be here at four."

"Hi, Babe. There must be some confusion. Jamie ran into Lizbeth Monday at a birthday party for Jennifer Aniston's cat's cat, and according to her, the dinner is tomorrow night, so we changed his schedule accordingly."

"Fuck my ass, are you kidding me, Sara!? The dinner is tonight! Can you please get Jamie here right away? I'll push the meal back an hour or two."

"Unfortunately, no. He's now booked to show up at a charity auction in downtown LA tonight."

"Enough!" I screamed as I slammed the phone into the receiver.

Karma can be a nasty bitch. Goddamn you, Lizbeth, and your fucking networking at celebrity pets' birthday parties! This was a complete and total disaster. My dad was going to be home in the next thirty minutes and I was celebrity chef–less, and therefore dinner party–less, and I was starting to have a meltdown. Then I got a really fucking cute text from Roman.

Roman 7:07PM: Got day drunk in Malibu with Gen. Not gonna make it tonight but tell your dad that we love him soooooooooo much. Don't hate us!!

Babe 7:10PM: I always knew you two would betray me. Have TONS of FUN getting another DUI.

To top it off, I had an e-mail on my BlackBerry from Elton saying the weather in Nice was shit and he was stuck there for a few more days. So now it was going to be myself, my dad, and his stuffy work friends sitting around a table with no food on it. Perfect. I cracked open Pinot Noir from Oregon, or somewhere else far away and expensive, and started drinking straight from the bottle. I must've called and disinvited my dad's partners at some point, but that memory is kind of fuzzy. Either way, they didn't show up, thank God.

I was three sheets to the wind when my dad walked into the dining room. I was sitting at the head of the dining room table with all the lights off and a single candle burning next to me.

"I'm sorry, Dad. I ruined the party," I whispered.

"What party?" he asked.

"Your surprise promotion dinner party."

"You sneaky little fuck, you planned a dinner for me? That's sweet, but I don't need some big to-do party. It's okay, darling."

"No. It's not okay. It's inexcusable."

"It's not inexcusable. Who cares?! Plus, I fucking hate socializing. Pass that bottle, darling," he said.

"I tried to get Jamie Oliver here to cook for you, but my plan was foiled because I lied to Lizbeth and told her the dinner was tomorrow night instead of tonight because I didn't want her to come." I handed him the wine. "I can't even do one nice thing for the person I love most." This sounded sappy dripping out of my mouth, but the sad part was that it was true.

"I know you think this night is just a big cock-up but it's not." He smiled, taking a swig from the bottle. "We have wine and we have each other's company. That's good enough for me."

"Do you hate me, Dad?" I winced.

"Babe, I love you more than I've bloody loved anyone or anything else in my entire life. I'm glad that we are here right now, just the two of us. We haven't spent any quality time together since Tai Tai's funeral."

"I know, but I've been happy doing my own thing. Plus you've been working harder than a stripper and spending all your free time with Lizbeth."

"I understand that you're adjusting to Lizbeth. That's fine. She can seem like a real twat when you first meet her, but once you get to know her, she's great. You'll see." He was trying to make me feel better.

"Whatever. I'm kind of too busy to be making new friends right now anyways, so tell her not to hold her breath."

"What are you busy with? Shopping? Cutting your hair? Deleting entire food groups out of your diet?"

"Yes, exactly."

"Don't you want more for yourself, Babe?" His eyes were getting serious. "University didn't really work out in the way that we had all hoped." He took another sip of Pinot and passed me the bottle. "You've been home for a bit, you've had your shits and giggles, you've fucked around. Shouldn't you be settling in? Maybe thinking about working?"

I hated where this convo was going. My dad continued. "It's been three months since your grandmother passed away, and to be perfectly shitting honest with you, you haven't seemed like yourself. You have no direction, no passion. You're floundering, Babe. I can tell when you're floundering."

"Dad. I'm gonna try really hard not to be completely offended right now." I took a deep breath, repeated my mantra twice in my head, and said, "I decorated my room, I acquired three vintage Alaïas last month, I read style.com every day, I planned this whole party! My life is a lot more work than you think."

"I know you can fill a calendar, but you're missing the point. You're playing around and wasting your time. None of your appointments or purchases are going to fulfill you if you don't earn them for yourself. Your spending habits have gotten ridiculous by the way." He was getting heated, so I fired back.

"Oh, really? Well maybe you should come to my next appointment with my shaman, Steve, because he seems to think I'm *very* fulfilled. And who are you to talk about ridiculous spending? You buy whatever the fuck you want! Last week I saw a bill on your desk for that new fish tank. Thirty-seven thousand dollars? Come on, Dad."

"I spend money that I work my bloody arse off for, so I *can* buy whatever the fuck I want. I've *earned* that right. You, my dear, have not. It would behoove you to get a job."

I stood up and put my hands on the table. "Okay. It's been really great spending this *quality time* with you, but FYI, I'm over this convo!" I yelled.

I stormed off to the kitchen. This conversation was

completely stressing me out. I grabbed Mabinty's giant tub of Häagen-Dazs ice cream out of the freezer, got the biggest fucking spoon I could find, walked over to the sink, and proceeded to scoop large spoonfuls of ice cream and angrily flick them directly down the drain. My father followed me to find me in the midst of my binge/purge.

"Tai Tai told me that I shouldn't have to work to make a living, and she was right. I like the way things are. I'm happy with my life. I command a lot of respect in the places where I conduct my business."

"Well, I can't let you just float through life, all la-di-fucking-da. You're bloody better than that. You have so much goddamn potential when you put your mind to something. Your sketches are brilliant and you made such good marks at fashion school. That kind of drive is what makes you really fucking special."

"Then what should I do?"

"Find something you love to do. I love my job, and I know that you have it inside of you to feel the same way about something. But it's not just going to fall into your lap. You need to get it sorted."

I stopped scooping ice cream and looked at him. Until that moment, I'd assumed that my life would just go on as it had been going. I'd buy a lot of clothes, marry Leonardo DiCaprio, get divorced, get scary skinny, get fat, and then die. I never saw myself as a career girl. Now that my dad was forcing me to get a job, it was obvious that I was going to have to rethink my life path. No one had ever tried seriously leveling with me about my goals, and it felt wrong, dirty even, like it was a subject that I wasn't supposed to talk about. What the fuck was I going to do with my life?

Maybe people would take me seriously if I weren't so hot.

To keep my dad off my case, I started waking up early and making him coffee every morning before sending him off to work. I literally had no reason to be up this early, other than the fact that I needed him to believe that I was super-motivated and actively seeking employment, which was easy for him to buy when I'd bound down the staircase all happy and rosy at 7 A.M. Once he was gone, I'd go back to sleep until twelve or one, but getting up that early for thirty minutes was a great way to keep his nagging at bay.

Then one afternoon, while napping in my sauna, I had a dream that put my entire life's purpose in perspective. It started off with me floating through space in a truly unflattering spacesuit. And I've worn a lot of spacesuits. Trust me. There was a week in 1998 that was all about spacesuits for me.

I knew I was dreaming, because I had a French manicure, which I would NEVER. Suddenly I started hurtling toward Earth at light speed. It was like skydiving but way more intense. Like if you took two Ambien and then went skydiving and forced yourself to stay awake the entire time. I thought I was going to die, and then I remembered I was dreaming and you totally can't die in your dreams, so I went with it. I landed somewhere in the Kalahari Desert. My spacesuit must have burned off when I entered the Earth's atmosphere, because I was naked, covered in sand, and my hair was really beachy and wavy. I stood up and started walking.

I had no idea where I was going, but I knew I was on a mission of some sort. After what seemed like aeons of trudging through the desert, I came to an oasis. A blue pool of water surrounded by lush, green palm trees. I knelt down to take a drink of the ice-cold water, when all of a sudden a figure arose from the middle of the pool. It was my Tai Tai, and she was wearing a dashiki.

"My dumpling," she said. "You look great."

"Thanks. I've lost weight. You look good too, but why are you wearing that?"

"Because it's beautiful. It's simple."

"Um. What are you talking about? Can I have your vintage Goyard luggage? It wasn't in my part of the will, but no one else wants it."

"You're missing the point, my love. You don't need any more baggage."

"Tai Tai, who *are* you right now?"

"I'm your guardian angel, and I'm trying to tell you that your life is in dire need of direction. Simplify, and you will find balance."

"Can you please be a little more specific? What am I supposed to do with my life?"

Then there was a low rumble that started erupting into an upbeat, drum-heavy song. A tribe of beautiful African children ran up to me. They took my hands and started dancing with me. They danced around my Tai Tai too, singing and laughing. I looked closer and saw that they were wearing the cutest, chicest little dashikis I had ever seen in my life. In an array of colors. Gold, magenta, tangerine, cerulean, sparkles. I gasped, and then I woke up in my Missoni bikini, covered in sweat, screaming.

I knew then, at that moment, that my Tai Tai had infiltrated my dreams to finally give me my ultimate purpose, my reason for being on this Earth: To design a high-end line of children's dashikis with matching kufi hats. (I'm pretty sure Leo had something to do with this inception. Leo, if you're reading this, yes, I'll marry you. But you already know that because you've been inside my brain. Blushing!)

My idea would be a breakthrough in child care/baby fashion. It was ethnic, fabulous, and original. An idea that would not only establish my talents, but also make me a worthy contributor to the global community at large. Perfection. I peeled myself off the bench of the sauna and immediately got to work writing up my business model.

Babe for Babies

INITIATIVE

Babe for Babies is a for-profit nonprofit organization. The mission is to create a line of high-end children's apparel inspired by traditional African dress. 50% of the net proceeds will go to Small Babes, a charity that focuses on providing needy African children with upscale, fashionable-yet-functional clothing. The other 50% will go to me, Babe Walker, as the CEO, President and Head Designer of the line.

PRICING

Infant (size 0m–24m) $695.00
Toddler (size 3T–5T) $1295.00
Kids (size XXS–L) $1775.00

TARGETED VENDORS

Barneys New York, Fred Segal, Madison LA, Creatures of Comfort, Opening Ceremony, Maxfield, Colette Paris, Shopbop.com, Net-A-Porter.com, "Babe for Babies" Pop Up Shops.

MARKETING STRATEGY

Thanks to a pristine production process, mixed with an array of ultra-luxe materials, these dashikis will practically sell themselves. There should also be ads in *Vogue/Harper's Bazaar/*

Elle/British Vogue/French Vogue/Vogue Nippon/Vogue Italia/any other major fashion publications.

I had to create a mood board to set the tone for my collection. I started with images of my favorite celebrity mothers and their adopted offspring. Angelina Jolie and Zahara Jolie-Pitt, Madonna and David Banda/Mercy James, Sandra Bullock and Louis Bardo, Woody Allen and Soon Yi. I added luxurious swatches and textiles, sequins, patterns, ikat, rainbow, photos of Alek Wek, most of the spring/summer 2011 Lanvin collection, and for good measure one shot of Natalia Vodianova making the same face that the Afghani girl from that famous *National Geographic* issue did. You really need to be all-inclusive when mood boarding.

I sketched out an entire collection, thirty-four looks, inspired by the creation of the Earth and the natural elements. The collection began with basic muslin dashikis in black, then muslin dashikis in white, then an explosion of space-print dashikis in rich satins, and then an earthy, woodsy vibe with bark-colored cashmere dashikis and green kufi hats. Then I transitioned into a sky, air, and water vibe ranging from the lightest blue silk dashikis to deep oceanic silk-organza blend dashikis. The final seven looks were inspired by the hot Kalahari sunsets. I'm talking sheer linen dashikis in blazing oranges, corals, and fuchsias. The collection was beautiful. It was inspired. It was everything. It was my baby.

I needed a backer to help me produce my vision, so I scheduled meetings with some well-connected family friends. Namely, Diane Von Furstenberg, Marc Jacobs, and Rachel Zoe. I perfected my pitch:

Smash cut to you as a baby in Africa. You're naked, you're starving, where are your parents? Who knows. You're alone in the world. What would really come in handy? Food, water, shelter, and a gorgeous dashiki.

Now smash cut to you as a baby in the United States. What do you want more than anything? You want to be hip. And nothing's more hip than being fashionable and charitable. Enter Babe for Babies. Our dashikis are luxurious, they're handmade, they're day-to-night, they're expensive, they're sustainable. Fifty percent of the proceeds of your dashiki have gone to providing our friends in the motherland with an equally expensive and gorgeous dashiki. Think about how confident you'll feel, slipping the luxurious fabric over your little body, knowing that you are providing a baby in a faraway land with all the resources they need to live their lives and look fabulous doing it.

Babe for Babies is not just a clothing line, it's a lifestyle. It's a worldview. It's a solution.

Surprisingly, they all turned me down. This just goes to show you that even visionaries can be shortsighted sometimes. They were basically telling me that they didn't want the world to be a better place. It's fine, people did the same thing to Gandhi, Moses, and Joan of Arc. I decided to approach my father and offer him the opportunity to be an investor in my line.

"Dad. Here's the deal. Clothing. Luxurious, beautiful, African clothing. For children. By me."

"Babe. What the fuck are you talking about?"

"Daaaaaaaaaaad. Can I have ninety-seven thousand dollars?"

"What?!"

"That's what it's going to cost to produce this line. Who's going to bat for African orphans in the scope of children's fashion?! Sure, girls like Suri Cruise can carry their expensive, mini designer handbags, but when are they going to represent for their fellow earthlings living in squalor? Help me help everyone. I can do it for eighty-seven thousand if I cut the beaded clutches."

"If you think I'm going to invest in a fashion start-up, you're out of your bloody mind. I'd never see a return on my

investment. And eighty-seven thousand dollars? For baby clothes? My God!"

The fact that my dad foolishly passed on the opportunity didn't stop me. I knew if I was going to see my vision come to fruition, I would have to take matters into my own hands. This unfortunately meant I would have to take the money out of my own trust. Annoying but necessary. I went into full-scale production mode, hiring a design assistant and six interns. I repurposed the guesthouse to be my live/work space. This is an absolute must for young designers on a budget. It was my little factory of dreams.

These dashikis were not the easiest thing to manufacture. I mean, I thought they would be because they're small and I expected that I (my interns) could throw at least ten together per day. Nope. The Italian silks that I had flown in were so fucking delicate that we ended up ruining half of the supply within the first week of production. After three weeks of literally doing nothing but work on my line, my team and I had managed to complete two full dashikis, and were $11,000 over budget. The interns looked dead—they all had really greasy hair and dark circles. I was fatigued. I was only getting seven hours of sleep a night and had a paper cut on my left ring finger. Nothing is easy in the world of fashion.

Although we were thirty-two looks short of a full line, I started putting feelers out via e-mail to buyers I had relationships with, just to get a sense of how many dashikis we would need to produce once orders were placed.

Dear ______,

You look great! Now it's time to make a difference. Attached is my business plan and order form. Feel free to e-mail me with any questions you may have.

Best,

Babe Walker

CEO, President, Head Designer

Babe for Babies

Babe@BabeforBabies.com

A few weeks went by, and no one had responded. I didn't get it. I decided to call up my friend Xander, an assistant buyer at Barneys, to see if he'd gotten my e-mail.

"Hey Xanta Claus, it's Babe Walker."

"Babe—my God, you are such a crazy bitch. That e-mail you sent last week had us all in stitches. Where do you come up with this stuff? Hilarious! Those sketches? Too much. Loved it."

"Amazing! When can I expect your order? I'm doing a fabric buy later today, so if you can give me an estimate of how many pieces you're going to take, that would be super-helpful."

"AHHHHHAHAHAHAHAHA!!! You should come by the store soon. All the new Proenza stuff is in. Love you. Mean it."

He hung up. Confused, I called Linda, another buyer friend, at Fred Segal.

"Hey, Lindyyyyyy," I said.

"Hi, Babe. Got your e-mail last week. Kind of offensive. I spent six months in Ethiopia after high school, building schools and educating families on sustainable farming."

"So you totally get it. I never got your order form though. Want to just tell me what you need over the phone?"

"I won't be ordering anything. Personally, I found the whole idea to be pretty tasteless. So fuck you."

"Okay. Um, wow . . . what are you trying to say?"

"But you should totally come by the store and check out the new Proenza stuff. It's insane. Tons of neon." And then she hung up.

After reaching out to some more buyers, it was apparent that nobody wanted anything to do with my passion project. No one was on board with Babe for Babies.

What the fuck?! Where had I gone wrong? My idea was completely organic. It had come from a good place—a place of love and wanting to help the less fortunate. One hundred and eight thousand dollars and all that hard work down the drain, and all I had to show for it were these two stupid dashikis and no one cared. I didn't know what to make of it. I thought I was following my dreams and honoring my Tai Tai's wishes. How could she have led me so astray? I had unresolved anger at all the buyers for not placing any orders, but they were spot-on about the new Proenza collection. It was major. I bought most of it. So, lesson learned, I guess.

Every job I've ever had is the worst job I've ever had.

So, as it turns out, everyone really does have a job. Even people who seem like they don't have jobs, like the President and Ryan Seacrest, do. Sometimes you can't tell that someone is actually *at work*, but they totally are. Like lifeguards and taxi drivers. I was starting to notice that the pool of my friends that could meet me for lunch at 3:00 P.M. on a weekday was drying up. There were days when I literally called everyone I knew within a five-mile radius to see if they wanted to get lunch with me, only to be met with defeat. It was becoming a real issue. I even offered to take Mabinty to lunch one day and she straight-up refused.

"Dis laundry's nah gwaan fold itself, gyal. Plus, mi sick of eating salads wid yuh white ass."

"Mabinty. Chill with the laundry talk. Can't you just roll

yourself a blunt, work up an appetite, and then I'll drive us to La Scala? What is the f-ing *problem?*"

"Either mi steam dis dress for yuh, or we go to lunch together. Yuh decide."

"Fine, steam the dress. Just know that I'm really annoyed."

As I walked away, I stopped and turned back to her. "Should I get a job? Why do people really have jobs? Does no one value free time? I wonder if I'd like working. Wouldn't that be so weird if that's the turn my life took right now? I'm not even hungry anymore."

I knew if anyone could help me figure out what I should do, it would be my shaman, Steve. Since I'd never had a job, I didn't have a clue as to what profession would best suit my talents, and I trusted Steve to pull it out of me like only a shaman can. He shook his rattle over me and asked, "How does your father spend his days?" I explained that my dad was *the* entertainment attorney to the stars, and Steve replied, "Your soul rests in your father's footsteps, my friend."

OMGivenchy, I'm a lawyer.

After an intense no-contact massage, I walked myself out of Steve's shaman den with all the certainty in the world. I had found my calling. When I asked my dad if I could join his firm, he was thrilled and told me to arrive at his offices at 8 A.M. Monday morning. Cheryl, his secretary, would set me up for my new, entry-level position, which I'm pretty sure is how all new partners enter a law firm. I went straight to Barneys to find the perfect work bag and an ensemble that proclaimed: *Power.*

Monday

I arrived at my dad's offices in Century City at 8:45. Turns out, rush hour traffic is a real thing. I thought it was just an urban legend. Then, of course, there was no valet, so it took me ten minutes to find parking. Unscathed by the morning's obstacles, I strutted into the office with my latte in hand, ready to take on the day. I was wearing a printed Balenciaga shift dress, an oversized Yohji Yamamoto blazer, six-inch purple suede Yves St. Laurent pumps, and a massive work Birkin. Today, I was all about the power of positivity, so I approached Cheryl's desk with a warm smile.

A little background: Cheryl has been my dad's secretary since I was a baby Babe. Whenever my dad brought me to the office, she was in charge of keeping me happy, be it taking me shopping at Barneys when I was four or ordering my ahi tuna salads when I was seven. Basically, she hates me.

"Hi, Cheryl, how are you? Long time no see! Cute boots."

I was lying. Cheryl's boots were an epic disaster, a tsunami of the 2012 variety. Think patent leather, with a kitten heel, and not a Prada kitten heel, but a kill-yourself kitten heel. Her personal style has always screamed Shania Twain summering on the Jersey Shore circa 1998, and I just don't get it. After all these years working around chic individuals, you'd think that Cheryl would have figured out how to present herself in a way that says, "I may be kind of fat and rude, but at least you'll think I'm cute from twenty feet away."

"You're late," she said, flatly.

"I'm so, so sorry."

Another lie. I am a lawyer!

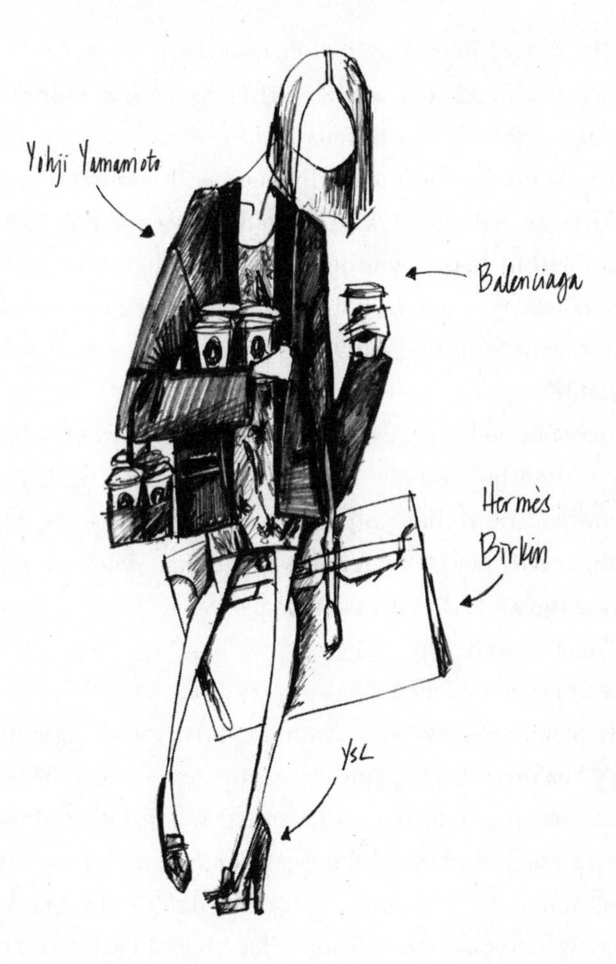

"Traffic was awful this morning, as I'm sure you noticed."

"I've been here since seven-thirty."

"Oh. Hate that for you." I cringed thinking of Cheryl in her sensible Toyota. "Why so early?"

"Because you were supposed to be here at eight o'clock."

"Oh yeah. Which way to my office?"

"Excuse me? Your office is right over there."

Cheryl pointed to a boxlike structure that couldn't have been bigger than three- by four-feet.

"That's funny. I'm not really good with confined spaces. Where is my real office? My interior designer and my feng shui master will be here any minute, so I should get a feel for the space before they arrive. I'd also love to check out the blueprints for the building. Will there be a zoning issue for a small koi pond?"

Cheryl smiled. I noticed that she could really benefit from laser whitening, and she should focus on opening her eyes more when she smiles, to make them look less beady. Also I couldn't really put my finger on what her hair color was trying to say to the world, but it wasn't happy.

"This is your desk."

"But my dad told me I'd be an entry-level, so . . ."

"Welcome to entry-level. There's a partner meeting at nine-thirty. You're in charge of picking up the coffee every morning. You can use the company card for that. You'll also need to answer the phone and forward the calls to the appropriate extensions. You're on mail duty every Monday, Wednesday, and Friday. When you get back from coffee, check in with me. I have a stack of license agreements for you to copy, collate, and file for the paralegals."

I pointed to my latte. "Oh, I already got my coffee, so I'm all good, thanks. Also, I love that you just told me all that fun stuff, and you sounded really confident during your monologue, but do you want to just go ahead and shoot me a quick e-mail with all that info? Also, when you e-mail me, make sure to flag it as 'urgent,' otherwise I won't even see it. You'll get the hang of my nuances once we've been working together for a while. It's so exciting having my own assistant!"

"No. Babe, you need to take the elevator to the ground floor, walk two blocks east to the Starbucks at the corner, and pick up the coffees for the partners. First you'll need to take everyone's order."

Cheryl was clearly testing me. I understood, and I too could play this game.

I proceeded to make my rounds through the office and typed all the coffee orders into my BlackBerry, which took forever. Then I walked over to Starbucks. By the time I got there, my feet were killing me. I was cursing myself for forgetting to have Mabinty take my YSL pumps for a test run to break them in. We have the same shoe size (a must for a maid/best friend). It was 9:20 when I placed the order for eight coffees and was 9:31 by the time they were all ready. My BlackBerry started ringing. It was Cheryl.

"Where are you? The partner meeting is starting."

"Um, how in God's name do you expect me to carry all these coffees back to the office?

"Figure it out. Get here now please."

She hung up. What the fuck?! Now it was 9:43. Ugh. After staring at the coffees for another five minutes, a barista offered me a couple of heinous beverage totes and sent me on my way. I limped into the office at 9:55. Cheryl was standing at her desk waiting for me. I approached her, glaring.

"Why did you hang up on me? You're fired for that, but now I'm rehiring you because I'm all about second chances. That was your first lesson in forgiveness. So embarrassing that I'm late for my first partner meeting! Where is my seat? Do you want to take these coffees in?"

Cheryl's face did its best impression of a confused gremlin.

"Babe, let me clear a few things up. You are not a lawyer. You don't have an office. You are an entry-level office assistant. Assistants sit in cubicles, and assistants do everything I tell them to do. And right now you are wasting everyone's time. Get in there, now, and put the fucking coffees on the table!"

"Rude. Okay, fine. But you're still on thin ice."

So far being a lawyer was really stressful.

I finished handing out the coffees at 10 A.M. I was exhausted. Normally I wake up around ten, so it was extremely frustrating to have my sleep schedule thrown off just so I could get to this stupid office and deliver a bunch of wrinkly lawyers their coffees. Did anyone even care to ask me how I was doing? I mean, I was sweating, for God's sake! I knew lawyers had to be rude to do their jobs, but I didn't think that meant they had to abuse the entry-level lawyers. I headed to my desk to take a breather and check my e-mails. I sat down and took three cleansing breaths. A fresh start.

I had canceled my appointment with the interior designer and the feng shui master, and was about to reply to a message from my astrologer, Jackie, regarding the Ophiuchus sign and how it would affect my menstrual cycle, when the phone in my cubicle starting ringing in the most jarring way. I turned and stared at it, hoping it would stop, which it did not. I got up and walked over to Cheryl's desk.

"Hey, Cher-Cher, the phone in my office will not stop ringing, and the ringer isn't really giving me the best vibes, to put it lightly, so is there any way you could order me a new phone? Oh, and definitely order one for Dad too. Oh, and for sure order one for yourself. I think Bang & Olufsen should have something great." Being a lawyer is all about delegating responsibility; clearly my strong suit.

"Are you kidding?"

"Are you kidding? It's giving me a migraine."

"Babe, you're not getting a new phone. That was me calling you. When your phone rings, you need to answer it. Because you were late, you're already really behind schedule. When I give you a job to do, I need you to get it done quickly and with a smile." My migraine was so painful at this point that I lowered my head into my hands and focused on massaging my temples. I don't remember exactly what else Cheryl said, but it was something along the lines of "Blah, blah, blah, rules are rules, you can't tell me what to do. I'm power hungry and I wouldn't be so mean if I liked the way I looked. You're so pretty. I wish I could be you . . . etc., etc."

Cheryl ended her rant by handing me a huge stack of files and telling me to get to work. I put them on my desk and took a much needed thirty-minute bathroom break. I met a little intern girl in the bathroom who was supercute in a J.Crew kind of way. She had this really eager look about her, so I felt comfortable asking her to tackle some of my duties.

"Hi, Jane, (I didn't know her name, but trust me, she was a Jane) is there any way you could help me file and coagulate a stack of documents for Cheryl? I'm due in court in ten. Cute tie!"

"My name's not Ja—"

"Thanks. You're a lifesaver." There's no "I" in team, so why should "I" be forced to do any of this work by myself?

Now I was freed up to spend a couple hours doing what I should have been doing as a lawyer: getting to know my clients. I chatted with a glamorous lesbian couple (the DeGeneres/de Rossis) in my dad's office, about the necessity of owning a property in Sardinia as well as a property in Dubrovnik. In case you don't already know, Dubrovnik is the tits right now—previously war-torn but now it's EVERYTHING (Google it).

Lawyers love power lunches, and I had planned on meeting my personal shopper at La Scala to split a chopped salad—that is, until Cheryl The Demon practically assaulted me on my way out the door and commanded me to stay at my desk and answer phones while everyone else in the office went to lunch. Even though I usually welcome a chance to skip a meal, this was downright rude. Had Cheryl forgotten about all those Hanukkah and birthday gifts from my father that I had picked out for her over the years? It's not easy to find something chic for a dowdy secretary with small teeth/big gum disease. Where was her loyalty? How quickly they turn.

I decided that with everyone being out of the office for lunch, this would actually be a great time to meditate. Lawyers need to clear their minds every once in a while. I popped in my headphones and listened to the soothing sounds of monks chanting. I must have retreated to a deep space within myself, because when I opened my eyes, Cheryl was standing over me looking bloated and angry.

"What are you doing?"

"Namaste, Cheryl. I was meditating. You should try it sometime. It's really good for people with low self-esteem."

"Go home, Babe."

"What?"

"You have done absolutely nothing all day. Go home."

"That is so not true." I said, taking my headphones off. "I've been swamped. I got the coffees, and I entertained clients. You canceled my lunch, so I couldn't do that, which was really stressful because Melania is really sensitive about me canceling plans at the last minute and—"

"Who is Melania?"

"My personal shopper at Barneys! Lest you forget, I also had to cancel with my interior design team, which is *so* unprofessional. Cheryl, I have been busting my ass all day at this firm being a lawyer, and I don't think I need to explain myself to you any further."

"Babe, you're fired."

"You can't fire me. You're my dad's secretary. And I'm a partner, so you're fired."

"No! YOU ARE NOT A LAWYER! And yes, I am your dad's secretary, but I'm also the head of HR, so you're fired. Please leave the premises."

I stared at her for twenty seconds, until she turned to walk away.

"No, Cheryl. Actually, I'm the CEO of HR, so you're fired. I think *you* should leave."

But she didn't budge. How could she do this?! What the hell is HR? Obviously she was so jealous of me that she couldn't stand for us to coexist in the same environment. I gathered my

Birkin and my office supplies (headphones, iPad, BlackBerry, iPhone, white iPhone, and Montblanc fountain pen) and made my way out of the building.

I had tried so hard to be a lawyer, but the universe simply didn't want my law career to take flight. The gods were against me. Nature was against me. Jane was against me. How could this be when I had been so convinced of my calling? Then I thought back to something that Ellen and Portia had said to me when we were talking in my dad's office. They'd explained how they didn't choose to fall in love with Dubrovnik. Dubrovnik had chosen them. It was the one place where they truly felt at home. There needs to be that special connection. Well, I had chosen to be a lawyer, and clearly, the law had rejected me. It was simply not in the stars. I don't do "fired," so tomorrow I would tell Cheryl that I quit.

After driving around listening to the entire *Born This Way* album, thinking things through, and stopping at Barneys to pick up a pair of Lanvin flats because my feet were killing me, I was back home getting a massage and trying to rid my psyche of the day's horrors.

Tuesday

I showed up to the office to hand-deliver my letter of resignation to Cheryl, but she wasn't at her desk. It was 9:15. Jane walked by with a pen and paper in hand. She was experimenting with a sweater-set-and-skirt-combo moment.

"Jane, are you doing today's coffee run?"

"Um—"

"Great. Cheryl will have a venti, peppermint mocha Frappucino with three extra shots of sweetener, whole milk, whipped cream, sprinkles, chocolate syrup, and white chocolate shavings." (Estimated calorie count: 400,000.) I left my letter on Cheryl's desk and got the fuck out of that hellhole.

Dear Cheryl,

After careful consideration, I have reviewed the pros and cons of practicing law, and have woefully decided the cons outweigh the pros. Please accept this as my letter of resignation.

Best,

Babe Walker

P.S. I realize now that as a lawyer, it was my obligation to be under oath at all times. So yesterday when I told you that I thought your boots were cute, I perjured myself. Best of luck!!!!

WHITE GIRL PROBLEM #22

I'm never drinking again, except for the occasional glass of white wine, vodka sodas, on holidays, or my birthday month.

Crowds are never a good look. Crowds are hell. I'm a very body-conscious person, so when my personal space is invaded, I feel threatened and sometimes act out. Therefore, it's important for me to position myself at a corner table when I'm at clubs in Hollywood. If I end up stuck in a crowd, I need to find the quickest way out possible. Sometimes I pretend to cry and scream "MOM!!!" until people move out of my way. I have a rule that clubs on weekends are off-limits. It's too much scene, and not the good kind. But I do break this rule for one person: Roman. If he wants me to show up for a night that he's promoting, and I'm not on my period, I'll go. I'll be on more drugs than Burning Man himself, but I'll go.

I was with Roman and his new boyfriend, Uri, and Gen and her new boyfriend, whoever, at a club called Lash, for a party called Lush (which was all about models, trannies, and trannies who are painters, connecting with each other over delish, high-priced cocktails). We were celebrating my voluntary departure from my career as a lawyer by getting shitfaced and playing Shoot, Marry, Fuck at a corner table. We weren't actually communicating though—too loud, too much work. When I'm at a club, especially a Hollywood club, I only hear about 5 percent of what's actually being said to me. The rest of the time I just nod my head, laugh, and make meaningful eye contact to let someone know I "got it" and they can stop talking.

So there we were at our chic little VIP corner table. I was feeling safe, we were sipping shots of tequila, dancing, and discussing the difference between sleeping with someone and fucking someone, and Roman was trying to find guys for me to make out with.

"Babesicles," Roman slurred, drunk and trying to dance like Beyoncé, "Okay, okay, I have a good one—shoot, marry, fuck: me, Uri, and um . . . ," he pointed to a cluster of Italian/Spanish/Whatever male models, "those models over there in an orgy."

"Well, let me think. You're a dick who likes dick, Roman, so I could never marry you, and we *have* fucked, remember? So I guess I'd fuck you again, marry Uri, and shoot those chaunchy models over there trying not to look like they didn't just blow ten lines of bad coke in the bathroom. Gen, what would you do?"

"Ugh I don't know. You're all too young for me." She motioned to her boyfriend. "Butch and I have to go. There's this show on the History Channel tonight about World War II planes that he's obsessed with. We'll see you guys later." They both got up to leave.

"Bye, Gen. Bye, Gramps. Try not to get too wild tonight."

As I hugged Gen good-bye, I caught a glimpse of the DJ. The dim lighting was accentuating his sinewy neck muscles and his hair was amazing and I was in love. I'd never seen a guy move with such graceful body awareness. It was an energy thing—he was playing good music and looked so happy to be making other people happy.

"Roman, what is that?" I said, pointing to the DJ booth. He and Uri had their tongues down each other's throats and were clearly having a *blast* not paying attention to me. I tugged at Roman's collar.

"What, Babe? What!?" Roman screamed.

"What is that *thing* over there? In the DJ booth. I'm kind of dying for him."

"What?? I can't hear you! It's so fucking loud in here."

"I said HELP ME FUCK THE DJ!" I screamed directly into his brain through his ear.

"Oh! THE DJ?! THAT'S CAMERON. SO FUCKING HOT, RIGHT?! MY FAVORITE IN TOWN FOR SURE. LIKE TOTALLY THE BEST UNDERSTANDING OF WHAT YOUNG PEOPLE ACTUALLY WANT TO LISTEN TO. I JUST LOVE CAM SO MUCH. IS THAT WHAT YOU WERE ASKING ABOUT? YOU LOOK SO GORGEOUS, BABE. I MISS YOU."

I didn't hear 90 percent of what Roman said, but I did take a mental note of the DJ's name. Cameron. I could work with that. I was on enough (insert any club drug here) and was so superdrunk from bottle service that I thought it would be a good idea to walk right up to my new obsession and let him know that I was ready to go home with him whenever he wanted. I pushed my way past three men with tight up-do buns, six shitty at-home blowouts, and a pair of faux-snakeskin Nine West pumps. I climbed into the DJ booth and sauntered up to "Cameron." He smelled amazing.

"I want this song inside of me," I think I said.

"Yeah, right? Shit like this is solid gold."

He was even more beautiful up close, but in this, like, androgynous way. His eyes were a shimmering light blue, and his dark roots were singing a melodious tune with his bleached shaggy locks. And those full lips? So my type. So New York circa April 1998. I wanted to jump his bone structure.

"I'm Babe. Roman's friend. I mean, Zeppelin mashed up with Kanye mashed up with Rammstein mashed up with 2 Live Crew mashed up with Salt-N-Pepa mashed up with Pavarotti? It's like you're playing the soundtrack of my life."

Cameron winked at me, and gestured to his turntables. I'd clearly caught him at a bad time, because he was kind of busy DJ-ing and wasn't really paying attention to me. I took this to mean I should talk louder. I tugged a little at Cameron's belt loop and winked back at him. I leaned in close to his ear and yelled, "OKAY, YOU'RE OBVI BUSY, SO COME SAY HI WHEN YOU'RE DONE WITH YOUR JOB, OR WHATEVER." Then I pointed to the corner table where Roman and Uri were now dry humping, and stumbled back to the VIP area.

It must have been a while before Cameron came over to us, or I should say me, because Roman and Uri had gone home and left me asleep in the booth. Those assholes. This always happens when I go out with those two. Cameron woke me with his gentle touch and his sweet angelic voice.

"Let's get you home, Babe," he said as he lifted me up and onto my feet.

He may have looked like a heroin addict, but I could tell Cameron was a good guy. He was not your typical sleazeface Hollywood DJ. He was a gentleman. A real, old-fashioned kind of guy. He even helped me find my bag (a *major* royal blue Celine zipper clutch), which was in my hand, and my jacket (a *really fucking major* vintage giraffe-print DVF cropped smock), which was in the men's bathroom for some odd reason.

He got me in his car, which was a pleasing 1973 Porsche 911S Coupe with a matte black finish, and I was all over him. I could tell he liked it but didn't really know what to do with my immense passion for life, and my fingers in his mouth. I told him to drive us to his place, but he said I was too fucked up. Oh, please.

The next thing I knew, it was Saturday morning and I was in the special corner of my closet where blackout Babe likes to sleep, naked and gripping a bottle of open champagne. Typical. What was not so typical, however, was Cameron sleeping next to me, fully clothed. He was snoozing like a little angel muffin. This was a big deal for me. I had never shared my blackout den with anyone. I guess I had asked him to stay with me? All I can say is I was pleasantly surprised to find him there in his perfectly baggy T-shirt, loose A.P.C. raw denim jeans, and a Rolex. He was so skinny.

I snuck into my bathroom, making no sound at all, to brush my teeth and hair. I slipped into a cute pair of black La Perla boy shorts and my fave vintage Rolling Stones tee and wedged myself right back next to Cameron. Then I set my alarm for

11:05. It was 11:02. When my alarm went off and woke Cameron up, I rolled over to face him, yawning.

"Hey, Cameron. Sorry about that alarm. I always wake up and do yoga on Saturday mornings."

"Morning, Babe."

"Thanks for getting me home last night. I never get that wasted."

"Dude, I know what you mean. It's cool. One time I was so wasted that I made out with Lindsay Lohan and she totally stalked me for like two weeks."

"Ew. Um . . . did we fuck? It's totally cool if we did, I just need to know."

Cameron looked a little taken aback by this, and he laughed at me. He had the best laugh. And great teeth.

"Nope, we didn't fuck. We drank a lot of champagne, smoked a joint, and then you told me about your charity work with deaf cats. All in all, a tame night. I dig charitable girls. Come here."

We made out on my closet floor for twenty minutes. I was crushing so hard on this rando! What had come over me? I *never* go for DJs. I just don't. Do not. I swear. DJs always have a zillion girls texting them, they go to work at a club (which I believe I've made clear is not my happy place), and they rarely have good taste in music. But Cam was different—he was no bullshit. When it's on, it's just on.

"Should we get brunch?" he asked, running his fingers up my arm.

I normally expect people to gather from my image that I'm not really a brunch-food kind of girl, but I forgave him because his offer clearly just meant that he wanted to spend the morning with me. And so began a perfect day with my new boyfriend, Cameron.

I threw my hair up in a messy, half-up/half-down style, added a little body with a curling iron and some hairspray, and then messed it up again to make it look really natural, put on a pair of distressed J Brand jean shorts, and strapped my feet into a fabulous pair of vintage Salvatore Ferragamo platforms that I'd been saving for a special day-date situation. We hopped in his Porsche and took off on Sunset Boulevard heading toward the beach. Cam suggested we opt for coffee and cigarettes instead of brunch (sigh!). Traffic was slow as hell, but Cameron was a pro and got us there solely on side streets. Not an easy thing to do, trust. There is nothing sexier than a man who takes charge on the road. Am I wrong?

We spent the afternoon cutting our way up the coast. We talked about our families, we exchanged opinions on the *Lost* finale, and we made out, a lot. He had the perfect answer to every question and he really listened to me. It was bliss. Simple and sexy. I deserved it. Our day ended with a delicious meal back at my place. God, we were becoming such homebodies! I had Jean-Raphael put together an all-macrobiotic plate of leafy greens and protein alternatives that we could share. It's always kind of awkward when your chef/ex-BF has to meet your new BF, but whatever. To drink: 100 percent Blue Agave Organic Tequila, splash of lime.

"Thanks for today," I said, taking a sip of Cam's drink.

"No prob, Babe. I had a lot of fun. I feel like we were, like, connecting and shit."

"Totally connecting. It was amazing, and our hair looked so

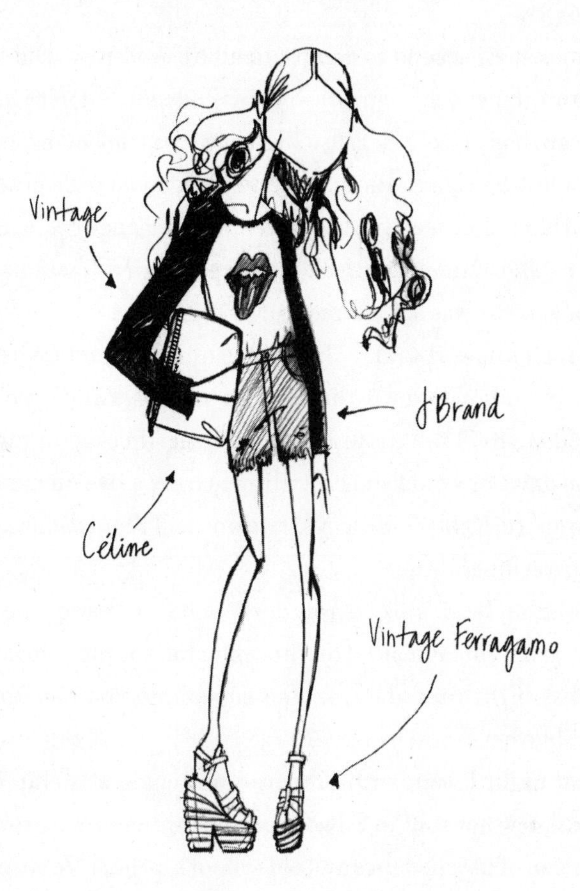

good. Your car is the perfect height off the ground for the wind's trajectory to create a healthy and natural blowout. I feel so lucky to have you in my life. Is that psycho?"

"No way. Not as psycho as what I'm about to ask you."

"Yes. This is my real nose."

He laughed. "Do you want to move in with me? I mean, I know it's way fast, but we're vibing so hard. I think we should just go for it."

It took me a second to comprehend his question. Did he actually want me to move in, or was this code for "I don't want you to see anybody else"? Because I've used this trick on people before. With some guys, the second they know you're dead serious about them, they feel like they owe you some huge gesture. And they do. But Cameron wasn't that type of guy. I could tell he meant what he was asking me.

"I don't know," I said. "That's a big question and I have this, like, connection to my bathroom and my closet and my chef." I winked at JR. "I'd have to make huge sacrifices with my diet. Do you have, or would you be willing to hire, a live-in maid who is easy to train? My folding restrictions and regulations are not easy, even for Mabinty."

"Babe, Babe, it's okay. You don't need to answer me right now. I just wanted to put it on the table. I'm so into you."

"Okay, I'll think about it. I'm super into you too. You're a freak. I love it."

That night I went with Cameron to his gig at a club called Loser, a new hot spot in Silverlake where hipster met hippie in a collision of psychedelics and old school hip-hop. We ate mushroom chocolates—well, Cam ate the mushroom chocolates, and I ate the mushrooms and discarded the chocolate, naturally. I hung out behind the DJ booth all night, featuring shoulder dances and closed eyes. Lots of arm waving and fancy finger pointing at Cameron. Just getting really into the beats and loving myself. If you saw me that night, you would have seen a girl in love with life. By the time Cameron carried me out of the club, I was tripping my ass off.

"You know what we should do?!" I shouted.

"Drive to Vegas and get married?"

"Duh! And then we should take the bus home! I've always wanted to ride on the bus, ever since I saw that Keanu movie! I fucking love Keanu! Let's get married and have Keanu officiate!!!" I was scream-laughing. "Will the bus take us to your place?!"

I was really able to let my hair down around Cam. He just made me feel so comfortable. That was our thing; we loved each other for who we were. I was realizing now more than ever that the key to a good relationship is acceptance.

We slept at his place that night, but nothing really happened because I was too busy trying to find the sea animals that were swimming in my hands and talking about how I was the founding member of the Illuminati. The next morning, I woke up to the sound of a shower running. I had no idea where I was for a second. Cameron's room. It was so fucking chic for a guy. Minimal. Exposed brick painted white. A well-curated wall of black-and-white photographs. Understated and delightful. Then I heard his voice from the bathroom.

"Yo, Babe. I'm in here. Come take a shower?"

Without saying a word, I slipped out of my underwear and sauntered to the open bathroom door. "Okay," I said to myself. "He's gonna see you naked. He's gonna love it. Your thighs are in perfectly respectable shape. Just do it." I threw my hair around a little bit and walked in.

There, standing in the shower, was someone who looked exactly like Cam in the face but had boobs, and a vagina. And by boobs and a vagina, I mean tits and a pussy. Cameron was a girl. I stood and stared at Cam for about a minute. She was staring at me too, confused. It was awkward.

"So . . . you're not a boy?" I asked.

"Is that a joke?"

"Yep."

Silence.

"Are you coming in?" she said.

"Hmm. I'm going through a lot right now. It's kinda dark for me. I'm gonna go. Great vagina."

I turned around, grabbed my shit, got dressed in the hallway, and called a cab. I felt bad about leaving Cameron in the shower, and I wanted to want to get in, but I just couldn't. I texted her from the cab:

Babe 10:39AM:	Hey it's Babe (from earlier). I didn't mean to leave you standing there, naked.
Babe 10:40AM:	But I was expecting you to have a penis. My bad.
Babe 10:40AM:	You couldn't have been cooler about it.
Babe 10:41AM:	You're such a sweetheart.
Babe 10:42AM:	I'm excited for us to be friends now!
Babe 10:50AM:	Your apartment is so chic. xxB
Cameron 10:51AM:	Ok...

Not the most graceful of breakups, but I had to follow my heart.

A lot of drugging and drinking had happened that weekend, but still . . . how could I have missed the fact that Cameron was biologically female? If you were to ask me now if I was gay, my answer would be no, but sometimes, as evidenced by my weekend with Cameron, it's unclear. I mean, Cam was an amazing kisser and I was super-turned-on by her, but I couldn't see myself fully committing to a guy that didn't have a penis. I didn't know what to think.

I bottomed out at Barneys.

In times of need and confusion, I almost always take myself to Barneys to collect my thoughts with a healthy dose of retail therapeutics. Some people turn to drugs, others turn to drinking, I turn to Barneys.

Fred Pressman, son of Barney Pressman, founder of Barneys, is quoted as saying, "The best value you can offer a customer is personal attention to every detail, and they will return again and again. Ultimately, the customer cares the most about how he or she is treated."

So true. Unless your life is a serious shit show like mine was on this fateful day that changed my life forever—or for at least twenty-eight days.

Having the panic attack to end all panic attacks and ultimately bottoming out at Barneys was not entirely my fault. My life hadn't exactly been a breeze leading up to my demise. The American workforce hated me, I hadn't found a trainer who could give me the same results as Anthony, my therapist had just betrayed me by falling asleep during a really important session, I was on the sixth day of a text war with Genevieve, Roman was in "love," Mabinty had been on vacation all week, and my new boyfriend had turned out to be a girl. I couldn't trust anyone. And then I got a text message that sent me over the edge.

Unknown Number 9:36AM: Hi B. Been a while. Made your famous kale smoothie last night. Hope you're well.

Unknown Number 9:37AM: This is Robert, btw.

What a total mindfuck. I never thought I'd hear from Robert again after we broke up. Did he not remember how I'd completely botched our relationship? Did he not remember the part where I got a tattoo of his dad's name? Or the fake pregnancy I made him endure? Was he trying to destroy me as payback? I didn't know what to think, but true love is strong, so, after carefully weighing all the options, I decided Robert must be coming to LA, in an attempt to win me back.

Oh my God, I thought. *He's making kale smoothies? He's texting me? He must be coming to LA. Oh, he's for sure coming to LA! He's probably going to call me and arrange a romantic dinner this weekend at a chic restaurant. I wonder what hotel he's staying at? Hopefully Sunset Tower. I need something to wear. Goddammit, Robert, you are so tricky. I love you for that.*

The morning hours at Barneys are the cleanest, the body traffic is at its lowest point in the day, and the store's energy is positive because the snappy employees on the makeup floor aren't depressed yet (that happens at about 3 P.M.). So I got there at 11 A.M., ready to find the perfect outfit and ready to drink a Valium martini for my nerves. The sun was pouring into the store, making everything look shiny and beautiful, yet I still felt a cloud of pressure and angst about my looming weekend with Robert.

I beelined to the second floor (Women's Ready-to-Wear) breathing heavily and trying to remind myself that I would soon be in a better place. "Just get there, Babe," I was whispering under my breath. A little mantra, if you will. I got to the top of the stairs and stood there for a moment with my eyes shut tightly, concentrating. Sometimes I allow my inner compass to direct my body toward the right designer. I walked with my eyes closed, hands sticking straight out, allowing myself to be drawn by magnetic force to the rack that called to me. After knocking over a mannequin and accidentally punching someone in her fake boobs, my intuition said to stop. Stella McCartney!

I wrapped my arms around the entire rack of clothing, squeezed everything together into one big bunch, and lifted the entire collection off of the rack, turning around to call for assistance.

"Melania?!" She's my girl at Barneys.

No response. I tried again, which made me nervous because Melania's always right there when I need her.

"Melani— uh . . ." That's when I noticed that out of thin air had popped a strange girl with some kind of braids thing happening in her hair, standing right next to me. She smelled like the Bath & Body Works oatmeal soap that she'd probably used as face wash that morning, and the whole thing was very unclear to me.

"May I help you?" I said to it.

"May *I* help *you*? I'm Kelly. Can I start a fitting room for you?" it said to me, smiling.

"Hi, Keely. I'm in a pretty serious situation here, I'm not trusting people right now, and I'm afraid that you're about to tell me that Melania isn't here today. If that is, in fact, what you're about to tell me, please just blink twice instead of actually saying the words. I will lose control, drop these clothes, and slap you if you say those words out loud."

One blink. Two blinks.

For fuck's sake. What had I done to make the universe so pissed at me? I dropped the pile of clothes on the floor and walked away, pulling my phone out of my bag. I called Robert.

"Hello?" he said. I missed his manly voice.

"Hey Rob, it's me. I'm having a piece-of-shit day—piece-of-shit week and month actually. I'm so glad you're reconsidering us. I know you're probably trying to surprise me by showing up in LA this weekend, but I'm kind of psychic, so I figured out your plan. Let's try this new raw place on Larchmont when you're here? I know you hate raw, but—"

"Whoa, whoa. Babe. I'm not coming to LA. What are you talking about?"

"What are *you* talking about? You fucking *texted me*!" I yelled into the phone.

"Yeah, to say hi."

"Exactly!"

"Didn't mean anything by it, just a simple hello."

"NO! NO, no, no, Roberrrrrrt!?" I screamed, before hanging up on him and throwing my phone back in my bag. People in the store were staring at me like I was some kind of a psycho, but they had no fucking clue that I was going through the worst breakup of my life, for the second time.

I marched back over to Keely. "Hi, Keely. Don't look so scared, it smushes your forehead. Okay. What's going to happen now is that I'm going to calmly collect myself by taking five sips of kombucha and tapping my third eye twenty-one times. Then I'm going to slowly walk over to the dressing rooms, where I'd like to find a comprehensive array of chicness waiting for me. I'm talking shoes, accessories, and prêt-à-porter. These are my needs. I just really have to buy something right now, you understand."

"No problem," she responded quickly. "Also, my name's not Keely, it's Kell—You know what? Never mind." And she scurried away.

The dressing room was full of hanging clothes by the time I got in there. The shoes were lined up in ascending heel heights, and the accessories were coordinated by color. Keely must have read my mood, because the garments were telling a murky story about a girl on the edge. She was smarter than she looked. I rifled through everything like an animal, trying things on and throwing them to the ground.

I didn't allow Keely into my dressing room, because I was vulnerable, and she was not to be trusted with my emotions. Plus I was ashamed of the huge mess I was making. I usually re-hang everything as soon as it's been given a test run, but that day I was moving through the outfits so fast that everything ended up on the floor. Complete loss of control. I was a murderess.

"Keely!" I called out. "This stuff is great. I think I'm going to take some of it."

"Great. Which items?" she asked.

I was fiending, and I refused to let any of the garments out of my sight, so I'd bitten off the price tags to give to Keely, bless her little soul. I slid two handfuls of price tags under the door.

"These items. You can charge them to my account."

Over the next hour, if I tried something on and I liked it, I'd bite the price tag off and slide it under the door to Keely, who'd charge it to my account. I bought fourteen sweaters, thirteen pairs of black jeans, twelve going-out tops, eleven long skirts, ten day dresses, ten pairs of sunglasses for driving, ten pairs of sunglasses for walking, ten pairs of platforms, ten T-shirts, nine pairs of flats, eight blouses, seven formal gowns, six short skirts, five pairs of sandals, five necklaces, five bracelets, five rings, four pairs of day trousers, four blazers, three pairs of stilettos, two pairs of wedges, two motorcycle jackets, one fur jacket, and a pair of socks.

Normally I am able to maintain some semblance of composure when shopping, but today I was a ravenous she-beast. I couldn't stop spending. After six hours of trying clothes on, Keely passed my receipt under the door for me to sign: $246,893.50

"Fuck," I whispered to myself. My breath was short and my vision was getting hazy. I started panting. I looked at myself in the mirror, only to see a zombie-faced girl with bloodshot eyes

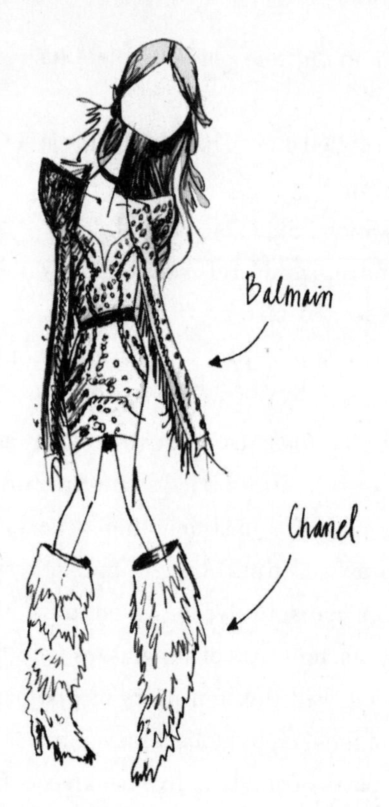

and wild hair staring back at me. She was all alone, in a dressing room at Barneys, and she was one pound overweight. I threw a studded Louboutin at the mirror and collapsed.

I must have passed out, because I woke up to loud knocking on the door and Keely asking, "Babe? Are you okay in there?"

I sat up, looked around, took in the scenario, and realized that the dressing room was destroyed. The mirror was broken and the floor was covered in clothes, shoes, and purses. Not an inch of carpet was visible. I was lying amidst a knee-high me-

lange of the fall's finest pieces. I had written "I LOVE HIM" in red lipstick on the wall. I noticed an indentation in the middle of the mess where I'd been lying. And then it hit me. My eyes filled with tears. I'd been *nesting* at Barneys. I was horrified. I had never nested anywhere besides my own closet after a bender. How did it come to this? Who was I? My shopping had spun out of control.

"This has got to stop!" I wailed.

I looked up at Keely standing by the now open dressing room door with a key in her hand.

"Oh my God," she said under her breath. For a split second, I could see the terror in her eyes, and then it was gone as quickly as it came. She handed me a Pellegrino. "Honey, it's okay. Here. Drink." I took three large gulps and collapsed again, sobbing in the center of my nest. *This is the end of the road*, I thought.

Tears poured down my cheeks as I began digging a hole in the pile. I was going to burrow, and then die. As I was furiously digging, I found a giant Balenciaga bracelet in black lambskin with rose gold hardware. I held it in my quivering hands and softly whispered the four words that you never want to have to say to your Balenciaga.

"I can't quit you."

Rock Bottom, meet Babe Walker.

I turned to Keely, who was now on her knees rubbing my back. "I think I have a serious problem," I said, tears streaming down my face. "I should probably go to rehab, right?"

"Or . . . you could return all the stuff you just bought?"

"No. I don't think so. I really love all of it, like, *really* love it. It's too late for me. I need rehab. I need to go to Cirque Lodge. In Utah. Now."

Without missing a beat, Keely wiped my tears with a $3,000 Mary Katrantzou dress, jumped to her feet, and was immediately on the phone with Cirque Lodge arranging my transportation and check-in. I was in the presence of an angel. We went through my purchases and selected the perfect wardrobe for my time in Utah. I decided on three pairs of sensible Lanvin flats, an array of chunky Prada knits, and an Isabel Marant rainbow fur. Rehab was starting to look super-cozy, and super-fun. I felt so much better already.

On the way out of the store, I said something to Keely that I'd never said to any employee of any establishment in my entire twenty-three years.

"I fucking love you."

"I fucking love you too," she replied.

"What's your name again?" I said, looking at her face for the first time. She was a perfect mix of beautiful and plain.

"It's Kelly."

"Oh right. I knew that," I said. "Keely, you will be my new personal shopper/fashion sherpa. See you on the other side, I'll send you a postcard. P.S. you have the nose of a Disney princess."

"No, you do."

"Shut up. Thanks. You're the best," I said, walking away.

"Oh, and Babe? You still want me to wrap up the rest of your purchases and send them to your home address, right?"

"Duh. Of course I do, you little muffin."

We air kissed and I climbed into the waiting black Escalade that Keely had waiting for me. "This is gonna suck," I said to the driver. "Do you have any blow?"

"Sure do," he said. And off we drove into the rest of my life.

I surrender, aka excerpts from my rehab diary.

Day 1

I'm on my bed, sitting across the room from another bed, which I guess means that I have a roommate? Unclear. Don't really know anything about her yet. She seems to be a minimalist though. Nothing on the walls above her bed. No books. No photos. Who are you, roommate? Are you my age? I don't especially like girls my age, so I really hope not. Will I be able to heal properly if I don't have personal space? These people have got me all wrong if they think I can share a sink with someone for an entire month. The last time someone tried to give me a roommate, I turned right around and walked to the next available university, but the closest rehab facility is over five hundred miles away, so that's definitely not an option today.

Wait. There's a Birkin hanging off of my roommate's bedpost. Black with silver hardware, beat to shit. Are those tire marks?

Scars of a life thoroughly lived? I fucking love my brilliant and chic new roommate! But when will we meet?

Hey, I'm back. I just had to pee 'cause I was so excited. So, okay, while I was peeing I noticed that the maids hadn't folded the toilet paper into a triangle at the end, and there was a dead moth on the floor of the shower. Now I'm looking around and coming to terms with the fact that Cirque Lodge isn't exactly the wintry vacation scenario I was hoping for. I mean, the girl at reception was wearing a scrunchie, and the room I'm in is bare, not super-cozy like I had expected. Also, Cirque is mainly for drug and alcohol addicts, so I'm hoping that my new rehab friends will accept me for being the odd girl out. My spending addiction is way more interesting than any of their addictions, so they'll probably look up to me for being unique. I'm usually a hit when it comes to meeting new people.

Earlier today I had a meeting with some hippie named Jackson who told me that treatment should not be seen as a punishment, but rather a positive experience. Um . . . okay? This is rehab, not The Grove. I want to change my life. Not like, become a different person or anything, but I want to be open to the right suggestions that I need to take, or whatever. This is my moment to finally build a relationship with myself, a loving relationship. I'm standing on the snowcapped mountain of my life, and the horizon looks beautiful. I don't know, I just copied most of that from one of the pamphlets they gave me. I'm on a lot of Ativan right now.

Love,

B

Day 2

So, turns out there is a God, because my roommate is an ex-model!!!!!! One of my absolute faves who I totally wanted to be when I was six!!!! I can't write down her real name in this diary because I respect her anonymity. It just wouldn't be right for me to "out" her. She's making everyone here call her Gina, so I'll just stick with that.

Gina (the person not the name) is fabulous. A little ragged on the edges, meaning that she could get rid of the bottom inch of her over-treated hair. She could also go ahead and preempt her aging neck's fall from grace with a tuck job—nothing major. In general she looks great, for an alcoholic. Flawless skin and still thin as a rail. Nineties thin, not 2000s thin. It was such a relief to see Gina walk through the door. I literally gasped when she came in, not only because I was in the middle of my evening's nude, inverted chant, but also because I thought that she had died. She dropped off the face of the planet after an epic Gucci ad campaign in the spring of 1996. She is virtually un-Googleable after that date, trust me. But now she's my fucking roommate!! I think we'll get along famously, but for now she's feeling me out and kind of acting like a cold bitch.

Today I had my first group therapy session—a lot of freaks, a few crazies, Gina, me, and a hot older guy named Paul with amazing forearms and a Vicodin addiction. Jackson, my counselor, spent the first part of the session putting me on the spot in front of everyone. He made me answer invasive questions like "Where are you from?" "What are you here to work on?" and the worst, "In this moment, what would you most like to change about yourself?" So . . . I spent the next thirty minutes discussing all of the changes I'd love to make to my wardrobe, until we were out of time. Sowwy.

Love,

B

Day 5

Fuck this place. I can't even buy a vintage Prada backpack on eBay without them revoking my Internet privileges. Rehab is bullshit.

Annoyed,

B

Day 7

I lost control of myself this morning, so they're making me spend the rest of the day outside in what they call "nature's classroom," which is just a few benches in the middle of the woods. It was a cursed day that began with me waking up from a nightmare, scream-crying. Scariest dream of my life. I was at Old Navy, wearing a magenta fleece "tech-vest" that I couldn't take off because the zipper was broken, and it was too small, and everyone around me was telling me how "cute" I looked.

So dealing with all of that, I did my best to participate in this morning's group session, but I was too full of feelings. I was still shaken up from the nightmare, I was having Barneys withdrawal, I was over not carrying a wallet, or a bag, or a phone, and I couldn't handle Jackson's prying about my past spending habits. So, I LOST IT.

I screamed at him, "You'll never understand my needs!"

Which is completely true, but I didn't need to raise my voice. I jumped across the room and tackled him like a panther, then I ran out of the room, grabbing anyone I saw in the hallway by the throat and demanding that they tell me where the "motherfucking gift shop" was.

It was not my best look, but it's okay. Rehab is all about being ugly. I get that now. So please, someone, get me out of the woods. I don't have any underwear on and I'm freezing.

Help,

B

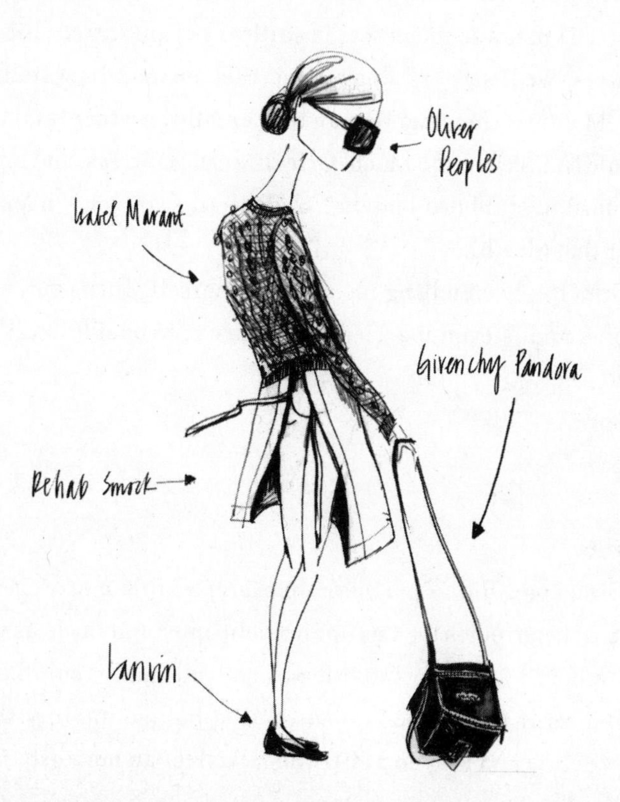

Day 10

Jackson and I totally patched things up, and I've accepted him into my life again. He just pushed me too far that day in group. Never in all of my years has anyone questioned the importance of devoting $2000 a month to sunglasses, and it baffled/completely overwhelmed me. There was no reason for me to get physical with Jackson and embarrass myself in front of Paul and the other little addicts. I don't blame myself for flipping out, but I will admit that I slipped up and had a scary moment.

In other news, my equine therapy starts this afternoon. I haven't gone near a horse since Mischa Barton broke my back in 2007. I'm not so much scared shitless as I am scared shit and pissless. We'll see. If I don't come back to you, diary, tell my dad, Mabinty, Gen, and Roman that I really love them and they shouldn't miss me too much. Grieving causes stress, and stress can lead to stubborn belly fat, and we all know what happens after that (death).

Gina has been telling me all about herself. Turns out, she's a lesbo and is even married to another ex-model lesbo. Ultra chic.

Love,

B

Day 12

Gina and I did a "partnership exercise" this morning. Two men in beige polos took us up in a helicopter and made us wear these horrible helmets and it was so loud that I could barely hear myself think. We landed on this big mountain-y thing where Gina and I sat on a cliff and talked for an hour-ish.

I asked her to tell me about her rise to modeling fame, and she explained how she forged past the typical expiration age for models (21.5) and became a star when she posed naked for Arthur Elgort. The fast-paced lifestyle of being a model was exciting, too exciting sometimes, and eventually Gina ended up feeling like a cog in the image machine. She started to wonder what she was contributing to the world besides trends. Uh, *what*? I hate it when people don't appreciate what they have.

Gina retired at twenty-seven, and she and her wife (who she calls "D") left New York City to move upstate and start a small, organic farm. They hired a small staff of locals to run the place and have been living like this for years. I got kind of bored when she started using words like "sustainable" and "dairy," so I may have zoned out a little, but it sounds like they had a lot of fun? That is, until Gina decided she was over being a farmer's wife and started taking trips to NYC to see old friends (photographers-turned-drug-dealers, drug-dealers-turned-photographers, other ex-models, and Sandra Bernhard). She was hitting the bottle hard, and her drinking spiraled out of control. D gave her an ultimatum: "Stop being a fucking drunk and go back to rehab or move the fuck out." That's love.

I told Gina about Tai Tai, and college, and my labiaplasty, and that week when I was addicted to huffing computer cleaner, that time that I dared myself to roofie myself, that time I fucked The Rock, and that time I dated a woman. We bonded over knowing what it's like to be totally bored with your life. I even recounted my bottoming out moment at Barneys, which was hard, but Gina was really sweet and nonjudgmental about it. She told me that the lowest points in a person's life hold the most opportunity for growth. Then we exhaled negativity and inhaled positivity. And hugged for a really long time.

I guess today was pretty major.

Love,

B

Day 13

Guys I Wanna Fuck When I Get Out of Rehab:

James Franco
Ryan Gosling
Banksy
50 Cent
Leonardo DiCaprio
Joaquin Phoenix
River Phoenix
Kurt Cobain
Jim Morrison
Howard Stern
Aladdin
Sandra Bullock

Day 16

Fuck this piece-of-ass day. Group was a nightmare. I thought I could trust these freaks, but once again, I've completely misjudged those who are closest to me. I was in the middle of a very important self-reflective moment about my final hours in the

Barneys dressing room on the day I hit rock bottom, when this woman, who only wears pale, had the impudence to interrupt me with "I'm sick of hearing about this bitch's white girl problems."

Oh, I'm sorry, Thunder Thighs, do you have somewhere to be right now? Am I keeping you from a super-important facial that you've needed for the last twenty years?? Because I don't have time for your bullshit either.

I thought my addict friends would have my back, but they all agreed with her! It was a full-blown Babe-otage. They taunted me, saying hideous things like "Poor baby!" and "What's a Barneys CO-OP?" One man even said that he wished he was in my shoes because my addiction wasn't even real!!!!!??????????
??

I immediately broke down in tears. It surprised me that I got emotional, because honestly who gives a fuck about these people that don't even know me anyway? I guess I shouldn't have gotten so upset, but their attack hit me like a ton of coke bricks. Gina was on stable duty, so she wasn't even there to slap someone for me, and Paul just sat there staring at the same point on the wall that he always stares at. He never says anything besides "I miss my girlfriend." Fuck he is so hot.

Luckily, Jackson came to my rescue. He told everyone to relax and let me have a second to work it out, which I took to mean that I was free to go. So I got up and stomped out of the room and Jackson followed me down the hallway. Annoying. He told me that my problems are very real and that he wants me to come to his office tomorrow for one-on-one. Whatever, dude.

Tomorrow is visiting day. Dad (and Lizbeth) and Mabinty are coming, if they even remember me.

Who cares? Not me,

B

Day 17

Well, today I met my mom. As in, my real mom, and it was a shit show. Interesting, but a shit show, nonetheless. I'm gonna do my best to recount everything that happened. It started like every day here at rehab. I was sitting with Gina on the porch, having a cup of black coffee and a cigarette, and talking about John Galliano, when one of the counselors came out to tell Gina that her wife, D, had arrived and was waiting in our room.

I was dying to meet D, so I went with Gina. When we got to our room, D was sitting on Gina's bed, rifling through her own black, beat-up Birkin. She was wearing all black, very casual, ripped Levi's jeans and a T-shirt by The Row. After they embraced for a cute amount of time, Gina introduced us. I immediately realized that D was actually Donna Valeo, another model whom I'd seen in magazines when I was a little girl. Two of my favorite models in *my* rehab room at the same time?! My eight-year-old self would be so proud of me. I had to contain my excitement by chewing the inside of my lip so that I wouldn't blurt out: "I wanted your legs so BADLY when I was younger! Teach me your ways!"

We all chatted for a little bit. Gina told Donna about my obsession with fashion (aka my addiction and the reason I was here in the first place) and Donna seemed sympathetic enough. When they started making out and whispering to each other, I felt like an intruder on their special lesbian island, so I gave them some alone time.

When I walked out of my room, my dad, Lizbeth, and Mabinty were standing in the hallway talking to Jackson. I was so excited—I didn't realize how much I'd missed them. I ran up and threw my arms around my dad. Mabinty was crying. She squeezed both of us, making for a totally embarrassing group-hug moment. Lizbeth stood there smiling supportively. Bitch.

I wanted to introduce my family to Gina, so I led them back into the lesbian jungle. She had become my rock over the last three weeks, and it was important to me that my family got to know my new best friend.

As soon as my dad walked into my room, he stopped dead in his tracks. Typically, my dad is the first person to break an awkward silence with a string of expletives, but for the first time ever, he was the one causing the awkwardness. He looked like he was in pure and utter shock.

"Dad? Please don't die in front of my new best friends," I said.

Smash cut to Donna's face—same fucking expression. Deer in Xenon headlights. Then, like I was living in some sort of ABC Family movie, Donna said, "Oh my God. Hi." Her eyes darted to me and then back to my dad.

Wait, how did they know each other?

"Excuse me, can you fill me in on what's going on?" I said. "Did you guys used to fuck or something?"

"Babe," my dad stammered, "this is Donna bloody Valeo."

"I totally bloody know that."

"And she's your mother."

Okay. Okay. Okay. I've obvi fantasized about what it would be like to meet my real mom, but I didn't see it going down like this.

Here she was. Donna Valeo. My mother. After all this time learning not to ask questions about her, not to even *think* about her, here she was.

"So, I came out of your vagina?" I said.

"I guess you could put it that way." Donna's eyes were welling up. She moved closer, and it almost seemed like she was about to hug me.

"Whoa." I backed away and looked around the room. My dad was standing there sobbing, Mabinty looked oddly touched, Lizbeth was smiling, genuinely thrilled that *The Mystery of Babe's Mom* had been solved, and Gina looked like she could use a scotch. As for me, I was numb. Thankfully, I was able to temporarily avoid some major awkwardness when Jackson came in and whisked everyone away to their respective family therapy sessions.

My dad was completely shell-shocked from seeing Donna for the first time in twenty-four years, so our session was a bit stressful. Jackson kept trying to talk about my dad's role (or lack thereof) during my childhood, adolescence, and formative years, and how that might have fucked me up a little bit, but my dad could barely focus. He just kept stammering "I'm sorry," over and over. I felt bad for him. I mean, he did his best. Trying to create a normal life for me by himself was probably a difficult task, but I think he did an amazing job. Of course he had a lot of help from Mabinty, Tai Tai, and MTV, but I would say that I've turned out to be a very well-adjusted and passionate young woman who has her head in the right place most of the time. But I'm also a Gemini, so yeah, there's a lot going on up there.

But honestly, besides my dad's dramatic waterworks, and the poems Mabinty wrote and read for me, my family sessions were kind of a bore. I'm not trying to complain, I understand that everyone cares and feels bad about enabling a completely helpless girl to the point that she had no choice but to send her own damn self to rehab, but after a month of talking about myself and hearing other people talk about me, I'm over it. Anyone would be.

Before he left tonight, my dad wanted to talk to me about all the craziness that'd happened this morning, but I knew he was gonna start crying and I couldn't go down that road with him again, so I tried to lock myself in my room, but of course, the doors have no locks on them, so that didn't work.

He let himself in, sat down on my bed next to me, and, just as I'd expected, totally fucking lost his shit.

"Babe, darling, this has been an absolute brain-fuck for me, so I can't even imagine how you're feeling right now."

"Dad, I'm fi—"

"This all has made me think about the goddamn past a lot. I just need you to know one thing before I go. You have a family that loves you so much and cares about you more than anything in this bloody world. Your mother wouldn't have been good for you, even if she was around to raise you."

"Dad—"

"When she left, I felt totally lost. Like a complete twat. I was a fool, a fucking mess, darling. I didn't know the first goddamn thing to do. I mean, a fucking baby? I didn't know what to do with a baby! And I was so mad at Donna. I'd gone absolutely mental. I thought she was a wicked fucking bitch back then, to do that to me . . . to us. If it weren't for Tai Tai and Mabinty, I don't know what I would've done. But over time, and once some of the dust settled, I realized how lucky I was to have you. You changed my life."

"Dad, look. I really appreciate that you're having a moment right now, but—"

"I realized that my life would have to be about you. I'd have to work my ass off to make sure that you were protected, and that your shit show of a mother didn't screw it up, for either of us. And the sad part is, I also missed her."

"Please! My brain is weak and I can't handle everyone's emotions. I love you, but can we talk about this when I get home?"

After blowing his nose for thirty straight minutes and wiping the tears from his eyes, my dad said, "Fine, Babe. That's all fine. We can talk about it when you get home. But please, darling, know that I'm here and I love you. Whether you and Donna talk again, or whatever happens with you all, remember that I'm here. I'm on your side."

"Thanks, Dad. I'm, um, glad to hear that."

I hated seeing him like that. It made me feel sick. But it also made me feel kind of good because he was being super sweet. Like, super, super, sweet.

My dad took a minute to pull himself together, and the two of us walked outside to meet Mabs and Lizbeth, who were waiting by a black SUV. Mabinty was examining her nails.

I kissed everyone good-bye (one-arm-hugged Lizbeth),

went out to the back deck, and smoked a full pack of Marlboro Lights.

Should I be freaking out right now? Should I be mad at Donna? I don't even know her, or at least not as well as I know the fantasy version of her that I've created in my head over the past twenty-four years. I mean, it's like waiting your entire life to be gifted that crocodile Birkin that you've always wanted, and then when it's finally sent to you from that Saudi prince that you've only met at, like, one or two parties, you look at it and say, "Maybe the crocodile reads a bit too *evening* for the rest of my look."

I don't know how Donna fits into my life. Now I really need to go to sleep.

What the fuck,

B

P.S. I saw Paul's girlfriend today. She was wearing pink UGGs.

Day 18

So, I thought all of the mama drama was over and I could wake up today in a slightly less stressful environment, but as per usual, I was terribly wrong. Donna is staying in town for the next couple of days, until Gina finishes treatment on Thursday. Of course, sneaky little Jackson took the liberty of arranging a one-on-one therapy session for Donna and me. Oh fucking great. Thanks buddy! This was just what I wanted to do after the barrage of force-fed therapy that I'd dealt with yesterday.

I did my best to remember what was said in the session, because when the honest and brutal portrayal of my life is presented as a film in five to ten years, the scene where I talk to my mom for the first time should play out exactly like the following. I might as well start writing the script now while it's fresh in my mind and I'm sober.

Jackson: I know we only scheduled the one session with your dad and Mabinty, but some pretty obvious and unexpected circumstances made me feel that bringing you and Donna together would be a good idea.

Silence.

Jackson: (*cont.*) I know it's not going to be a simple task to open a line of communication between you and your mother, but we ought to try. Leaving this unaddressed would not only be irresponsible of us, but it would also further some of your issues, Babe.

Me: I've told you before and I'll tell you again: I really don't appreciate your obsession with my problems. It's weird. Plus, this is not my issue. It's Donna's. She's the one who dipped out on my life. She's the one who fucked up. Not me. So make her talk about her issues.

Jackson: Well, we're here to help *you.* Why don't you start by telling Donna how you're feeling?

Me: I'm honestly over it. Seriously, I don't need a mom, okay? When I get married, I'll have my husband's mom to fill that role of "older woman to whom I have the absolute freedom to be a bitch." Until that day, no mom needed. Thanks so much, guys—great session. Are we done here? I'm trying to fit needlecraft in before my colonic at one o'clock.

Jackson: Babe, wait. Donna's here, right in front of you. She wants to talk with you, and I think it would be smart to talk back.

Me: I don't even like talking.

I stand to leave the room.

Donna: I wouldn't want to talk to me either. I get it. Being here is really hard for me too, but we've been given this chance to be together and you deserve to know why I decided to leave when you were born. Abandoning you is my biggest regret, but we all make decisions that we can't change. You have every right to hate me.

Me: I don't hate you, I just hate you right now. I mean, no, that's not it. I just . . . I don't know. You haven't been the best mom.

Donna: I know. When I met your dad, I was nineteen and an absolute fucking mess. I had just moved from Ohio to New York. The modeling industry was eating me alive. I was dealing with addiction and my sexuality and an eating disorder.

Me: Chic.

Donna: Not chic. I cleaned up and got sober when I found out I was pregnant with you, and I thought I could be saved by starting a new life with your dad.

Me: So like what kind of pregnant were you? Were you totally fat everywhere, or were you, like, superthin with a big round tummy? And who did I meet when I was inside of you? Donatella? Ohmigod, Gianni?!

Donna: I was the thin kind. And you met both. When you were born, it was too much for me. I was scared. I didn't know how I would be able to take care of you if I couldn't take care of myself. I was young. Way too young. (*Starts crying.*)

Jackson: This is great. Keep going, Donna.

Close up: My face, totally creeped out by how into this Jackson is, yet, at the same time, totally impressed at how well Donna hides the fact that she's from Ohio.

Donna: (*through tears*) I hadn't had a drink or a narcotic in nine months and I was losing my mind. The responsibility was too overwhelming. I took a ton of Klonopin, granted full custody to your dad, and ran the fuck away from it all.

Me: Kinda selfish.

Donna: Totally fucking selfish. I was a scared little girl, Babe. I moved back to Ohio, and the guilt was so intense that I couldn't get out of bed for months. After a year, I finally got my shit together and moved back to New York to start working—

Me: You were modeling?

Donna: Yes. But keeping my career afloat was a nightmare. I was trying to suppress my demons with drugs. It wasn't until I met Gina and we moved to the country that I was able to clear my head and confront my troubles head-on.

Me: Did you even try Googling me once you stopped being a psychopath?

Donna: Of course. There have been so many times when I thought contacting you would be a good idea. But I didn't want to mindfuck you, so I'd always decide just to stay out of your life.

Me: You look like me when you cry. It's sick.

Jackson: Babe, how does all of this make you feel? What's your gut telling you?

Me: Stop saying I have a gut. That's offensive.

Jackson: Babe, please.

Me: Jackson, please.

Jackson: Babe. Let's work here. Let's get it all out on the table.

Me: You guys, I'm soooooooooo tired.

I take one long, deep breath, slowly shut my eyes, and pretend to nod off in my chair.

Jackson: Babe!

Me: Fine! I'm up! That was a super-intense story, and I'm sorry to hear that I have ancestors in Ohio, but I'm not going to freak out about it, because I promised myself I wouldn't cry or scream at anyone today. Is that okay? I mean, what do you want from me? Donna, Mom, lady, whatever—you fucked up. I'm angry. The end.

Donna: Thanks for being honest with me, Babe. And I do hope that we can start to build a relationship.

Me: I don't know . . . I'm gonna be, like, the busiest ever when I get out of here. So we'll see.

Donna: Well, my door will be open to you from now on. You know, sometimes Gina and I go to church and pray for you. Not that I really believe in all of that shit. I'm sure that doesn't make you feel any better, but I thought you should know.

Long silence.

Donna: (*cont.*) P.S. Your jeans are really good. Are they Rag & Bone?

Me: Yeah, they're really old. So, you knew Karl Lagerfeld when he was fat?

Donna: I did actually. It was chic in person, believe it or not.

Me: Ew, really?

Donna: He was youthful, so the extra weight was working for him. I always loved walking for Karl. You know, it was fast music, great energy, short skirts.

Me: And he always featured his little black fan, right?

Donna: *(laughing unreasonably loud)* Yes!

Me: So, you walked for Chanel, or Fendi, or what?

Donna: Both. I did lots of running around in those years. It was a shit show. I think you would've liked it.

Me: Liked it? Are you fucking kidding? I would've disintegrated into a pile of mush to have been at his spring '94 shows. I've been scouring eBay for those crotch-emblazoned Chanel bikinis for five years.

Donna: You're kidding. Those are hideous!

Me: Speak for yourself, lady.

Donna: Well, Gina has one lying around that she's never worn because I forbid it. As far as I'm concerned, it's all yours.

Me: OHMYFUCKINGGOD THANK YOU!!!!!!

Donna: It'll be a hand-me-down from us.

Me: I accept.

Jackson: I'm really glad we did this.

Donna: Me too.

Silence. They both stare at me.

Me: What? Am I supposed to say something?

End scene.

And that's how it went down.

Love,

B

Day 19

Last night I dreamt that I gave birth to a baby version of myself at the end of the runway during Oscar de la Renta's seminal spring/summer 1987 fashion show. It was vile. Remind me to never give birth. My mind was racing and I couldn't get back to sleep after that, so I woke Gina up at 5:30 A.M. I dragged her out of bed, threw her in a lace slip that I found on the floor, and we left for the woods. I had a million questions about Donna/Mom. I needed answers. I'd gotten the story of why she'd left, but I didn't know the little details that made her the woman she is now.

Gina and I walked for about nineteen cigarettes, and I got to ask her all of the things that I wanted to ask Donna but couldn't. I found out what Donna's favorite color is (gray), who her favorite designers are (Azzedine Alaia, Calvin Klein, Hussein Chalayan), if she's good in bed (yes), does she eat white starches (no), what her favorite leafy green is (kale, which is weird because kale is my favorite leafy green too). I'm beginning to piece together who this woman is. This woman . . . my mom! That's so fucking weird to say. Ew.

Unclear,

B

Day 20

Gina completed her treatment program and left Cirque this afternoon. It's not like me to miss people, but I'm going to miss her a ton. What am I gonna do without her? She became my loyal confidante when no one else understood me. Every time my fellow rehabbers turned on me in group, I had Gina to bitch to over a glass of Pellegrino at the end of the day. When I wrote

Paul an anonymous love letter, sprayed it with my perfume, and slid it under his door, and he didn't say ANYTHING about it to me, Gina let me hold her Birkin and cry. Out of all the people in the world that have fucked my mom, she's my favorite, after my dad.

When I was walking Gina to the car, she stopped me as we were crossing the serenity bridge and handed me a little piece of paper with her e-mail address scribbled on it. She said that she wanted to be a part of my life, and that I was always welcome in hers. It was a total moment. I was crying, she was crying, and my hair was a mess from the wind. It was a TOTAL moment. I do hope that we can keep in touch. Is it bad that I kind of wish Gina was my mom instead of Donna?

I was expecting to get in touch with my demons and maybe drop a few pounds at rehab, but I found a new friend in Gina. Bye, bitch.

Love,

B

Day 22

I fucked Paul.

Whoops,

B

Day 25

Jackson and I had our last one-on-one session today. I wanted to talk about ways that he could refresh his look, namely with some Rogaine and a new jacket (preferably not from Patagonia). I even brought some before and afters that I'd mocked up for him, but all he wanted to talk about was my recovery and my dad and meeting Donna and how I was going to cope with life on the outside and the most annoying question of all: how I got to this place in my life.

Jackson has asked me this same fucking question literally twenty thousand times, and every time I say the same thing: "I am in rehab because I spent $246,893.50 at Barneys in one afternoon. It's embarrassing, I get it."

Today, Jackson refused to let it go. He kept trying to tell me that there were underlying issues that led me to this place in my life. He seems to think that I need to face these issues head-on in order to "make progress in my recovery." Also, now that all of this Donna shit has hit the fan, he keeps bringing her up and wanting to talk about my feelings toward her, and I need him to stop because I don't know what's going to happen between Donna and me! It's weird, the whole thing's weird! I feel like I have all of these unresolved questions about who she is as a person, but Jackson's the last person I want to talk to about them.

UGHHHHH. What's his problem? Was that therapy session he sprung on me not enough of an ambush? Why is he so obsessed with me?

And he didn't stop there. Jackson spat all kinds of nonsensical reasons why I ended up at rehab, like that my dad wasn't around to enforce boundaries so I made my own rules, and that my grandmother's death stirred up painful feelings of abandonment I had from not having a mom, and that I grew up with a dependence on material things, and blah fucking blah. Whatever.

I told Jackson that he clearly doesn't get my struggle and I'm out of here in three days anyway so it doesn't even matter. And then, AND THEN, he had the nerve to tell *me* that *I* needed to adjust *my* attitude because he was trying to help me?! Fuck you, man. I'm going to sleep.

Suck it,

B

Day 28

Today is supposed to be my last day, but after reading through everything that I just wrote over the past forty-eight hours, one thing is clear: I'm kind of a psycho and kind of a drug addict, and kind of toying with the idea of staying on for another twenty-eight days of treatment. The last month hasn't been ideal, and there were certainly moments when I thought rehab was hell, but maybe I just wasn't open to accepting the fact that I might actually need help? It wasn't all a wash. There were minor successes: I got back on a horse, I made a great friend in Gina, and I fucked Paul.

This morning, I was looking for my matches, and I pulled the little paper out of those jeans and saw that it read: **donna.v@newbridgefarm.com.** Turns out that the e-mail address Gina gave me wasn't hers after all. When she gave it to me, I slipped it into my pocket without even looking at it because I was too busy crying.

At first my heart kind of sank, because I felt like Gina expected me to reach out to Donna and I wasn't sure that I wanted to do that. But maybe it'll be good for me to connect with both of them. I could use some positive lesbian influences in my life.

Another thing I realized after reading through all the stories I'd written was that I clearly needed to make amends with a few people, so I wrote a really positive e-mail.

FROM: Babe Walker <BDubs@gmail.com>

SUBJECT: **Sowwy!**

DATE: July 11, 2011 11:37:43 PM EDT

TO: Dad <WalkerLawyer@GKLWLAW.com>

CC: Mabinty <Mabs@Jamaicalove.com> Roman DiFiore <RomeoRomeo310@gmail.com> Genevieve Larson <PropertyOfGL@gmail.com>

Hi guys-
Just wanted to drop you all a line and let you know how sorry I am that I've been gone all month. I didn't really take into account how you all would feel about me being absent from your lives for so long. It's clear that I had some growing up to do while here in UTAH! I'm not sure I've succeeded in doing so, but only time will tell.

Dad— I love you. I'm sorry that Donna ditched you when I was born, and I'm sorry you had to date a string of semiretarded models in order to get over her, but I am so grateful that throughout everything, we've had each other. I'm also sorry about the whole Barneys thing. I wish I could say that you taught me to know better than that, but...

Mabinty— Thanks for always letting me be myself and understanding my struggles. I'm sorry for taking my bullshit out on you. You don't deserve to be screamed at or bossed around, but I guess that's kind of what mother figures are for. I'm not saying it will never happen again, but I *am* saying that now I'll be able to recognize when I'm doing it, and that's progress.

Roman— Hey Ro, love your new FB profile pic (so ripped!!!?!). I miss you! How's Uri? Can't wait to see you when I get out of here! P.S. I'm sorry for being a cunt sometimes, but I'm working on it. Plus, you can be a cunt sometimes too. Love you!

Gen— I'm sorry that you never texted me back when I told you I was going to rehab.

I miss you guys and I miss my old life, but I'm kind of excited about my new life? See you all soon-ish. Prob staying for another 28 days. I'm feeling like treatment might actually be a good idea for me, it just took me some time to warm up to it!
LOVE,
B

I also wrote this . . .

FROM: Babe Walker <BDubs@gmail.com>
SUBJECT: (No Subject)
DATE: July 11, 2011 11:37:43 PM EDT
TO: Donna Valeo <donna.v@newbridgefarm.com>
CC: Jackhole <jackson@cirquelodgeweb.com>

Hi.

So, we'll see how all of that pans out. In the meantime, maybe my stories can help other people. My journey is pretty inspiring—I should try and turn it into a book. Everyone and their mother is writing a memoir these days. I mean, I realize that this wouldn't technically be a real memoir because I've never been molested or raped, but still.

Possible titles:

Babe Walker: Perseverance
I'm Fine: The Babe Walker Story
I'll Buy the Flowers Myself: The Babe Walker Story
Babe Walker: The Babe Walker Story
Walk the Line: The Babe Walker Story
Fashion: My Story

All really good ideas, but I have plenty of time to decide. I'll let it come to me organically. You can't force the creative process, especially when you're out of Adderall.

It'll be really interesting to see if I can get my shit together.

Love,

B

ACKNOWLEDGMENTS

This book (my life) would not have been possible without the love and support of the following people:

Dad, Mabinty Jones, Genevieve Larson,
Roman Di Fiore, Robert, Donna Valeo and Gina,
Jackson Whatever, Lara Schoenhals, Tanner Cohen,
and David Oliver Cohen.

And now I'd like to take a moment to mention all the people who should thank me for writing this book:

Butch Schoenhals, Linda Schoenhals, Jake Schoenhals, Kurt Schoenhals, Sara Schoenhals, Jennie Hunnewell, Chandler Hunnewell, Marcia Cohen, Stewart Cohen, Jessica Lindsey, Natalie Stevenson, Luce Amelia Stevenson-Cohen, Cristiana Andrews Cohen, Penelope Ziggy Cohen, Liz Newman, Frank Newman, Tristan Andrews, Byrd Leavell (a super-hot dad and the best agent a girl could ask for), Jill Schwartzman (my fearless editor), Samantha O'Brien, and the entire Hyperion team, Howie Sanders, Larry Salz, Jason Richman, Amanda Burnett, Wyatt Hough, Jenna Griffin, Carey Waggoner, Colette Kennedy, Eva Amurri, Rachel Schubert, Susan Sarandon, Audrey Adams, Leonardo DiCaprio, Ryan O'Connell, Olivia Wolfe, Celine Rixey, Megan Fulton, Chris Macho, Christine Ronan, Amanda Bynes, Emma Roberts, Steve Jobs, Princesca, Gizmo, Babe, Catcher, Oscar, Moose, Big Pudy, Little Pudy, Milo, Pepper, Tiger, Socks, Pudy, Nancy, Neko, Toby, Sophie, Biscuit, Rockwell, Panda, Martha, Orangie, Emily, Red Sox, Little Kitty, Tabby, Butch Jr., Madison, Little Black Princess, Wolf Girl, Dirty Nose, Whiskers, Cleopatra, Sophie, Maxwell George, Maggi, Samba.